**She was almost naked,
her skirt and blouse torn away...**

There were the parallel marks of fingernails across her left breast, and blood on the corner of her mouth. Around her neck was the necklace of Apache Tears. In the lower, inner swell of her left breast was a small, powder-burned hole.

He unhooked the necklace. He put it around his neck and fastened the clasp.

It would remind him of the debt of revenge he owed one Apache half-breed. As if he could ever forget....

"MacLeod is obviously a master....Unmistakably authentic. Few Westerns are so unsentimental as this, and fewer still are better."
—*Publishers Weekly*

"A superb book written with great knowledge but most important with great heart and spirit."
—Clair Huffaker, author of
The Cowboy and the Cossack and
Nobody Loves a Drunken Indian

APACHE TEARS
is an original POCKET BOOK edition.

APACHE TEARS

by
ROBERT MacLEOD

PUBLISHED BY POCKET BOOKS NEW YORK

APACHE TEARS

POCKET BOOK edition published January, 1974

Two minor historical events have been shifted slightly in time to accommodate the story. Several minor characters were actual historical personages; all other persons and events are entirely fictitious.

This original POCKET BOOK edition is printed from brand-new plates made from newly set, clear, easy-to-read type. POCKET BOOK editions are published by POCKET BOOKS, a division of Simon & Schuster, Inc., 630 Fifth Avenue, New York, N.Y. 10020. Trademarks registered in the United States and other countries.

L

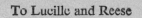
To Lucille and Reese

APACHE TEARS

CHAPTER 1

Camp Verde, about a mile from the west bank of the Verde River, was almost at the geographical center of Arizona, and about sixty miles east of the nearest civilization—Fort Whipple and the nearby town of Prescott, which had been the first territorial capital, but now, in 1875, was no longer.

Supper was over. Everything seemed to be hung up, hanging fire, in suspension; the sun still hung suspended over the pine-timbered Black Hills; Corporal Sullivan of Company G, 21st Infantry, hung drooping from the wagon wheel to which he had been spread-eagled for insubordination; a double pack hung from the agonized shoulders of Private Scanlan of Troop K, Fifth Cavalry, as he shuffled around the parade ground on double guard duty—four hours on and two off—for kicking an Apache Scout out of his path, and who was alive now only because Sergeant Neil Douglas had grabbed the Apache before he could cut the trooper's throat.

Although it was still daylight and golden dust hung in the sultry heat like a mile-long curtain draped along the road, a moon like a vast silver peso hung low over the Mogollon Rim—the great barrier reef of cliffs that crossed Arizona Territory diagonally, north and east of Camp Verde—the moon that silver-plated junipers and creosote bush and every imaginable thing that had thorns, and the canyons and cliffs where the Anasazi, the Old Ones, had built their starkly beautiful dwellings a thousand years ago.

9

Sergeant Neil Douglas hung back from joining his
five Indians in the wall tent because, while their smell
wasn't offensive, it was pervasively Indian—buckskin
breechclouts, rawhide-soled, thigh-length moccasins
rolled down to their knees, oily hair—and nobody would
say anything in English unless trying to wheedle more
of his tobacco; and the Apaches, Yellow Face, a Tonto,
and Chalk Eye and Chiquito, Mescaleros, would be
quarreling over a game played with three flat bone dice;
while Limpy, the Mojave with the bullet-scarred knee,
rocked on his heels humming an interminable chant that
Neil Douglas understood no better than he understood
the gobbles and hisses and vocal explosions of Apache,
and Chulito, Pretty Boy, a Mimbreño and the youngest
of Neil's Scouts, squatted on his heels examining his
chin for rare whiskers which he plucked with tweezers
improvised from a flattened cartridge case. All five
were adorned with necklaces of turquoise and coral and
amulets and good luck charms—pierced coins, bits of
petrified wood, little leather sacks of owl feathers, gold
bracelets, and silver rosaries, undoubtedly the profit
from murderous raids in Arizona Territory and down into Mexico.

For a while, for a couple of weeks, maybe, Sergeant
Douglas would have liked to bunk with white men in
the long adobe noncoms' barracks, eat with them there
at the long tables and join in the roughneck humor, the
dirty talk about women, and the nightly poker games.

Not that he didn't like his Indians—he did. Unlike
First Sergeant Eddie Burke, Douglas had lived with his
Indians almost night and day, ever since he enlisted for
service with the Indian Scouts, four years ago when
General Crook's campaign was just beginning. It was
a matter of the cultivation of mutual trust and interde-
pendence, which was great if you were hanging onto
a trail of "bronco" braves and women and old men
and children even after your horses played out. You
carried out General Crook's orders never to abandon a
trail, even when you knew the hostiles were going to
beat you to the border and escape into Mexico. It was

fine, for instance, the night of December 27, '72, when your Scouts discovered a big party of Chuntz's band holed up in the cave in the Salt River Canyon, and Major Brown and Captain Burns and Lieutenant Ross were going to take them out of there in the morning, or pry them out, or kill them; and they wouldn't surrender, and got themselves killed by bullets bounced off the cave roof, or by rocks rolled from above. You felt like one of your crew of skilled assassins then, one *with* them—for instance, the afternoon before you and them and Eddie Burke's bunch and the forty Camp Verde Scouts—Apaches, Navajos, Opatas, Pimas, Mexicans— waited until midnight, back there in April '73, to start climbing Turret Butte, and the dismounted troopers and the dogfaces waiting for somebody to cough or roll a rock down, and for the hail of lead straight down into your face, and the raging screams of the broncos on top and the terror screams of the shot, the falling—which didn't happen, and by a miracle you were all on top by first light, and caught them sleeping and killed them all, men, women, grandparents, kids, if they wouldn't quit. But most of them quit.

You bet! That was the life—you and old Chalk Eye with his scarred eyebrow and cheekbone and that white staring eye, and the other one like an obsidian marble; and Chulito, smooth skinned, womanish looking, deadly as a diamondback, checking over his Long Tom .45-70 in the tent, there; and Limpy grinning and lifting your Bull Durham sack out of your shirt pocket with never a grunt of thanks, and who had taken a slug in the right knee when he could just as well have left you, and dragged you from under your dead horse while carbines roared in the chaparral and hunks of lead screamed off the rocks. Yes, that made a life—but he wished he wasn't stuck with it right now, that without hurting his Indians' feelings, he could bunk in the noncoms' quarters. Like First Sergeant Eddie Burke, who was an inspired leader of Indian Scouts even while he despised them. Probably because Burke, himself, was half Tonto

Apache, and ashamed of it, and ready to deny it with profanity and fists.

Maybe that was why Sergeant Burke had only one close companion among the eight Indians in his own bunch—his and Neil Douglas's five being all that were still at Camp Verde. Burke's friend was really more protégé, audience of one, body servant, and dogrobber than companion. He was a white man more Apache than any Apache. Douglas thought this was why Eddie Burke tolerated him as a companion, went hunting with him and visiting the reservation. Maybe he felt his own stature greater in the eyes of others, as measured against such a white man. Maybe it told him that even with Indian blood he was better than a white man.

Troopers called the man Whitey, and the Scouts called him White Eyes, their insulting term for any white man. A twenty-five-year-old Dutchie or Swede, with white hair, pale blue eyes, a mass of freckles on arms, neck, and shoulders, forever greasing himself, forever sunburned and peeling, a man who didn't know his name or who he was. When he was very young, a party of Mangas Coloradas's raiders had shot down his pioneer father and gutted him because he had managed to kill one of them, and had done hideous things to his mother before she died, and had taken the child to the home ranchería and over twenty years made of him the most Apache of Apache warriors, with no memory of any other life. At least, that was the story a couple of old-timers told.

When an Indian adopted a son, the relationship was not merely symbolic, but as valid as any blood kinship, and was considered as such by the entire family and clan. Whitey was Apache, nothing more or less. From the standpoint of a white man, he had no morals and no scruples, but a hatred of all whites, and a talent for unraveling a trail, for deception, misdirection, and murder.

Neil Douglas despised him—for no assignable reason, because his own Scouts were capable of anything Whitey might do or had done—but perhaps because he *was* a

white man, however altered. Perhaps because of the
wedding rings he wore, one on each little finger, which
clearly had been worn by white women, and almost certainly were mementos of murder.

Douglas could almost hear the earth groaning and
cracking, like an old house contracting with the first cool
breeze of dusk. He rolled a smoke and was about to go
to the tent and bed down in his blankets and read again,
by lantern light, his month-old copy of the Prescott
Arizona Miner and the editorial that advocated dropping pills compounded of strychnine and brown sugar
where Apaches would find them, to hasten the extermina-
tion of the vermin. Then he thought he might go over
to Shanty Town, adjoining the post, for a couple of
slugs of skullbreaker whiskey and someone to talk to.

He didn't look very soldierly, with no natty service
blouse covering the nonregulation red flannel shirt
faded and out at the elbows. He wore the light blue cavalry pants with the yellow stripes down the seams,
stuffed into black field boots cut off square below the
knees, and the gray campaign hat, broken-brimmed and
sweated—but the pants were wrinkled and spotted, the
boots run over at the heels. Officers and noncoms attached
to the Apache Scouts were allowed great latitude in dress,
to avoid the demoralizing effects on the Indians of sup-
pression of individuality of the rank and file.

He thought sourly of First Sergeant Burke, meticul-
ously smart and military while on the post, who went
to the opposite extreme in the field, dressing to match
his Indians—loose red cotton shirt with the tails out, over
a long buckskin breechclout that hung below the knees
fore and aft, loose and baggy cotton drawers in winter,
barelegged clear to the crotch in summer, clumsy thigh-
high buckskin moccasins turned down below the knees,
a cartridge belt, a sheathed fighting knife—and although
his hair came down only around his ears, he even affected the red headband the Apaches wore to confine
their shoulder-length hair. Thus attired, Sergeant Burke
had got himself shot at a couple of times by troopers who

took him for a bronco, in the dust and smoke of battle. Too damn bad they hadn't knocked him off!

And here came Eddie now, stomping toward him
across the parade ground, sore about something, as
usual. First Sergeant Eddie Burke stopped, fists on hips,
a half snarl on his handsome face.

"Whitey says you was foolin' around with her again,
over on Suds Row," he accused.

"Who?" Neil asked. "Who was I foolin' around with?"

"You know damn well who! Molly Killian!"

"Foolin' around? Why, you goddamn jughead, I
took my laundry to her. That's what she's for, ain't it?
And anyway——"

"I told you before, I'll tell you once more, keep away
from her!" Burke yelled in his face.

Neil almost slugged him, but held back. He was only
technically Regular Army, and on a short-term enlistment at that, assigned exclusively to the Indian Scouts because he was a horseman, a packer, a marksman, a
native who knew the country and knew the Apaches;
but Eddie Burke was Regular Army, and therefore fa-
vored over Neil by West Point officers. He outranked
Neil, and could and did aggravate him with petty per-
secutions, hated him for his efficiency, his companionship with his Indians, whom Burke despised, envied him
his higher pay (Burke's original $17 a month having
been raised to $19 upon his reenlistment for a second
five years). Moreover, Neil had not concealed his eval-
uation of Burke as a blowhard. He knew it would gall
Burke now if he kept his temper instead of matching
Burke's bluster.

"Why do you bother?" he asked. "In six months,
you haven't made the grade, but any dumbjohn recruit
can pat her on the ass and roll her over. She just don't
like Indians, I guess."

He got set to lean inside a right-hand swing, and
hammer Burke's short ribs, but Major Trumbull and his
wife were strolling toward them, and Burke had to con-
tent himself with snarling, "Keep away from her or I'll
break your back! An' call me Indian again an' I'll

stomp the hell out of you, you grinning son of a bitch!"

Neil laughed at him. "What you ashamed of?" I got Piegan in me. From my grandmother. I'm proud of it."

Burke glanced at him in the fading light, snapped to attention, and threw a salute at Major and Mrs. Trumbull. Neil, hating the military forms, only said, "Evening, sir, ma'am," and turned indifferently away to go to his tent and his five Indians.

CHAPTER 2

Ever since Neil's enlistment in July, '71, he and Burke had been on the same campaigns. From the first, there had been a natural antipathy. Now, walking across the parade ground, Neil wondered why it all seemed to be coming to a boil—why he had almost welcomed a brawl with Burke. Come to think of it, this wasn't so strange. It was just Neil Douglas and Eddie Burke—and not only them. The whole camp was on edge, barn sour like a good horse too long in his stall.

There was simply nothing to do. General Crook's two-year campaign, his unrelenting pursuit—spring, summer, and winter—had broken the Apache uprisings, and stopped the raiding, the burning, the murders, and kidnappings and stock stealing that had gotten worse all through the war, and afterward. And now the Apaches were on the reservations, fifteen hundred of them, mostly Chuntz's and Alchesay's bands, and mostly Tonto Apaches, right here a mile from the post, each with a metal bangle on his wrist—crescent, square, triangle, disc—to show the band he belonged to, and stamped with a number to identify the individual and advertise that he was a "manso," a tame Apache, and not a "bronco." And Chuntz had been killed, and Del-She, and Cochise himself only two months ago, after his honorable surrender, and dishonorable and callous internment at the swampy and unhealthy Tularose reservation, to which the Bureau of Indian Affairs had solemnly promised never to send him, and from which he had escaped and gone on the war trail once more.

Except those who had fled to Mexico, only a few small bands of broncos still roamed free—Chiricahuas and Mescaleros in the Dragoon and Chiricahua Mountains. The rest, cheated by crooked agents and venal BIA officials conniving with the "Tucson Gang" and the beef contractors, robbed, starved, and despised, were making an effort at self-support under the guidance of the few sympathetic officers such as Lieutenant Whitman at Camp Grant, whose peaceful and fearful charges were, one fine morning, slashed and clubbed to death— old men, women, wives, children—by hite hyenas from Tucson and murdering Papago Indians.

General Crook, called Nantan Lupan, the Gray Wolf, whom the Apaches feared but trusted and respected, had put the defeated people to work farming, digging a five-mile irrigation ditch with makeshift tools furnished from Camp Verde, making a start toward self-sufficiency, only to have the crooks of the BIA and political pressure undo all his work and force the browbeaten Apaches to move to the barren San Carlos Reservation, where contractors could batten on them. The exodus was to start this coming August. That General Crook had been breveted Major General and was to be transferred to the Department of the Platte did not sweeten his bitterness at the government's breaking of all his promises to the Apaches.

Boredom was working on Camp Verde like an ulcer on a sour stomach—a couple of desertions each week, troopers brawling with dogfaces, both brawling with the town riffraff of gamblers, bootleggers, thieves, and pimps, and the Indian Scouts reduced to policing the reservaton.

Drill and fatigue duties were increased to keep the men occupied, but this only antagonized them further.

The enlisted men's pay of thirteen dollars a month was two months overdue, and no one could afford a slug of red-eye, or one of the middle-aged whores in Shanty Town. A few men with good-conduct records were given passes for a week of hunting. The adjutant, Second Lieutenant Underhill, was trying to organize a sort of track meet for the Fourth of July, to divert the men from their complaints, but was meeting only indifference.

The three laundresses, the "spikes" on Suds Row, the line of adobe shacks just off the post, permitted by the regulations, were quarreling viciously in their hugger-mugger enclave, overrun with mongrels, scrofulous chickens, and sickly kids whose fathers no one knew. Of the three, slovenly Molly Killian was the youngest—about thirty-five, and the only pretty one—red-brown eyes, creamy complexion, small waist, deep breasts, round hips—attractive despite her red hands and sloppiness of person. She had a dirtier tongue and no more morals than her sister laundresses.

Neil stood outside the tent, oblivious to the gabble of the dice players and the humming chant of the Mojave inside. Well, he thought, no wonder me and Eddie are at each other's throat, and the whole camp a powder keg on a short fuse. It's a damn wonder there's been no killings, no shavetail in the creek with his throat cut, no trooper with a slug in his gut and another high-tailing for Mexico.

Funny, he thought, me and Burke could almost pass for twins, same hair like black wire, same brown hide, almost the same build—only difference is he's a couple of inches taller and fifteen pounds heavier. Must be the Indian blood. Now why don't Molly go for him like she does anything else with pants? Maybe because sometimes he don't *wear* pants, but a clout like any Indian. She's sure let *me* know I'm welcome, any old night, and no charge. But she won't lay down for him for his month's pay. Must be our eyes, I can't figure anything else—him with those black glass marbles you can't see into, and mine gray. Maybe my Piegan grandma had a Scotch grandfather, herself.

He went into the tent and sat on the hardtack box by his blankets, where he kept his razor and soap and spare socks. The dice game was still going on and old Chalk Eye had a beaded headband of Chiquito's and a prized skinning knife of Yellow Face's. Limpy came to squat on his heels beside Neil and said, "Gimme tobacco, hey, flien'?"

Neil said, "Hell with it. Buy your own, sometime."

Limpy whined, "Me puss hoss, you 'membah, huh? No puss hoss you dead, huh, Sar'nt Duggles?"

Neil silently translated, "I pushed that dead horse off you that time in the middle of the fight, remember? If I hadn't you'd have been killed, wouldn't you, Sergeant Douglas?"

Neil said, "You goddamn lice ranch, you figure that earned you tobacco for the rest of your life?"

He handed Limpy his Bull Durham sack. Limpy rolled a cigarette and said, "Sar'nt Book, he talkin' launly woman she don' talk somebody."

He leered at Neil and made a one-handed gesture illustrative of copulation, then coughed and got ready to spit, and Neil said, "Outside, damn it!" Limpy looked at him like he was crazy and got up and spat through the doorway. Again Neil translated in his head: "Sergeant Burke was quarreling with the laundress, ordering her not to play fast and loose with anyone else."

The bugler blew tattoo. In the barracks the men would be lining up for roll call—but not the Scouts. They didn't stand formations or perform fatigue labor or run errands for the major's wife.

Neil thought of General Crook's order relating to the Indian Scout, which read about like this:

Headquarters, Fort Whipple, Department of Arizona, 17 March 1871.
    Daniel O'Leary, Commanding Indian Scouts.
Sir:
    The Department Commander directs me to furnish you the following instructions for your guidance in the management of Indian Scouts:

The first principle is to show them that we trust them. They understand thoroughly what is expected of them and they know best how to do their work. To try to direct them in details will disgust them and make them mere "time servers." Explain what you expect of them and let them do their work in their own way. Indian Scouts must not be required to stand post as sentinels or pickets. They are for scouting purposes only and are to use their own methods. Caution must be exercised lest the ambition of the Scouts be taken out of them by unnecessary labor. The question is how to get the most valuable service, hence the caution sought to be conveyed in this letter.

By order of General Crook.

Captain L. J. Andrews, A.A.D.C

Riding out from Prescott to Fort Whipple to enlist, Neil had passed a group of cavalry officers trotting behind a rider dressed in a linen duster, a pith helmet, brown canvas overalls, and wrinkled Apache moccasins, who wore great bushy sideburns plaited into braids, carried a double shotgun across the fork of his McClellan saddle, and rode a mule. A few minutes later, Neil was waiting in the administration office under the contemptuous stare of a spit-and-polish sergeant-clerk, to talk to the general, when the mule rider came in. The sergeant leaped up and saluted, and the whiskered man said to Neil, "I'm Crook. What do you want?"

Neil said, "I'm Neil Douglas. I wanta fight 'Paches, but I don't wanta march an' drill an' present arms an' all that horseshit. You still recruiting for the Scouts?"

"You a native around here?" Crook asked.

"Yeah. My grandfather was one of the first in the territory. Bear Douglas, they called him. He was a trapper for the Hudson Bay Company before he came down here. There was a lot of beaver around here, and he built a cabin over near Beaver Creek, and I rode and hunted with him from Utah to Mexico."

General Crook looked him over carefully. He said, "I expect he had an Indian wife."

"Yeah, brought her with him. My gramma. She was Piegan. General Crook, I've punched cows all over the territory, and I'm a packer, and I can follow a track. And I got a grudge against 'Paches. My mother died when I was fourteen, and me and my father were working a prospect hole, over in the Greenwood Mining District, and one day I found him stuck full of arrows. That was twelve years ago, when I was fifteen. Anyway . . . well, I been on my own ever since."

"Greenwood District," Crook said. "That's over by the Big Sandy." He paused. "You know, Douglas, Apaches never worked that far west, not more than a stray once in a while. The history of the Apache has been written by his enemies, the Spaniard, the Mexican, the American, and a lot of it is lies. That was Yavapais or Mojaves killed your dad. Apaches always get the blame. Well, how does this strike you? Sergeant's chevrons and fifty a month. That's, let's see, that's thirty-three more than regulation. Five-year enlistment."

Fifty a month was also twenty more than Neil was making pushing cows around on the Windmill Ranch. He said, "I guess not. Sergeant is fine, and fifty is fine, but five years is way too long. How about a year?"

"Three," General Crook said.

They settled on two years, and Crook said to the sergeant-clerk, "Sign him up. Give him a soldier suit. And a horse, and I mean a *horse,* understand? And turn him over to Dan O'Leary."

General Crook and the new sergeant had understood each other very well, back there four years ago. And Neil Douglas, new Sergeant of Indian Scouts, Department of Arizona, had ridden from Fort Whipple to Camp Verde in the company of the already famous Al Sieber, commanding the Second Company of Indian Scouts; and Archie MacIntosh, half Indian; Sam Bowman, American; Marijilda Grijalva, Mexican; and the deadly, wall-eyed little Mickey Free—most of them now at San Carlos, policing tame Apaches.

Neil was grinning at the recollection of his enlistment, when Limpy interrupted his reverie by filching the Bull Durham sack from his shirt pocket.

Limpy said, "Launly woman he gimme." As Neil figured it out, this meant, "The laundry woman gave me this."

From under his belted, greasy, buckskin breechclout, Limpy extracted a grimy piece of folded paper.

Molly Killian sure hadn't had much schooling, not as much as Neil. The crude lettering ran straggling uphill:

Seargant Douglis hony
Wy dont come for them shert after Tap wen nobody be here and that dam indin sargant not smelling arond here like tomcat in heet
You kno who!

The bugle blew Taps, long-drawn and sad and beautiful, and Neil's mind could see her—blowsy golden hair in a bun, strands of it stuck to her forehead by sweat, her rough red hands immersed in the washtub, her sleeves rolled, the deep cleft between her white breasts when she bent over the tub, the female womanness of her not disguised by the ground-sweeping skirts, the leg-of-mutton sleeves, and the bustle over her round and exciting rump.

Suddenly he was stirred. Excited and aroused as he had been before by Molly Killian—crudity, foul mouth, promiscuity, and all. It would be a joke on her—he was as much Indian as Eddie Burke, who couldn't touch her. And it would be a hell of a joke on Eddie! Nothing ever kept secret in this place, and Eddie would go up like a rocket when he found out!

That wasn't all of it, of course. Neil hadn't been with a woman in three years. He wasn't afraid of women—he was afraid of syphilis and the clap, because good women didn't fornicate with soldiers. And Neil Douglas didn't fornicate with Indian women. He'd have to be harder up than he had yet been, to bed down with a squaw.

So Sergeant Neil Douglas got up and went out. And in the tent, Limpy made that gesture again, and Yellow Face and Chalk Eye and Chulito and Chiquito grinned.

The moon had taken full charge, now. Shadows were black, the white-plastered adobe walls of the buildings on three sides of the parade ground—officers' quarters, noncoms' quarters, barracks, headquarters, commissary, tiny guardhouse and supply sheds—were luminescent. The sky was garish with stars, the Milky Way suggesting that God had ambled across the heavens carrying a bucketful of them, spilling them carelessly as He went. Dogs barked blustering challenge to coyotes squalling like maniacs not a hundred yards from the parade ground. Neil, crossing the area, hoped they were dividing up Major Trumbull's wife's snuffling pug dog which had a habit of messing in Captain Eastwood's wife's flower garden, and kept the feud burning between those ladies.

Molly Killian's dogs barked at him and cringed away, and she opened her door and pulled him inside hastily. Two small redheads peered solemnly at him from the other room, and she shoved them back and slammed the door. When she kissed him, he could smell the booze.

She was in a hurry, a lot more than he. She hugged him close, ground her loins against him, then shoved a sack of dirty laundry off the cot against the wall.

As he unbuttoned and pulled off his shirt, boots, pants, and long drawers, he watched in astonishment while, in the glare of a reflector lamp, she divested herself successively of high button shoes, a floor-sweeping wool skirt, a flounced, long-sleeved shirtwaist, a handful of bone hairpins that let her thick and frowsy hair cascade to her waist while her lifted arms disclosed tufts of reddish hair. Next came a long skirt-chemise, a flannel petticoat, black cotton stockings and the gartered, bone-strutted corset, a pair of bust pads and, last, a pair of baggy, knee-length drawers decorated around the bottoms of the legs with crochet-

ing. Yard goods being scarce on the frontier, the drawers,
like those of many a ranch wife, were made of flour
sacks.

How in *hell* could she work all day in that rig, over
a steaming wash boiler, elbow deep in harsh suds and
hot water!

When she stood naked in the warm light, her figure
had altered. Freed of restraint, it was no longer pinch
waisted, and round hipped. It was thick waisted, mot-
tled white, and that seductive, shadowed bosom, down
which he had peered avidly during business discussions
about dirty shirts, now resembled two large, round,
hardtack biscuits, each with a raisin in the middle. He
was repelled—but she was female and white, and the
urge was on both of them.

She panted and grunted under him, slippery with
sweat, and would have clung to him lovingly when it
was quickly over, for an interlude of loving chitchat
before another go at it, but he got up and dressed
and managed somehow to take his departure without
hurting her feelings.

Feeling unclean, he closed the door behind him and
stepped into the moonlight. And First Sergeant Eddie
Burke slugged him in the left eye and knocked him reeling backward against the wall, half stunned. Burke
made the mistake of taking time to call him filthy
names, and reiterate that he had warned Neil to stay
away from Miz Killian—and somehow Neil got set to
meet his charge. With fierce joy and gut-deep satisfaction
such as he had not got from Molly Killian, he leaned inside Burke's roundhouse right, pulled him close, butted
him hard on the chin, and ripped two savage right
hooks into Burke's belly, high, just under the ribs.

Burke grunted, stumbled back, sat down hard, and
vomited over his sprawled legs. He rocked, clutching
his belly, strangling for breath. Whitey came around the
corner of the house, and Neil caught the glitter of the
knife in his hand. He snatched up a chunk of firewood
and backed against the door, behind which Molly was
shrieking like a banshee. The stable guard shouted, and

a sentry over on Officers' Row answered, and running footsteps pounded toward Suds Row.

Whitey grabbed Eddie Burke's arm, hauled him to his feet and dragged him, bent over and staggering, behind the house. Neil threw the chunk of pine at them, and slunk behind Mrs. Bannon's next-door shack and went the long way around, back to his tent.

First Sergeant Eddie Burke wouldn't forget those two hooks to the belly for a while. The odds were that he was spitting up a little blood, right now.

CHAPTER 3

For two days, Eddie Burke got out of his bunk only to make his way painfully to the latrine behind the non-coms' quarters. Neil Douglas, with his purple left eye still swollen almost shut, happened to find him there.

In the four years of Neil's two enlistments, there had been many a time when he had held himself in check and endured Burke's provocations. Punishment would have been harsh had he broken a couple of Sergeant Burke's ribs, because any West Point officer inevitably would have been prejudiced in favor of the Regular Army sergeant against the cowboy with sergeant's chevrons who didn't give a damn about the hallowed traditions of the Cavalry branch.

Now in the latrine, Neil asked Burke, politely, how he was feeling. From the effect of those two terrible hooks to the belly, Burke must surely have been forced to the conclusion that twenty pounds advantage in weight and three inches in reach weren't enough.

Burke stood and pulled up his pants, grimacing when he buckled his belt. He went out, saying, "When I feel better, I'm gonna beat the livin' Jesus outa you. You ain't gonna catch me with no sneak punch, next time."

The man actually believed those two paralyzing punches had been lucky accidents!

It had never been timidity that kept Neil off First Sergeant Burke, heretofore; and now he was ridden by a reckless impatience to get it over with, to call Eddie out like some gunslinger, and wreck him. He knew well enough what was working on him and didn't give a damn that it was the same rot, the same breakdown of discipline that was eating like acid into every man in Camp Verde—the boredom, the restriction to the company of each other, the sudden irritation at the way a man chewed his rancid bacon, or maybe the tilt of his hat.

The weather only added to the sour dispositions—fat, white, cumulus clouds piled miles high in the northwest against a burning sky so blue it hurt the eyes; the ingrown world of Camp Verde hushed, tense, waiting for the stabbing violet lightning, the crash of thunder, the smashing downpour that would lift the weight of still, dead air and drop the temperature thirty degrees—but which held off and held off.

Even though the Camp Verde Indians were to be sent to San Carlos, there were thousands of Apaches on other reservations, and hundreds of Scouts still needed as police. Neil's second enlistment would be finished in three weeks, in the middle of July, and he thought he wouldn't sign up again, even though the major had offered him a first sergeant's hen tracks and five dollars more a month.

The paymaster brought the two months' back pay from Fort Whipple in an ambulance pulled by six mules with six troopers riding escort.

Two thirds of the camp got drunk in Shanty Town, and there were fights with civilians and brawls between troopers and dogfaces and soldiers and civilians and laundresses and whores: and the next day, the parade ground was occupied by men with brutal hangovers marching double guard duty, men bound and gagged with bars of yellow soap, men toting forty-pound logs for half a day, not permitted to put them down or to rest.

The morning of June twenty-sixth, Second Lieutenant Underhill's dogrobber came running for Sergeant Douglas with an urgent summons. Sergeant Eddie Burke, still sore in the belly, came trotting into the administration office right behind Douglas.

Second Lieutenant Wilbur Underhill was a shavetail fresh from West Point, and Douglas had wondered why the Army kept turning them out, while it was letting the old-timers go. Tall and gangling and pink-faced, Regulations and Manuals and the History of the Cavalry Branch were the be-all and end-all of his humorless existence. He was Major Trumbull's adjutant, that unlucky officer upon whom devolved all the details of command, of supply, of discipline, the slavey of the post, and now very important because Major Trumbull and Captain Eastwood and their feuding wives had fled to Fort Whipple to escape the depressing conditions at Camp Verde, and the lieutenants commanding Troops K and L were off somewhere on a hunting expedition.

Lieutenant Underhill was excited. Some reservation Apaches had brewed up a batch of tulapai, or a bootlegger had got to them. And Sergeants Burke and Douglas certainly were aware of what liquor did to Indians! Why, they even got to fighting among themselves! Killed each other even, sometimes! And fell into their fires, and threatened the agent and BIA officials, and stole stock, and ran away and killed miners and ranchers! And women and children!

Neil interrupted. "How many, sir? How long ago?" The lieutenant hadn't said the Apaches had jumped the reservation, but if it had been no more than a drunken brawl, the agent would have taken care of it with his Indian police.

"Now don't go off half cocked!" the lieutenant said.

"We'll go over your orders as soon as I write them up."

"Lieutenant, sir!" Neil said. "Minutes count, maybe. Are they armed? Have they got horses?"

Eddie Burke said, "You get the facts, Neil. I'll get my boys, and get word to yours."

They both knew their personal feud was postponed.

Burke saluted the lieutenant, did a fine about-face and marched out, with the lieutenant sputtering, "Sergeant Burke! Just a minute, there! Sergeant ——"

"Sir," Neil said, "I'll pass on your orders. How many broncos, sir?"

Lieutenant Underhill said, "I'll put that sergeant on report! Now, listen! Draw fifty rounds per man. Three days' field rations. Bring those renegades back, Sergeant! Dead or alive! They're dangerous! They took a shot at the agent! It has always been suspected that all arms were not turned in when they surrendered, and that——"

"Sir," Neil interrupted. "Sergeant Burke has been through this many times. Please, sir! If you know how many, and where . . ."

The lieutenant glared at him. "God damn you, Sergeant, don't tell me my job!" He waited to see if Neil would continue his insubordination, and Neil waited for the information. After a moment, the lieutenant said, "Five or six of them, that's the word I got. They have horses, two troop horses stolen from your stupid Indian police. And others." He was getting together printed forms, and pen and ink, while Neil stood fuming.

"Four copies," the lieutenant said. "Four of everything!"

Burke yelled his name, outside, and Neil said, "With your permission, sir," and trotted out, with Lieutenant Underhill squawking behind him, "Wait, damn it! I haven't written up the orders! Sergeant Douglas, damn it!"

Good old Chalk Eye was there on his Morgan troop horse. Instead of a saddle, he was sitting on a couple of grain sacks and a folded blanket strapped onto his mount: but offsetting the lightness of his gear were three full belts of cartridges for his Springfield Long Tom, one around his wrinkled old middle and one over each shoulder, crossing on his chest. He was holding Neil's big bay, which packed all the regulation gear except the two spare horseshoes, the curry comb and brush, and the picket-pin in the saddlebags. Chalk Eye would already have put spare magazines for Neil's Spencer carbine in the saddlebags, and coffee and canned fruit and vegetables. The thirty-foot lariat, wrapped around itself in the shape of a long sausage, hung from a ring on the near side of the cantle of the McClellan saddle. The blanket roll, with a two-quart can shoved over its end for making coffee, was strapped behind the cantle, and a canteen and tin cup were snapped onto a saddle ring by means of a short sling; but Chalk Eye had not fastened the regulation dog-tent roll across the pommel. Attached to the quarter strap on the off side was a small, open leather socket, to keep the carbine, slung muzzle down across the rider's back, from beating him black and blue. The saddle itself was cinched over a heavy, blue saddle blanket. The horse wore his halter under the bridle, its lead rope tied to the cinch ring. Neil's Indians often chided him for encumbering himself with all this gear; but no white man (except Whitey) could move and fight or even exist with as little as Apaches carried. When *they* lacked food and equipment, they ate their horses, made waterbags of their intestines, and kept going.

Yellow Face was there, and Chiquito, and Limpy came galloping up as Neil climbed into his saddle. Chalk Eye told him that Chulito was off chasing a girl, a Yavapai living over on Pinto Mesa. Five of Burke's Indians, including Whitey, as lightly burdened as Neil's, were there, mounted and restless and ready. Eddie Burke had managed to convert himself, in about ten minutes, into an Apache buck, even to turquoise earrings in his pierced lobes, all vestiges of regulation equipment discarded except his carbine. All he lacked was the tangled hair hanging to his shoulders.

He asked, "What he say, Neil? Where they gone? How many?"

"Hell, he don't know anything, only some of 'em jumped the reservation," Neil said. "All he said was there's six or seven of 'em, and some of 'em got drunk and took a shot at the agent. They got guns and horses. I didn't wait any longer."

He spurred his mount lightly, and the bunch of them went into a trot. It was about two P.M., and the two under-strength troops were sweating out monkey drill on the parade ground, and the dogfaces slogging around on foot, with the sergeants bellowing unintelligible orders.

They shortcut to the road across a gravelly flat where creosote bush grew spaced out as though by measurement. A gaggle of squaws scattered, dropping their digging sticks as the Scouts loped across a stony field of potatoes and squash. A dozen antelope went skittering away like dry leaves in a breeze. Neil spurred up beside Burke and said, "What you think?" He had no lack of respect for the First Sergeant's professional skills.

"We'll circle the reservation till we cut sign, I'll send Naquis in to find out maybe who it is and where they're heading."

Neil felt good, for the first time in months he felt good, with his Apaches ranging alongside him, and a job to be done. They were joking and laughing, their spirits as high as his. This was old times, again.

Chalk Eye, with the blind white eye in the deep, scarred socket, saw the smoke. He always saw it before anyone else, smoke, or tracks, or a twig that had been cut by a horseshoe, or one that had been only bent by an unshod hoof. All of them saw things before Neil did, and that included Burke. The difference was that none of them had as good judgment or solid horse sense as he did.

The smoke was a long way off, just a thread dispersing in the afternoon breeze somewhere in Smith Valley, where the road to Prescott and Fort Whipple ran.

The first thing they found was a pain-crazed mule bashing blindly around in the brush by the road. A hunk of meat had been hacked off its rump, and whoever did it hadn't bothered to kill the mule—and that meant Apache. Not wanting to alert their quarry, Neil didn't shoot it, but had to rope it before he could cut its throat, an act the Scouts and Burke considered chicken hearted.

A half hour later, they found the big freight wagon and trailer burned out, smoldering, grain sacks broken and spilled, new army uniforms strewn about, slashed and ruined, cases of canned fruit broken open, every can hacked with a hatchet, the harness of the ten-mule hitch cut to pieces, five dead mules; and the skinner tied upside down to a wagon wheel with his peeling head only inches above the coals of a fire, and twelve bullets in him, fired at point-blank range. They had amused themselves otherwise with the swamper—had let him run, and had galloped alongside him whacking him with a hatchet, letting him get up again when he stumbled and fell, seeing how long he could hold out.

The Scouts said there were eight of them, and two were boys, or maybe women—something about the weight the horses were carrying, some subtle indication invisible to Neil, but not for a moment doubted in his mind. They continued to follow the road west toward Prescott until they came to where the renegades had cut away into the chaparral, heading south.

Dusk was beginning to spill into the arroyos and washes. Eddie Burke said the renegades were obviously aiming to cross the Black Hills by going up Cherry Creek, and maybe raid the miners by Lynx Creek or the farmers in Chino Valley. The Scouts would go after them at daybreak.

Neil said the only thing obvious was that Burke didn't know what they were going to do. As for him, he wasn't going to let the Apaches lead him around by the nose, point him where they wanted him to go, which wouldn't be anywhere near where they were going. Instead of jumping to some damn fool conclusion, they'd better just follow the sign, in the morning.

His opposition made Burke stubborn, as always,

and Burke's anxiety to prove Neil wrong had been detrimental to his better judgment before now. He offered to bet that he was right, and Neil said, "Hell, I've bet you on jawbone before. You're broke already, and I'd never get paid."

Two Indians stretched lariats around a few junipers to make a corral for the horses, which would get no feed or water this night. Limpy made a small, smokeless fire of mesquite bark, in a hole beside a rock. While they pounded hardtack into powder, weevils and all, to mix it with coffee (which was the only way possible to reduce its rocklike structure to edibility), Chalk Eye motioned Neil aside without drawing attention and gabbled at him in Apache.

Neil said, "Talk Spanish," and the old boy switched languages. He said he had heard that old Gallo and his son and son-in-law had brewed up a batch of tulapai, in the brush back of their wikiup on the reservation, and that Gallo belonged to the Oak Creek Band, just below the mouth of Live Oak Canyon. He said Burke was stupid, and Gallo was leading them astray, and any damn fool should know that tomorrow his tracks would fade out in some rocky canyon or creek, and he'd swing north.

Long since, Neil had learned to listen to the ugly old man. He told Chalk Eye they would turn back in the morning, and the hell with what Burke thought or said or ordered.

The moon, huge and distorted, slid up the sky from behind the Mogollon Rim, diminishing rapidly in speed and size. The men rolled smokes and wrapped themselves in blankets wherever they could find enough clear space in the scatter of sharp-edged malpais. Burke peed the fire out.

Two or three coyotes, sounding like a dozen, cackled and squalled, announcing either the death of a cottontail or frustration at its escape. As if in answer, a wolf howled far away, deep and musical and hair-raising. Neil's elation at the break in the deadly routine of Camp Verde had dissipated. He lay lonely and depressed, alien to his companions, a bunch of stone age savages whose lives had been devoted to raiding and killing, and still were, and a half-blood who, out of envy, or who knew what, had always tried to ride him roughshod, and now hated him because of a promiscuous laundress who wouldn't fornicate with Indians, and a couple of blows in the belly. And that was it. Not a friend in the world.

The gray dawn was cold. The Indians stumped around, ill-tempered, clumsily making a fire and opening cans with sheath knives while trying to keep their blankets wrapped around themselves. Neil had a long drink from his canteen, and poured the rest of the water into his hat and gave it to his horse—the only animal to be watered that morning. He found a patch of coarse grass and picketed the horse there, while he ate a mush of hardtack and coffee, a can of rubbery sliced peaches, and two slices of rancid bacon. Burke kept yammering at everybody to hurry up, that the renegades would be long gone. The Scouts ignored him. When they had eaten and mounted, Neil said, "Chalk Eye, Yellow Face, Chiquito, Limpy . . . come on. This is a false trail. We'll have a look along the river. Find out where they doubled back."

Eddie Burke said, "Cut out the crap! We're losing time!"

Neil thumped his horse with his left heel, turning it, and began to pick a way through the rocks and chaparral, with his four Indians following. Burke yelled, "God damn you, you're under my orders, you hear?"

Neil made a noise like a horse breaking wind, with his tongue between his pushed-out lips. Chalk Eye did the same, and giggled, and the five of them rode away north.

They crossed the road about nine o'clock, and made their way through very rough going to the Verde River, and turned to follow it northwest. They rode in the shallows to avoid the brush, and kept watching for tracks entering or crossing the stream, but found none. Neil didn't expect any yet. If Chalk Eye was right, and the

fugitives were Gallo and his family, and they were going
to try to make it to Live Oak Canyon, they would still
be back there, south and west somewhere, and the best
thing was to push on fast, stay well ahead, and lay an
ambush at Grasshopper Flat, which was hemmed in by
red rock cliffs and would force any riders to cross the
open area.

They turned north along Oak Creek, but soon had to
leave it and make a wide swing west because the creek
ran out of a canyon, past Sugarloaf, that was so steep-
walled and boulder-strewn, even a man on foot could
hardly have traveled it. They found a wagon track that
led them north, out of the rough going, and a little
past noon, with horses and men in a lather of sweat,
they were loping through knee-high grass. There were
low hills ahead, thick with round juniper trees and
piñón pines. Neil called a halt to rest the horses.

On the wagon track again, they went at a steady
lope until they were through the hills and looking down
onto the flat valley, Grasshopper Flat, with Oak Creek
cutting through it, lined with cottonwoods, sycamores and
willows; and north, the vertical cliffs of red sandstone
topped by four hundred solid feet of white rock. They
took to the talus slopes at the foot of the cliffs on the
west, and rode slowly, threading their way among fall-
en blocks of rock and spiky maguey and prickly pear
until they came to a ruin, a thousand-year-old cliff dwelling, three rooms of ancient adobe and stone, with the
pine roof beams still there, the structure on a ledge
against the base of the cliff at the top of a high talus
slope. Like every prehistoric dwelling Neil had seen,
this one commanded a magnificent view. His Indians
had a horror of such places and the ghosts of the Old
Ones that occupied them. They tied their horses to junipers, and settled down to wait.

Neil tied his horse out of sight of anyone traversing
Grasshopper Flat, and climbed the forty-five degree
slant of the talus up to the ruin, at the last going on
hands and knees up a steep, natural ramp, then climbing a vertical sandstone wall by means of the "Moqui"

handholds cut there by the ancients. Had there been time, he would have examined the two metates and a scattering of manos and potsherds and chips of flint, the refuse of arrow point manufacture, but now he settled himself to watch.

They came, about four o'clock, winding in and out the cottonwoods, following the convolutions of Oak Creek. For concealment, they had stayed with the creek and not followed the wagon track along which Neil's party had come. There were five of them, not eight, as Chalk Eye had said yesterday. They were leading four mules loaded with loot from the freight wagon, and they had been pushing their horses too hard. The mules must have slowed them down in the rough going along the creek, and kept them worried about pursuit. The horses were about done, and the renegades were pounding their rumps with gun butts and heavy sticks.

Neil tossed a pebble down the slope, and Limpy peered up at him from his concealment under a fat juniper tree. Neil pointed down toward the renegades, then waited until they disappeared into a thicket of willow before he got down from his vantage point and carefully descended the vertical rock face, and made his way down the talus to his horse. He got two extra, tubular magazines of seven cartridges each from the saddlebags and tucked them under his belt, in back where they wouldn't interfere with bending over or running. When he got to the bottom of the long slope, going carefully to avoid starting rocks rolling, his men were already out of sight, flitting along the base of the cliff to get ahead of the renegades and find a wash or arroyo that would lead them, unseen, to the creek. Their horses were left tied, because no Apache fought on horseback unless he had to. Neil followed as fast as he could go, scrambling, slipping on the loose gravel and the poor footing.

Firing broke out before he could get into the fight. He took two hurried shots at a man clinging to the neck of a stampeding troop horse, which went plunging in great leaps through the brush by the stream. The horse went crashing down, and the rider didn't appear. The firing was heavy, and Neil was sure he had missed—but someone must have got him. In five minutes, it was over. Of Neil's band, only Chiquito had been touched, a shallow gouge across his left cheekbone.

As Chalk Eye had predicted, the dead men were Gallo and his son and son-in-law. There was another man of the Oak Creek band, and a Tonto—Number C-18 —according to the triangular wrist bangle he wore. Gallo's son couldn't have been more than twelve or thirteen.

One of the stolen troop horses was dead, the one Neil had seen go down. The other was so used up, spurred and bloody and beaten beyond any chance of recovery that Neil shot it. The three underbred Indian ponies were in better condition, and Yellow Face tied them to trees, as spoils of battle. The mules were in bad shape; but being mules, they would recover.

The Indians were dispersed in the brush, searching the five bodies, and Neil called them together. He said in Spanish, "We'll camp here and rest the mules and horses all day tomorrow. Next day, we'll pack the bodies back to Camp Verde. I'll go upstream, now, and find a good camp spot. You drag them all together and pile brush on them so the coyotes won't get at them."

Yellow Face, looking sullen, told him the bodies would be stinking too much if they lay in the heat all day tomorrow. "Anyway," he said, "who wants them? Let the coyotes have them! We know who they are, and we have the identification tags."

"No," Neil said. "The smell isn't anything new to you. It won't hurt you. But the tags aren't enough. Major Trumbull won't believe us, without the bodies. They could have bought us off and headed for Mexico. Now go ahead! Cover them up! And unload the mules and water them and picket them on good grass."

None of them moved. They looked as stubborn and pigheaded as only Apaches could. Neil went back for his horse and led it a quarter mile upstream and found a pleasant spot where there were grass and wild flowers, and a huge old cottonwood hanging over the creek. He built a small fire and set coffee on to boil.

In a half hour, his Indians rode in, dismounted, stripped their horses and picketed them on the lush turf. They were still sullen. Neil asked, "Did you cover them well?"

Chalk Eye took five wrist bangles from a fold of the sash that held up his breechclout, and dropped them beside Neil, where he sat on a rock, drinking coffee. The old man walked back to where he had tied his horse, called to Yellow Face, and each picked up one of the grain sacks Chalk Eye had brought along for a saddle pad—but the sacks were no longer empty. The Apaches lugged them over and dumped out five tangle-haired, bloody Apache heads.

Neil gulped and got to his feet.

Yellow Face was spouting Apache, an angry outburst of grunts and gutturals. Chalk Eye said in Spanish, "You think Major Trumbull will believe these?"

There were times, with Apache Scouts, when you damn well just keep your mouth shut. And things such as severed heads weren't entirely new in Neil's experience. He said, "Hang them in a tree, but not here. Over there somewhere."

They had eaten, and shadows were lengthening across Grasshopper Flat, and Neil had passed his tobacco and papers around, when they heard the horses on the wagon track. In seconds, no one was in sight around the dying fire. The only sound was the metallic, double click of the hammer being eared back on a Springfield Long Tom— and another—and another.

Down the wagon track, First Sergeant Eddie Burke yelled, "Neil! Don't get scared! It's us!"

In a few minutes he rode in with his men. Whitey was carrying a grain sack like Chalk Eye's two, with a similar load—the heads of a very old man, a woman, a girl of fifteen or so—all relatives of the heads in Chalk Eye's sacks.

With a contemptuous look at Neil, Whitey rolled them out of the sack. Burke turned them over with his foot, so that the faces were uppermost, the girl's eyes staring straight up. He said, "So I was right, huh? You goddamn stupid go chasin' off when I tell you keep goin' this morning. So we got us three goddamn 'Pache, huh? An' you got nothin' but sore ass from ridin' nowhere all day, huh?"

"Yeah," Neil said. "Fine bunch of fighting men you got there," and Burke's dark face flushed a little darker.

Whitey mistrusted the expressions on the faces of Neil's Scouts. He glanced hastily around, then muttered something to Burke and pointed with his outthrust lower lip at Chalk Eye's sacks, hanging from the limb of a sycamore thirty yards downstream.

Neil's men were laughing at Burke now, and doubt spread over his face, comically, like the expression of some amateur actor registering consternation. He turned away, turned back, started to speak, and stalked away. Yellow Face and Chiquito and Limpy and Old Chalk Eye were roaring with laughter, harder than Neil had ever heard Indians laugh, and yelling taunts after the Burke faction, which, sullen and glowering, had mounted and turned its horses downstream.

Shortly after dawn, Neil was lying sprawled in his blankets, his shoulder supported by a round boulder, cigarette in one hand and cup of coffee in the other, as he contemplated the luxury of a full day lying around in the shade before returning to the bickering and boredom of Camp Verde. Then Chalk Eye came trotting into the camp, nearly inarticulate with rage. He yelled at Neil in Apache, and Neil said, "Talk Spanish!"

Chalk Eye screeched, *"They're gone!* That Whitey! I know his footprint! Burke, too!"

"Who's gone?"

"The heads! Our heads!"

They saddled hurriedly, and Neil led them at a gallop to where Burke's bunch was camped, a quarter mile downstream. All Burke's men knew was that Burke and Whitey had slipped out of camp very early—the moon was still up—had come back a little later carrying Chalk Eye's sacks, and got their horses and rode out.

Neil yelled, "Come on!" and his men charged through the camp, scattering Indians and the coffeepot and the fire, and galloped a mile down the wagon track before Neil held up his hand to stop them. They couldn't leave four government mules and assorted loot from the burned wagons at the mercy of Burke's Apaches.

Anyway, it was less than twenty miles back to Camp Verde. They'd never catch Burke and that white freak of his.

CHAPTER 4

During the twenty-mile ride back to Camp Verde, Douglas's Indians gabbled and gobbled. Their hand talk, which Neil understood better than their speech, was plain enough, adding exclamation points to their vilification of Sergeant Burke and his thieving gang. There was going to be a hell of a row—and if his Indians killed a couple of Burke's, there might be such an uproar as would resound clear back to the General Staff in Washington. He couldn't let anything serious happen. But Eddie Burke was going to learn a few facts of life, out behind the enlisted men's barracks.

There'd be no use in crying to Lieutenant Underhill about Burke, himself, being bamboozled by the renegades, and then stealing Gallo's head and the other grisly evidence. It would be Burke's lies against Neil's claims, and Burke had the proof. And it would never enter the minds of Neil's Apaches to protest to authority—it wasn't Lieutenant Underhill that filched those heads right out from under them, like a gopher snake stealing eggs from a broody hen; it was Sergeant Eddie Burke and his semi-slave Whitey.

Neil yelled, "Keep those jugheads moving, you baboons!" and his Indians quit chattering, wondering what he was sore at *them* for. The four worn-out mules were being pushed to the limit already, the Scouts whacking them with quirts as automatically as they kept thumping their spurless heels into the ribs of their horses. When they rode across the parade ground, the welcoming committee was out in force. Neil had been hoping that Major Trumbull and Captain Eastwood would be there, returned from their strategic retreat to Fort Whipple—but only Eddie Burke and Second Lieutenant Underhill stood on the veranda of headquarters, Burke grinning and Lieutenant Underhill looking very severe indeed. Troopers were standing around, grinning too, and Burke's savages were as close to open laughter as an Apache ever allowed himself to come, in the presence of white-eyes.

Underhill couldn't wait in dignity for Neil to dismount and come to him. He strode down the two steps, and Chulito dropped off his horse onto the back of a Burke Apache, hauled him down, and had a knife at his throat in a half second. Neil swung his leg over his pommel and dropped onto Chulito with both feet. Indians were yammering at each other; troopers, itching for any excuse, were punching Indians; mules were squealing and kicking. Neil pulled Chulito off his victim by the hair. The lieutenant bawled for the guard and grabbed Neil's collar, jerking at him. Chalk Eye, reeling from a blow, stumbled against Lieutenant Underhill, and Underhill, still clutching Neil's collar, kicked the old man in the ribs. Chalk Eye crouched. There was a skinning knife in his hand, held low and edge up. He shuffled toward the lieutenant, hissing softly like a boiling teakettle, and Neil swore at him, stopping him, while he grabbed the lieutenant's thumb and bent it back, breaking his hold. He doubled Underhill's arm behind his back and shoved him out of the melee. The lieutenant was digging in his heels, but Neil moved him as far as the steps of the veranda and let him go, saying, "Lieutenant, you're a half-wit! You're lucky to be alive!"

"I'll have you court-martialed!" Underhill snarled. "Failure of duty! Refusal of orders! Laying around in the shade at Oak Creek while Sergeant Burke brought me the heads of those savages!"

He was so nearly out of control that he raised a hand to slap Neil's face.

"I'll knock you on your ass!" Neil told him, and Lieutenant Underhill's face went white at the shock of such disrespect—but he lowered his hand.

"That old man was going to kill you," Neil said. "For God's sake, couldn't you see it?"

Slowly the realization came to the lieutenant. He stared into Neil's eyes, while the racket behind them subsided, the guard having separated the two groups of Scouts, who stood shuffling around threatening and insulting each other.

"I'll put him under arrest," Underhill said. "You, too, Douglas! For threats to me. For insubordination, for dereliction of duty! Sergeant Burke told me. You disobeyed *him,* and went off on your own, taking half the force. And after he killed the renegades, he found you comfortably camped at——"

"My title is Sergeant," Neil said. "And you won't put Chalk Eye in the guardhouse, nor me, neither."

"I'll not only put you both there," Underhill said, "we'll spread-eagle you on a wheel for a while, just to——"

"Lieutenant," Neil broke in, "if you never read General Crook's order concerning the treatment of Scouts, you better do it. In the first place, you try anything like that and you'll have some dead men on your hands, and they won't all be Apache. The rest of 'em'll just disappear like smoke . . . and won't Major Trumbull be pleased when he comes back and finds no Scouts, but only a pink-faced shavetail that messed up the whole stinking camp while he's gone!"

The lieutenant's face went from white with shock to

red with rage. He stuttered incoherently and pulled his
fist back again. Neil shifted his feet half an inch,
dropped his chin behind his left shoulder and cocked
his right fist. Sergeant Eddie Burke grabbed his shoulders from behind and pulled him off balance. While Neil
fought the sergeant's powerful grip, Burke said, "He's
right, Lieutenant. But when Major Trumbull gets back,
you just tell him about Douglas's little rest camp by
the creek, while me and my men was——"

Neil drove his right elbow back, hard, under Burke's
breast bone, precisely where he'd hit him with those
two hooks that had put him in bed for two days. Burke
fell backward down the two steps and scrambled up,
gasping for breath, trying not to show it. Tears of pain
were in his eyes, and he hunched his shoulders and drew
a long, gagging breath.

Neil said, "Underhill, Fish Eater here is a liar. All
the way, he's a liar, and you're going to find it out too
late."

Underhill started to speak, stopped, started again, and
Neil swung around to Burke. "You wanta go behind the
barracks and have a little talk, Fish Eater?"

Burke wasn't scared. Too cocky for that, and bigger
than Neil, and likely he really believed those two hooks
to the belly had been only lucky accidents. But his
belly was full of shooting pains and he still could hardly
breathe. He managed to say quite steadily, "Tomorrow
morning. I don't wanta take no advantage. You been
ridin' all day."

Neil said, "All right, Fish Eater, if you can climb out
of your bunk. Just so you don't get there late, like at
Oak Creek."

"I'm gonna kill you, Neil," Burke said. "All legal,
with my hands."

Grinning, Neil turned back to the lieutenant. "He
don't like that 'Fish Eater.' It's the worst thing you can
call an Apache. Something in their religion. I'll give
you a tip, Lieutenant. Some time when you catch a
bronco and want information, you'll never get it by
skinning him slow or pulling his fingernails out. Just

catch a catfish and pry open his mouth and tell him you're gonna cram it in. He'll spill his guts. He'll give you his daughter and his right arm."

"Burke's no Apache," Underhill said. "He's Irish. He told me himself!"

"My God!" Neil said, and stared at him as though he were an imbecile. "You ain't *weaned* yet!"

"You listen to me, *Sergeant* Douglas!" the lieutenant said. "I can't allow grudge fights! You know the regulations! But you can put on the gloves, and I'll referee. I used to box, you know! I was light heavy champion of West Point! And we'll go by the rules. I'll see to that!"

Neil said, "Light heavy champ of West Point? Man, you *really* ain't weaned!"

He shoved Burke aside and collected his five savages and herded them to their tent.

Major and Mrs. Trumbull and Captain and Mrs. Eastwood returned from Fort Whipple that evening.

The next norning Neil stood in clean clothes, shaved and clean in person, but slouching and unsoldierly as a point of honor, before the major, seated at his desk.

Major Trumbull said, "Well, Neil, Underhill put in a pretty bad report about you, and your part in catching old Gallo and his boys. I straightened him out about trying to discipline any Indian Scouts, and read him General Crook's order. No trouble there. But about you . . . well, you know that even as a civilian scout, you can't talk to a U.S. Army officer the way you did, and you can't push him around, the way you did when he stepped in to stop that brawl. And if you can't keep your Indians under control, I'll have to take steps. And don't think I won't."

"Major Trumbull," Neil replied, "my time's up on the fifteenth. I'll behave. But don't push me, either. Because you I'll obey. You I respect. Same goes for Captain Eastwood. But don't put me in that lieutenant's path. And that's all I got to say."

The major pushed an ink stand back and forth on his desk, then looked up at Neil. "What about a transfer?"

he asked. "Raise in pay. Rank of first sergeant, over at San Carlos, with Seiber. He can use a man like you. And that gets you away from Lieutenant Underhill and Eddie Burke both."

"I guess not, sir," Neil said. "Field campaigns, they're fine, but not this garrison duty. All the Scouts are doing at San Carlos is stewing in their own juice, like here, and once in a while bringing in some renegade, like we did Gallo and them other three."

"*We* did, Neil? Don't you mean Burke did, and you let yourself get sidetracked? According to Lieutenant——"

Neil interrupted, "Sure, Burke brought in them seven heads. But haven't you got *any* idea at all what triggered off that ruckus between Burke's Indians and mine? You think it just happened, like two bull elk running together by accident? And you think I jerked the lieutenant around just for nothing at all? What would you think if I told you that he'd've had his guts spilled all over the yard there, if I hadn't dragged Chalk Eye off him? And that Lipan of Burke's, why you think I pulled Chulito off him when Chulito was about to slice his windpipe? No sir, this camp has gone to hell, Major, and I'm sick of it, and while there's nobody else around to hear me, I'll tell you if you got no ideas about what happened, why then I'll tell you I *used* to respect you."

He turned to go, but the major called him back. "Sit down," he said. "Too early in the morning for a drink?" He got a bottle of good whiskey and two glasses from a drawer in his rolltop desk.

They downed their shots, and Major Trumbull poured two more. "I'll think it all over," he said. "You do that, too. Now here's something else. Everybody knows you and Eddie Burke aren't exactly wallowing in brotherly love, and the word is that you're going to beat each other's brains out, later today."

"The word's wrong," Neil said. "I'm gonna beat *his* out."

The major smiled. "If I hadn't heard a few things in Prescott, I'd think you were . . . well . . . I can't watch it, as it stands. But I put a hundred dollars on you, with Captain Eastwood. You want to tell me if I'm wrong?"

Neil thought it over. "Well, all right," he said. "I never said anything, because if I did, every goddamn Irish trooper on the post would wanta try me, and the way I am, sir, I'd never back down. Once I thought I might make a pile of money and quit punching cows, that's all. And I got nothing to prove to anybody. Only to Eddie Burke. I *owe* it to that son of a bitch to beat the living crap out of him."

He had a sip of his drink and Major Trumbull said, "A sergeant over at Whipple said you knocked down Gunboat Latvik. Said he saw you and Latvik on the same fight program, down in Tucson, and Latvik got a second-round knockout over the best heavyweight in the Army, and you fought a pro middleweight. And he couldn't come out for the third round."

"Well, sir, somehow I got a natural knack for hitting, some way my muscles and bones are put together. I mean nobody ever showed me how, not even Gunboat Latvik. He said nobody had to teach me how to hit, with either hand. He come to Prescott, well, that was almost six years ago, just traveling, betting on himself, and taking on all comers. He was a middleweight, and he was fighting light heavies and heavies, anybody at all, and he'd give a man ten dollars for every round he stood up to him . . . I don't mean just ran away from him, but would stand up and fight him.

"Well, I was kind of wild, you know, and brawling in the bars, and people got so they knew I could hit. So they got me to go against him. I really thought I was gonna take him, and I damn near did. Because, well, he was a tough boy, Major. I mean past his prime and a little potty around the belly and near blind in one eye and his ears like wads of dough . . . but you couldn't *hit* him! He'd weave and duck and slip punches and cross a right over yours and beat you to it. People used to yell at him to quit dancing, and they'd go to whistling waltzes. And whoever was in there with him would get excited and think if he could just hit

him once, and go charging at him, and that was it.
He'd stun you, coming in. He wasn't no one-punch
killer, but he'd club you and maul you and close your
eyes and step on your feet and butt you under the chin.
I mean *big* men, miners and muleskinners and loggers."

"Well, then," Major Trumbull said, ". . . here, let
me sweeten that for you." He reached for the bottle,
but Neil said, "No more, thanks. I'm gonna go find
Burke."

"But how did you——" the major asked, and Neil went
on, "Well, he just got careless, and I tricked him. Just before the first bell, I held up my right fist and pointed at
it, and I guess maybe he'd heard I hit pretty good with
my right. Because he kept circling to my left, circling and
playing with me, dodging my right-hand swings, never
taking his eye off my right hand . . . and just when he
was getting tired of fooling around with me, I hit him a
left hook he didn't even see. And honest, Major Trumbull, I thought for a minute there that I had killed him.
But he got up. He hauled himself up by the ropes, and
I hit him again, but not square, and he hung onto me
like a leech. Then he put his hand into my face and
shoved me away, grinding the heel of his hand into my
eyes, and when I rubbed my eyes, he hit me in the belly
like a horse kicked me. I got up, too. They told me I got
up four times, but I don't remember, except I got these
souvenirs."

Neil pointed to his scarred and thickened right eyebrow, the hump on his nose, and a crescent scar at the
corner of his mouth.

He told the major how Latvik, impressed by Neil's
punching power, had taken him on tour, brought him
along slowly, taught him to feint with head and hands
and shoulders, to shift and circle and stall and to hit in
linked combinations. Neil had won a dozen fights and a
good deal of money betting on himself and Latvik and
had taken a memorable beating from a huge miner in
Wickenburg after he broke his hand on the man's jaw.
That was before Latvik, drunk, got himself knifed in
an alley in Tucson. Neil had had enough. He had re-

turned to Prescott, and worked as a rider on the Windmill Ranch, and then enlisted in Crook's Indian Scouts.

Major Trumbull said, "You know I can't allow this brawl with Burke. It's my duty to prevent it."

"Now, Major, you never stopped one before, down back of the barracks."

The major said, "They're good for the boys. Let off steam. Let off pressure."

"Well then——" Neil began, and the major said, "First off, I couldn't watch it, and I wouldn't miss it for anything. Second, it's Lieutenant Underhill's duty, as adjutant, to do everything he can for the morale of this camp. He hasn't been able to do much . . . it's nearly impossible under the conditions. But he came up with one good idea . . . a sort of athletic competition, a track meet, for the Fourth of July. A fifty-yard foot race, and a hundred yard race, and a high jump. Tug of war between troopers and infantry, things like that. Might even have a couple of horse races."

"Yeah," Neil said. "He's been around trying to sign men up for it, and nobody gives a damn. All they want is to go into the town and get drunk, on the holiday. What do they care about the old Army spirit and that? Not the way this camp is now."

"It's different, now," Major Trumbull said. "Captain Eastwood and I and Lieutenant Mayer put up some prizes . . . two dollars for first, and a dollar for second . . . and a gallon of whiskey for the tug of war. And if you tell that to anyone, you'll cost me my rank."

"Well, it sounds fine, Major Trumbull," Neil said, "but I know what you're getting at, and I won't do it . . . not stand up there with a referee and all and box with Eddie. I told you, I got nothing to prove and I don't want to prove it to every dumbjohn Irish trooper that wants the glory of beating up an ex-pro, between now and July fifteenth."

"Well, you might as well have another slug," the major said, and poured the fourth one, "because if you fight him behind the barracks, I'll strip you of your hentracks. But I'm a fair man, and if you'll just box him an exhibition, let's say, to help out with the entertainment on the Fourth of July, so that Eastwood and I and the other officers may legally be present, I'll go quid pro quo, if you understand me. This feud between you and Eddie Burke . . . I'm afraid of it, and how it might wind up. So, if you fight—that is, if you'll box Eddie on Lieutenant Underhill's entertainment program—win, lose or draw, I'll give you your discharge and pay, predated to the fifteenth."

Neil grinned. "Has Captain Eastwood got any more loose cash? Will you lay another hundred with him for me? I'll bring it around later. Sir, take all the bets you can on a first round knockout."

Eddie Burke had been apprised of the plan, which suited him very well. It was not hard for Neil to needle him into a hundred-dollar bet, and double if Neil got him in the first round. Eddie borrowed and bullied the money from a number of troopers. Neil also laid out the last of his money at two to one, over three hundred dollars of poker winnings. Every civilian and soldier and officer from Prescott and Fort Whipple who could get there would be there.

The morning of the Fourth of July, 1875, dawned brilliant and hot. The camp was full of bustle and noise until noon, with no duties assigned to any soldier. The last of a dozen wagons and buggies and a sizable cavalcade, civilian and military, arrived from Prescott. About two P.M. the athletic contests began, and Neil, lying alone and relaxed in the tent, heard the catcalls and encouragement, and concerted roars of the spectators. About four P.M. Lieutenant Underhill came for him.

As Neil got up, Underhill said, "Well, God sakes, man, get ready! They're all there, waiting. Sergeant Burke and his second are already in the ring!"

"I'm ready," Neil said. "What's bothering you?"

"Well, my God," Underhill said, "Burke is stripped to the waist and in fighting togs, I mean the shoes and a sash and everything somebody brought from Prescott, but you——"

"I ain't gonna raise a sweat, Lieutenant," Neil said.

The only difference from his normal shirt and pants and boots was the substitution of tight-fitting moccasins.

There must have been three hundred people jammed around the makeshift platform of rough planks, twenty feet square, with the posts at the corners joined by three strands of heavy rope. A third of the crowd was civilians from Shanty Town and Prescott, sweltering in their hard hats and stiff collars that came almost to their ears, and being very gallant to a half-dozen overdressed fancy women. With Lieutenant Underhill forcing a path, Neil followed and stepped through the ropes.

Eddie Burke had seen some professional fighters. He was bouncing on his toes, squatting and leaping up, flexing his arms and shoulders. A broken-nosed trooper sat on his heels in Eddie's corner, beside a bottle of water and a bucket of water with a sponge in it. He had a towel draped over his forearm.

A hush settled, broken only by the maundering of a few already drunk soldiers. The two factions of Indian Scouts were behind the corners of their respective champions.

The crowd made a lot of noise, and the major held up his hand until it subsided. Before he could announce the rules, Neil said, "Sir, I asked you to hold stakes. Have you got it all?"

"Right here, Neil," the major said, patting his shirt pockets, both bulging.

He raised his voice: "This exhibition will continue until one man can't or won't answer the bell. Each round will continue until one man is knocked down, after which there will be an interval of one minute. Captain Eastwood will keep time, and handle the bell. Lieutenant Underhill will referee. Both fighters ready? Sergeant Douglas?"

Neil nodded.

"Sergeant Burke?"

"Let 'er rip!" Burke said.

There was a ragged cheer, a shuffle of excitement.

Neil held up his right fist, shook it, pointed at it, and the crowd went quiet. "Here's Taps for you, Fish Eater!" he yelled to Burke.

Trumbull looked at Captain Eastwood and said, "Ring the bell, John!"

Captain Eastwood struck the cowbell in his hand with a drumstick, and Sergeant Eddie Burke leaped from his corner, charged, and threw a vicious right hook, which Neil easily slipped, letting it whistle past by an eighth of an inch.

Neil shoved him back, grinding the palm of his left hand on Burke's nose and mouth, then grabbed the back of his neck and with his head shoved under Burke's uptilted chin, he growled, "You're a bag of wind, Fish Eater. You still think it was an accident that put you to bed for two days?"

Burke snarled, "I'm gonna beat your brains out!" and Lieutenant Underhill shoved between and pushed them apart.

He shook his finger at Neil and said, "We'll have no more of that butting!"

Neil missed a wild swing with his right, Burke danced and backed away with Neil following, telegraphing that wild right again and again. Burke had no trouble dodging, and began to circle smartly to his left to minimize the unlikely chance that one of the clumsy swings might land. Catcalls came from the crowd. Lieutenant Underhill made disgusted sounds, and Neil heard Captain Eastwood say, "That's a *pro?*"

Neil threw a quick glance at Major Trumbull, standing by Captain Eastwood. The major had a grin of unholy anticipation on his leathery face.

Burke's natural-born cockiness swelled into enormous self-confidence, and he began to amuse the spectators with fancy boxing on his toes in what he considered a very professional style—left fist extended, right fist against his chest cocked and ready, teetering back and forth, bobbing his head, and snorting explosively. He was grinning, too, in anticipation as delighted as that of Major

Trumbull, while he toyed with this clown who somehow had got the reputation of a fighter. He kept watching that wild right fist swing at his head . . . swinging . . . swinging . . . missing . . . missing . . . and Neil hit him with a left hook he didn't see coming, so hard that Neil felt the shock, himself, clear to his shoulder.

Neil turned away toward his corner, with Burke still on his feet—and behind him Burke smashed face down onto the planks.

In the stunned silence, Neil climbed through the ropes and held out his hands to Major Trumbull. Pandemonium erupted.

Major Trumbull put two handfuls of bills into Neil's hands, and Neil stuffed them into his pockets.

They threw a bucket of water over Eddie Burke, and rubbed the back of his neck and slapped his face. Neil shoved his way roughly through the crowd. Burke groaned, rolled over, sat up, realized what had been done to him, and bawled an obscenity. He got onto his hands and knees and tried to stand, but his elbows buckled, and he fell again onto his face. His bloody nose was flattened from that fall onto the planking, and his jaw was beginning to swell.

Neil walked away trailing admirers like the tail of a comet.

That evening, Neil went to the major's quarters and turned in his cap-and-ball six-gun and the Spencer carbine, the only issue items he possessed except his ruined pants and battered hat, and got receipts for them, and two weeks' pay in advance, which added to his bets and his winnings made nine hundred and sixty dollars, more money than he had ever owned at one time.

Major Trumbull gave him his discharge dated 15 July, 1875, eleven days early, and told him he could catch a ride in the morning, in a wagon returning to Fort Whipple.

They shook hands, and Major Trumbull said, "Sergeant . . . well, not anymore, huh? But Neil, seriously, you watch out for Eddie Burke. No man was ever more humiliated, and he'll never leave it at that. And that ratty white Apache of his hates you for what you did to his hero. You know *them* . . . it's all in the family, if you're Apache."

CHAPTER 5

Ex-sergeant Neil Douglas had no luggage. He owned a good skinning knife, a pair of razors and a shaving brush, and the faded clothes he wore—not even a pair of boots, only knee-high Apache moccasins under his yellow-striped pants—and a little more than nine hundred dollars in a money belt. He didn't have any friends to say goodbye to, either.

As the gray light of dawn filtered into the tent, only Chalk Eye had given him one limp, up-and-down handshake. Limpy had begged a smoke, grinned crookedly, and said, "You gone be cowboy, huh? Maybe Limpy gone put *you'* head in sack!" He considered that possibility very amusing.

After 5:30 reveille and breakfast, when 6 o'clock stable call sounded, Neil walked along with the troopers headed toward the stables, and stopped beside an escort wagon which had "U.S." and a number stenciled on its once-white canvas top.

Corporal Peter Paul Maher was cursing four mules as he tried to hitch them to the wagon. The mules, wall-eyed and nervous from the corporal's savage mood and clumsy handling, were ready to blow up. Neil talked to them softly and held the heads of the leaders steady, while Maher managed to untangle the off tug chain and hook it to the doubletree.

Neil asked, "You going to Whipple?"

"So if I am?"

Maher was about two hundred ninety pounds of belly and extra chins and fat thighs, surmounted by a bulbous head. His graying hair resembled a clump of rusting iron wire. It was said that he fastened his chevrons to his sleeves with hooks and eyes, so many times had he been busted for drunkenness—but the Cavalry kept its enlisted people so long as they could be used: the one-armed, the one-eyed, the rheumatic, the lame, and the halt.

"Jaysus!" Maher groaned. "The head I've got, I need an extension on me arm to scratch me ear! Ye wouldn't have the likes of a bottle would yez? No, that ain't the luck of Corporal Maher."

Neil looked into the feed box hung onto the tailgate. It was empty, and he went into the barn, lugged back a sack of barley, and dumped it in.

"Could yez handle a four-up hitch?" Maher pleaded. "I'm that sick I'm dyin' and no priest within a million miles."

"Where's your swamper?"

"In the guardhouse, where else? He won a month's pay on yez, an' we drunk it up. Peter Paul Maher can hold his liquor, an' that squarehead Dutchie can't."

"You water and feed these hammerheads?" Neil asked.

"Listen, ye miserable little squirt, drunk or sober, Maher's a teamster, an' don't yez forget it!"

Disgustedly, Neil said, "Go on, climb up if you can make it, and drive me over to Shanty Town before we start for Whipple."

Maher made no objection. There was booze to be had in Shanty Town. He seized the grab iron on the seat of the wagon, got one foot onto a wheel hub, and hauled himself aboard. He managed to unwind the reins from the brake arm and fell backward onto the spring seat, which canted to the right under the burden, like a ship with its cargo shifted. He freed the brake, yelled profanity at the mules, lashed the rumps of the wheelers with the rein ends, and almost went over the back of the seat as the mules hit their collars. Maher hauled the rig to a stop in front of the first saloon in Shanty Town, where a sign nailed to the sleazy shack of warped boards and dirty canvas roof announced: "GOOD WHISKEY, RUM, GIN, BRANDY, and tolerable water."

They had to wake the unshaven proprietor by pounding on the door and yelling. He swore and grumbled, until Neil told him what he wanted. Corporal Maher bought two double shots of "coffin varnish" and Neil told the owner to put it on his bill. Maher glowed with gratitude, while Neil began to haggle for a contraband Spencer Carbine and a Blakesly case of ten loaded tubes of cartridges. Almost every deserter sold his rifle or carbine for traveling money before decamping, and every honky-tonk and hog ranch in Shanty Town had them for sale. By the time Neil had checked the action and opened the breech and looked down the muzzle to find the rifling bright and unpitted and had haggled the man down to twenty-five dollars, Corporal Maher was beating time on the bar, and singing in a high, nasal tenor:

> "When the drums would roll
> Upon my soul
> This is the style we go,
> Forty miles a day
> On beans and hay
> In the Regular Army-O."

Somehow Neil managed to get the corporal into the wagon over the tailgate, where the fat man collapsed face down upon a heap of canned food, folded tarpaulins, a shovel, the wagon jack, an ax, mule halters and chain sidelines, a greasy flour sack that wrapped a half-slab of rancid bacon, three full canteens of water, and a fusty heap of empty grain sacks and filthy blankets.

In the seat, Neil took the reins, released the brake, and did his utmost to swear at the mules in imitation of all teamsters and skinners, because mules expected it, considered it a personal attention and their privilege. Some actually wouldn't start without it.

He didn't push the mules, but he didn't let them loaf along, either. Soon they were past the flat land around Camp Verde, and beginning the long climb up the increasing grades and tortuous switchbacks of "Crook's Road" running west across the Black Hills. Piñón pine began to appear among the round junipers with their sky-blue berries. Quail scuttled into the brush, a jackrabbit the size of a small hound leaped lazily ahead of the wagon, then took fright and went away in tremendous, stretching leaps.

Just to the south rose the hump of Squaw Peak, and beyond it the rugged Mazatzal range, sere and dry and forbidding. The grades got steeper and the turns sharper, and Neil pulled off the road to let a ten-mule jerkline freight rig pass, the mules on the inside of the curve nimbly skipping over the "Fifth Chain" as it tended to straighten out, then skipping back over it as the hundred feet of mules, wagon, and trailer, having negotiated the turn, swung back into line. The skinner riding the nigh wheeler let the jerkline lie slack in the collar rings, and the swamper released the brake pole of the trailer.

Before the sweet bells on the hoops fastened to the collars of the leaders had faded into silence, traffic began to overtake the escort wagon, coming from Camp Verde, people who had made the trip to see the one-punch fight yesterday; first, a captain of Cavalry in a hurry, pushing his horse intelligently to get the most out of it without hurting it; a couple of smart buggies with red wheels, drawn by magnificent horses; a couple of light wagons, canvas topped; and finally, a gaggle of over-dressed, overpainted fancy women, laughing, half drunk, parceled out among three surreys and their fashionable male contingents.

A long nooning to feed and water and rest the mules, at a spot of brilliant greenery where a spring welled from mossy rocks; a small fire, and coffee and crackers and canned peaches, and Corporal Maher emerging briefly to sit on a rock, struggling to get the bottle from under his sweat-blackened and reeking shirt, after which, sick and white-faced, he finished its contents, refused food, and had to be helped back to his sanctuary.

Neil buried the fire and the peach can and drove on slowly, passing the juncture with the rough road that ran south to the mining towns of Big Bug and Bumblebee, and camped early at Cherry Creek, not far below the six-thousand-foot crest of the Black Hills.

A circle of blackened rocks and a heap of rusted cans showed that others had camped here just off the road, under a large piñón pine not thirty yards from Cherry Creek, whose waters at this season were no wider than a man could step across, and lukewarm.

The mules were nickering softly, asking for water, and Neil, wary of shod hooves, unbridled and haltered them, and fastened the halters together mule to mule, with the six-foot halter chains. They wouldn't run off before they were watered and fed, but he took the precaution of shackling one of them with the Army's substitute for hobbles—a short chain fastened between one front and one hind cannon. Thus hampered, the four of them moved to the creek and drank. Neil admired mules. Horses, left to their own devices, would drink too much, too fast, after a hard haul up the mountain, bloat themselves and die. If Neil had let them, the mules would have had a good, back-easing roll, then a little water and a little grain, then a rest, another small drink, and repeat until they were satisfied. He fed them barley in their nose bags.

He built a small fire, found a coffeepot and coffee in the jumble in the wagon, and a half slab of bacon so old it was all stringy lean meat with no fat, wrapped in a greasy flour sack.

From the stink in the wagon, Corporal Maher had wet his pants. The odor of frying bacon stirred him out of his torpor, and he tried climbing backward over the tailgate and fell, lay for a moment as though dead, then struggled to his knees and managed to stand. To Neil's surprise, he had a full bottle.

He waved it at Neil and said, "Never downgrade

the luck of the Irish, son. I jist happent to find this under me hand whilst you an' that bloodsucker was hagglin' over that carbeen, back there in the gin mill." He pulled the cork with his strong teeth and had a huge gulp of whiskey.

As Neil finished eating, Corporal Maher, unable to climb back into the wagon, crawled under it, and lay in drunken sleep.

Before Neil climbed into the wagon and arranged a pile of grain sacks for a bed, he covered the great hulk with a blanket, hoping it wouldn't be attacked by scorpions, tarantulas, or more likely a Walapai Tiger, which insidious black beetle could insert its cone-nosed snout into a sleeper without waking him, suck blood, and leave as mementoes great suppurating yellow lumps that resembled fried eggs. Neil had never seen a drunken Walapai Tiger. Might be quite a sight.

In the morning, Maher drank coffee, threw it up, and managed to climb into the wagon with his half-empty bottle.

On the long road winding down the east side of the Black Hills, only one straining jerkline team of sixteen mules and a huge freight wagon, and one cavalcade of two prospectors and four pack horses passed the escort wagon. Corporal Maher wakened occasionally and cursed, only to resume snoring.

Neil Douglas had time for some reminiscences of his immediate past, and some bitter reflections about the way things were going in Arizona Territory that you couldn't do anything about; the treatment of humans that other humans considered subhuman; the crooked Indian agents and the bloody Tucson Gang hand in glove with the entrenched and heartless Bureau of Indian Affairs, battening off the Indians, fighting every effort by a few such men as General Crook to extend a hand to the defeated Apaches and help them to become self-sufficient; keeping the Indians idle in internment camps instead of farming and raising stock; crooked ranchers and contractors cheating in the supplying of rations and beef to the reservations, and cold-bloodedly stirring up trouble for the sole purpose of keeping a large military force in the field so they could sell it hay, grain, beef, and firewood.

But what the hell! Neil himself had had a bellyful of campaigning and starving and thirsting and risking the only neck he owned, and living with a handful of Indians, themselves killers by nature and inclination. If he had to be honest about it, there was a great majority of decent and humane whites, only they weren't organized like the thieves; and it was not by coincidence that "Apache" meant "the enemy" to all other tribes, and they had been murderers and raiders long before the miners and the ranchers came. It was too easy to get righteous and wrong about either side.

Now down on the level, the mules lifted into a trot, passing through Point of Rocks, the weird jumble of house-size, weather-rounded, granite boulders just east of Fort Whipple. After passing the post gardens, where men toiled who had never enlisted to hoe weeds and tend potatoes, beets, cabbage, and melons, and where thumped away a steam-driven pump pulling good, cool water from a well, the fort itself came into view—the administration buildings, the hospital, the quarters and barns and stables, all neat and military against the background of rounded hills black with piñón and ponderosa pine, all a vast improvement over the unpeeled log buildings and the falling-down log palisade and the one, unpainted board house that had been General Crook's headquarters four years ago, when Neil enlisted.

Troops were at monkey drill on the parade ground and foot soldiers slogged around in ragged formations in the heat, which was oppressive in mid-afternoon, even at Fort Whipple's five-thousand-foot altitude.

The mules were determined to turn in at the fort, but Neil wasn't, and there was a struggle, not so much of wills as of sawing reins and profanity versus muleheadedness. Neil won. He forced them to keep going to a roadhouse midway on the mile between Fort Whipple and the town of Prescott, a hangout of tough infantrymen, brawling cavalrymen, hard-nosed freighters and muleskinners, fractious cowboys, and miners with parched throats, just down from the mountains. Halfway House, part chinked logs and part adobe bricks, had wide, roofed verandas, a bar and dining room dark as a cave, several bedrooms for rent, a dormitory of cots in the attic, a hay barn, a blacksmith shop, corrals, and three girls in cribs down by Granite Creek, a short walk through the pines. A man could get a drink there, a fair meal, and a bed if he didn't mind sharing it when business was brisk. On occasion, Neil Douglas had made use of all its facilities.

He hadn't shaved in three days, his garb was a mixture of faded civilian and grimy Army, his hat a sweat-stained wreck, his tangled hair below his ears. When he set the brake and got down beside the line of bored horses at the hitch rail, it was perhaps not unreasonable of a drunken young trooper, a private, to step in front of him and inquire profanely what such a human liability as Neil might be doing with government mules and a government wagon—but Neil recognized the real motivation as the urge for a brawl, liquor-inspired. And suddenly and bitterly he hated uniforms and drunken Army teamsters and whisky-brave troopers and men on the veranda of a roadhouse beginning to stand and shove for vantage points to watch the fight. In earlier days, he had been well known at Halfway House and he knew that if he were recognized now as the man who, only yesterday, had knocked First Sergeant Eddie Burke stiff with one punch, there would be no respite from those who, brainless as gamecocks, had that incurable itch to find out. . . .

He reached into the wagon and got the Spencer carbine and its cartridge box and turned to walk around the challenging drunk. He nodded his head toward the wagon and said, "Driver's inside. Ask him, amigo, when he sobers up . . . say in about twelve hours."

The trooper grabbed his arm. "Not so fast, there! You didn't answer me. An' I don't like your looks none. Not none at all!"

Neil sighed, turned to the watchers on the veranda

and said, "Somebody mind these for me, will you? For about thirty seconds?"

He laid the carbine and the cartridge box on the ground.

The trooper grinned. "Ho *ho*! Thirty seconds is it! Will you listen to the man! Why mister, I'm gonna———"

A trooper on the veranda said, "Ho *ho* it is, Olson, ya half-wit! You never heard what happent? That fight at Camp Verde yesterday? Captain Barnes, he rode all night to get back here an' take the duty, an' he says it's the God's truth. Now that there is Sergeant Douglas of the Indian Scouts. So wade in boy. Hit the man!"

The trooper's eyes wavered to the faded chevrons on Neil's sleeves. He said, "I never yet been crazy enough to hit no sergeant. I'll let ya go . . . but you sure don't look like no sergeant I ever saw."

Neil grinned at him, not in friendship. "I never was the real thing, fat mouth, just a civilian employee. And I got my discharge yesterday, so you ain't in no trouble with the Army. just me."

He waited. The man's sunburned face flushed a little darker, then he grinned. "I wouldn't get caught hittin' no civilian, neither. So you stay an' *I'll* go!" He walked unsteadily to his horse.

Neil picked up the carbine and cartridge box and went up the steps to the veranda. The disappointed group made way for him, but reading the speculation in the eyes of several, he knew peace would be of short duration for him, here. Well, he'd move on tomorrow. Catch a ride to Prescott, or walk it, buy some clothes and a hotel room, play a little faro and poker, do a little drinking, and be in no hurry about his immediate future. Maybe he'd have a shot at prospecting when the edge wore off his new freedom. A lot of gold had come out of the Bradshaws, and there must be a lot still there.

He crossed to the bar and said to the apron, "Set me up six drinks in a row, and a glass of water. While I'm working on them, fix me up with a place to sleep and a bath."

CHAPTER 6

In the morning Neil's head was not of the dimensions of Corporal Maher's the morning before, but it felt as if his brain had shriveled to walnut size and was rattling around in a large, empty barrel. His mouth tasted like a brass cartridge case green with verdigris. The corner of his mouth was swollen. It came back to him slowly—the feisty, jeering miner, about his own size, calling him a fake whose gas-filled reputation he was about to explode, yelling that he had lost ten dollars on the fight with Burke, that the fight was fixed, and he was going to take ten dollars worth out of Neil's hide, and the others urging him on. Neil's refusal to fight had only increased the clamor. Then the big, ugly teamster in the filthy red flannel shirt had shoved him at the miner, who hit him in the eye. Neil couldn't remember the rest, but whatever the outcome had been he was going to get out of Halfway House, just to dodge trouble.

He washed his face, combed his hair after a fashion, discovered skinned and sore knuckles and went down the back stairway and out to a privy, then to the combined barroom and dining hall, for a shot of whiskey to help reduce the pounding of his headache.

There was a stud game going on at one table and various denizens of the Halfway House breakfasting at others. A stir went through the room as Neil walked in, and a couple of grinning men came to his table when he sat down—but he snarled at them, and they went back to their seats. The bartender-waiter took his order for a steak, eggs, fried potatoes, and coffee, lots of black coffee.

The man wanted to talk about the fight last night, but Neil looked him over and said, "Seems like I remember you sort of pushing at that miner to start something, along with some stinking freighter in a red shirt."

The man's face stiffened, and he hurried to the kitchen.

Neil ate slowly, and when the man came to clear the table, he said, "Now where's that fighting miner? Still around?"

"Uh, no, he ain't. I mean, he's still up in the dormitory where they carried him. You busted his nose, and some say his jaw . . . leastways, I picked up two teeth this morning. Man, I never saw nothin' like that, an' you not too sober, neither! That skinner that helped start it, he got out of here. Hooked up his team and got his wagons outa here, right there at two A.M. this mornin', after you said you was gonna look him up again."

The waiter looked at something behind Neil's chair, his eyes widened. and he backed away. Neil, with the big freighter in mind, slid sideways out of his chair and turned, ready for trouble.

"*Mickey*!" he said.

Mickey Free stood laughing at him. "You sure touchy, Neil!"

Mickey Free—Miga-n' la-iae—son of Maht-la, a Pinaleño Apache warrior, and Josefa Salvador, a captive Mexican girl, had number F-1 in the Indian Scouts, and was the first man to enlist under Dan O'Leary. He could look you straight in the eye with his black right eye, while his left wandered way off somewhere to the southeast. He owed loyalty to neither Indian nor Mexican nor white, only to the Scouts, and he was a first sergeant, and they paid him $150 a month. Fluent in English, Spanish, Apache, and other Indian languages, he was the most impersonal and efficient tracker and killer of any Scout yet. Not a man in the territory but knew of him, respected his deadly efficiency, and feared him if he wasn't on Mickey's side.

On his tangled, shoulder-length hair was a shapeless wool hat. A red scarf around his neck was tucked into the collar of a greasy corduroy jacket which concealed the six-gun and the knife at his belt. He tucked his pants into knee-high, old style moccasins turned up at the toes to prevent the entrance of thorns. He and Neil had bunked together, frozen and burned together, and fought many a battle and unwound many a trail together.

He allowed his hand to be shaken, although reluctantly, like the Apaches.

"What you doing here, Mick?" Neil asked. "I thought you were at San Carlos, with Seiber."

"Oh, I got some business here. Letter for the general. Seiber don't trust nobody else to bring it. Hell, it ain't nothin'."

"You read it?" Neil asked.

"Sure. Might be somethin' in there about ol' Mick, huh? I steam it open. Well, come on."

"Where to?"

"Georgy Crook, he know you're here. He know you got discharge. He wanta see you. I got you a horse."

"Huh-uh," Neil said. "I'm in no shape to go calling on the general. I'll take the horse and go to Prescott for some clothes, first."

"Sounds good," Mickey Free said. "Mick'll go with you. Maybe we'll hit a couple bars on Whiskey Row, eh?"

"Not me, Mickey. I had enough for a while. And I wouldn't show up in front of General Crook half drunk. Anyway, you have to report back. Tell him I'll be there this afternoon."

"Aw, you know Mickey, Neil. Do what he damn please, 'less some job to do. Mickey ain't been to no town in months."

He looked around, saw a corporal sitting in the poker game, and strolled to the table. The house man stopped dealing and said, "Hello, Mickey! Wanta set in?"

"Huh-uh," Free said. "Goin' to Prescott." He pointed at the corporal. "What you doin' off the post?"

"Adjutant sent me to find out about a escort wagon drove in here yesterday. That feller was drivin' it." He poked a thumb over his shoulder, pointing at Neil. "A trooper drove it to the fort last night, an' Corporal Maher was in it, drunker'n a polecat. He ain't real sober yet. Adjutant just wants the facts 'fore they bust Maher to private again an' put him on permanent latrine detail. Only they told me here that your friend gets a little touchy, an' I better wait till he came down for breakfast, not go wakin' him up."

Neil said, "He was drunk before we started from Camp Verde day before yesterday, and got drunker all the way. Somebody had to drive, huh?"

"Well, you know . . ." the corporal said, "Army property, mister, an' you a civilian an' all . . . well . . ."

"Just tell 'em it was Sergeant Neil Douglas of the Scouts," Mickey Free said, "an' if they don't like it, they can shove it where Paddy put the dollar. An' tell 'em me an' him's goin' to Prescott. He'll come see Georgy Crook this afternoon."

The dealer said to Neil, "You got any gear, just leave it with the bar, Sergeant Douglas."

"Thanks," Neil said. "A Spencer carbine an' a Blakesly case and a couple of razors up in the room."

He paid the apron a dollar for the room and waited while the man retrieved his few possessions and stowed them safely behind the bar.

He hadn't been in the saddle since they brought in the heads of those Apache renegades, and it felt good. They took the half mile to Prescott at a lope, and there was only one exchange of conversation.

Neil asked, "What's General Crook want me for?"

"How you 'spect me to know?"

They passed two great bull teams coming into Gurley Street, twenty oxen each, maybe more, and the ponderous wagons and huge trailers up from Sonora with barrels of flour, the Mexican bull whackers in their steeple hats and ragged sarapes gazing at the neat clapboard and brick homes, the gable roofs, the white picket fences. Except Flagstaff, Prescott was the only town in the whole of Arizona Territory that wasn't built of mud bricks and tiles and thatch and flat roofs.

Gurley Street pitched steeply down to pass The Plaza, where there was a painted bandstand, and a well, and a line pump on each corner for fire protection. It crossed Montezuma Street—"Whiskey Row"—where there were more than thirty saloons, each with its 24-hour-a-day, 7-day-a-week faro layouts, roulette wheels, chuckaluck cages, poker tables, and maybe a few girls upstairs for the high class trade that scorned the "restricted district" with its ten-by-twelve-foot cribs lining both sides of Goodwin Street, and housing about any nationality a man could name.

Traffic was brisk—ranch wagons and buckboards, long jerkline outfits bringing in mining machinery from Ehrenburg, two hundred miles west on the Colorado River, smart buggies and surreys, Indians and cowboys and miners crowding the sidewalks, horses lining the hitchracks, riders coming and going. A sawmill shrieked behind the brewery, and a man could feel the thump of some nearby stamp mill through his boot soles, always there but unnoticed, like the beat of a heart.

The saloons were segregated to some degree, stockmen frequenting the Cabinet House and the Palace Bar, miners hanging out in their chosen places, soldiers patronizing still others by a sort of unspoken agreement, violation of which was a frequent cause of brawls, but Mickey didn't give a damn about protocol. He swung his horse onto Montezuma Street and turned in at the Palace Bar.

Neil said, "See you, Mick," and kept going to Cortez Street and Cram's Variety store, next to the county offices.

He bought two pairs of Levi's stiff as stove pipes, two suits of red wool longjohns, a double-breasted blue flannel shirt, two blue cotton shirts, two red bandannas, a yellow silk neck scarf, a pair of fine wool dress pants, gray with a brown stripe, a blanket-lined Levi coat, socks, a rakish, flat-crowned black hat with a four-inch brim, a yellow oilskin slicker, a saddle scabbard for the Spencer carbine, a fine pair of flat-heeled boots that a man could walk in. Along with such things as Pear's soap, a shaving mug, the luxury of a toothbrush, sulfur matches, Bull Durham and cigarette papers, the bill came to a hundred and thirty-eight dollars, which made him wince. But a man that had spent four years living in a tent, or worse, with a passel of Apaches owed himself a little luxury for once.

He changed into his new finery in the stock room, and told Mr. Cram to burn the discards, put what he wasn't wearing in a sack which he tied to the cantle of the saddle, slung the carbine scabbard in place, and rode to the Palace Bar.

Mickey Free, at the bar, had a half-emptied bottle in front of him, a space four men wide on each side of him and no expression on his face. Without speaking, he poured a shot for Neil.

Neil tossed it down and said, "You ready to go, Mick?"

"I stay a while. Tell ol' Nantan Lupan Georgy Crook I come back some time."

"All right, Mickey."

When Neil walked out, Mickey Free, paying no attention to his departure, stood as steady as though rooted there; but he had a good grip on the edge of the bar to steady himself.

Neil considered getting a room in a boardinghouse, but already he was keeping the general waiting. He stopped at the Halfway House for the carbine and his razors, then rode on to Fort Whipple, passing at the entrance the only adobe buildings—the white-painted departmental offices, and just beyond, the hospital. To his right, to the north, were the troop quarters and a library, and behind the barracks, Suds Row. To the south of the wide parade ground were more offices, and on the west, the detached houses of the officers and that of the Commandant of the Department of Arizona, General George Crook.

Neil dismounted in front of the house, and a striker came hurrying to take the horse, curiosity and a touch of animosity on his face, seeing a civilian on that good troop horse. As he started to lead the horse away, Neil said, "Hold on, there, soldier boy! Where do you think you're going with my sack and my carbine? That's about all I own in the world!"

The recruit, red-faced, was framing a hot reply when General Crook called from the door, "Son, bring that gear in here, then take the horse to the stables. Come on in, Douglas. You're pretty late . . . but then I suppose, being a civilian now, you had to show your independence."

Neil hurried up the walk and took the general's outstretched hand. "No, sir, it wasn't that! Not with you. But I looked like . . . I mean I couldn't show up here——"

The general laughed. "I know. I got Mickey's message. It's good to see you, Neil. Sorry to lose you, but I guess I can't blame you. Did Mickey come back with you?"

"No, he was hanging on to the bar like grim death, to stay right side up, but he was all right. Could I say hello to Mrs. Crook?"

"She's visiting friends down in Tucson. Captain Bourke escorted her for me. She knows Tucson in July, but, well, she would go."

The orderly carried Neil's gear into the hall, and left.

General Crook said, "I have a dinner engagement. Old friend I knew a couple of centuries ago, when I was your age. Out here on a visit. I put him in Major Moore's quarters. Moore's on leave. Granville's got a bee in his bonnet about prehistoric ruins. Got a daughter, too, that I hadn't seen since she was about ten. Well, we'd better go."

"We, sir? Why, I couldn't think of——"

"You're invited. Matter of fact, we've been waiting all afternoon for you. You're looking pretty fancy, in all that new gear."

Pale eyed, straight, broad shouldered, six-feet tall, the general was a fine-looking man, except, Neil thought, for his beard, outstanding in an era of outstanding facial pelage. Long, peppered with gray, brushed outward both ways from his chin into wings of at least six inches' extension, running into a very full mustache, it was a wild contrast to his close-cropped hair which stood straight up like the bristles of a grooming brush. This was one of the few times Neil had seen him in full uniform—the dark blue serge blouse with its twin row of brass buttons and its upstanding collar, torturous in the heat. The gold epaulets shone on his shoulders, echoed by the wide yellow stripe down the lighter blue of his trousers. In an Army of hard drinkers and a whole territory of boozers and smokers and chewers, Crook neither drank nor smoked nor swore, which fact some considered weakness, some saintliness, and others a multiple falsehood.

They walked the hundred yards to the temporary quarters of Dr. J. Granville Whitman III, ethnologist, archaeologist and anthropologist, on a sort of sabbatical leave from the Smithsonian Institute in Washington, D.C. Neil was impressed as the general explained, because so far as he could remember, he had never heard those words, let alone known what they meant.

Warm lamplight glowed in the windows as they stepped onto the veranda. The doctor greeted them at the door. "Well, General! At last! Jennie has been having her troubles keeping the roast from drying out in the warming oven. Well-well-well! So this is our good man! Welcome, sir! Welcome! I hear most interesting things about you. I will be most happy to employ you, if half what I hear is true. Do come in!"

Employ me! Neil thought. He didn't even know yet what kind of doctor this big, portly, ruddy-faced, bearded man was—sawbones, pill roller, patent medicine hawker, vet, or what. The heavy gold watch chain across his protuberant belly, the gold fob hanging from a lower vest pocket, the Masonic ring with a ruby in the center of the square and compass, the polished boots, the wing collar, the diamond stick pin in the cravat and more than anything else, the air of total self-assurance, all indicated wealth and position. Well, if he was a friend of General Crook's, he had to be all right.

Dr. Whitman hung their hats on a rack in the hall. He said, "I'm afraid there is no time for the amenities, gentlemen. Shall we be seated at the dining table, for the relief of my poor Jennie, who has been slaving all afternoon in the kitchen?"

He ushered them to chairs at a well-appointed table in the warm light of coal oil lamps in wall brackets—where Neil was ill at ease. In the first place, he was in shirt sleeves—and there were white linen napkins in napkins rings, and a water glass and a stemmed goblet at each place except the general's; not only that, but a little plate beside his coffee cup (which was on a saucer!) with a short, blunt, silver knife beside it, and beside his plate, not only a knife, but *two* spoons, one large and one regular, and on the other side two forks, one regular and one smaller.

He jumped when Dr. Whitman called sharply, "Jennie! We're waiting!"

The swinging door to the kitchen was bumped open by a round feminine rump covered by a bustle, whose owner turned and came in bearing a bowl of soup in each hand, one of which she set at the doctor's place and one at the general's. Before Neil could get a good look at her, she went back, then returned with a bowl for him and one for herself.

General Crook rose to greet her. Dr. Whitman didn't, and the general hurried around the table to pull her chair out, and Neil, next to her, thought, well, that's a dodge I never yet saw.

The general said, "My dear, you look charming!"

Dr. Whitman said, "My dear, this is Mr. Douglas, Mr. Nate Douglas, who is to be the general factotum on our expedition. My daughter Jennie, Mr. Douglas."

"It's Neil, not Nate, Granville." Crook said.

Neil half standing, half sitting, bobbed his head and said "Pleasetameecha, ma'am," and sat down. General *who?* What the hell was Whitman talking about!

Jennie Whitman said, "Father and I are very pleased, Mr. Douglas. General Crook has spoken so highly . . ." Her voice trailed off to silence and she looked down at her soup. Neil wasn't sure whether the pink that suffused her face was embarrassment, or heat from the kitchen range. Certainly that strand of dark hair stuck to her forehead was damp with sweat—well, he guessed you said perspiration, for a lady, not sweat, or maybe "glow." Because she certainly was a lady—you knew that without thinking about it—even if a rather plain one.

"I ain't quite . . . I mean, I don't know what this is about," Neil said. "General Crook, what's the——"

"May I suggest," Dr. Whitman broke in, "that we discuss it over the cigars, after dinner. The soup is getting cold. In fact, it *is* cold." He cast an accusing glance at his daughter, who lowered her head, and blushed deeper.

By observation, Neil learned what the larger spoon was for. The salad was good, although Jennie apologized for the dressing, saying you couldn't get anything really needed in Prescott. The roast, also, was delicious, brown all the way through, the way Neil liked his beef; but Dr. Whitman said, *"Rare* beef, my dear! The only civilized way! Not burnt to a cinder! Rare, for red-blooded men! Don't you agree, Mr. Douglas!"

Neil started to say, Hell No!, but caught himself, and said, "Matter of fact, this is just the way I like it, sir!" The biscuits and honey were a treat. The pie, made of dried peaches, was superb. Neil ate hugely and complimented Miss Jennie loudly and sincerely, which made her blush. Dr. Whitman kept fishing for compliments on the wine, which Neil obligingly produced, although the thin red liquid tasted to him like vinegar. But, anyway, he'd found out what those stem glasses were for.

The girl said little, responding only to direct questions. Her father held forth on various subjects, but Neil sort of closed off his ears and furtively studied Jennie. Eating at the same table with a woman had been denied him for several years. Sitting next to a real lady from the East, eating delicate and unusual fare, was a privilege indeed! Suddenly, he thought of Chalk Eye and Limpy and Chulito and Yellow Face and Chiquito, greasy, smelling of leather and Indian and tobacco, squatted in the patched tent tearing half-raw meat held by greasy fingers, or squatted over a tiny fire eating a ground squirrel that had been gutted but not skinned, merely singed to burn the hair off. And himself, Sergeant Neil Douglas of the Indian Scouts, no different, no better —and now, here he was. He laughed suddenly.

Jennie started, looking at him with wonder; Dr. Whitman, interrupted in a long-winded monologue, looked injured, and stared hard at Neil.

The general seized the opportunity to push back his chair and say, "Thank you for a wonderful dinner, my dear. A rarity and a privilege, even in the relative civilization of the post. And when you consider what my men put up with in the field——" Suddenly he grinned at Neil. "Sergeant, was that perhaps what you were laughing about?"

"Yes, sir. A kind of a picture come into my mind— Old Chalk Eye and Limpy and me, trying to cook a . . . well, it was after dark and we had a little hole in the ground and a fire about the size of a match, and Limpy was holding a blanket over it 'cause we didn't want to be seen, because Chuntz's band was on the prowl around there somewhere. Well, Miss Jennie, this is the best supper I ever had!"

She really blushed at that, and got up and began carrying dishes to the kitchen. Neil hastened to hold the door for her, then picked up the meat platter, but she hurried back and said, "Oh, no, you mustn't! You're a guest! And Father's waiting in the drawing room . . . he wants to tell you——" She took the platter from him and hurried into the kitchen.

In the drawing room, seated on a horsehair sofa, Dr. Whitman tapped a finger impatiently on its arm. General Crook sat slouched in a rocker. Whitman said, "Mr. Douglas, please be seated. Over there." Suddenly, he raised his voice— "*Jenni-i-ie!* You forgot the port! *And* the ashtray, Jennie!"

Jennie, perspiring again, came hurrying in with a small silver tray on which was a decanter and two small, stemmed glasses. Her hands shook as she set the tray on a taboret.

She began to pour the dark purple wine into a glass, but her father said, "The *ashtray*, dear! I shall serve Mr. Douglas and myself."

Flustered and awkward, the girl hurried back to the kitchen. Neil was beginning to think he'd like to kick Dr. Granville Whitman III in the ass. Jennie hurried back with a copper ashtray, set it on the taboret, and turned to leave.

General Crook said, "Wait, Jennie. This concerns you. You don't have to leave just because it's customary in the capital. This is the frontier, and we think our women are important."

She looked questioningly at her father, who nodded, and she sat on the edge of a straight-backed chair against the wall, feet together, hands folded in her lap.

Dr. Whitman took a cigar from a box on an end table, clipped the end with a cutter on his watch chain, was about to light it, and remembered his manners. He offered the box to Neil, who took a cigar and bit the end off before Whitman could offer him the clipper. While Whitman looked on, pained, Neil extracted the cigar end from his mouth and put it in the ashtray. He dug a match out of a vest pocket, lit it with his thumbnail, and ignited his cigar and the doctor's.

The cigar was a pure delight, almost as good as the dinner.

"Now!" Dr. Granville said, and made his proposition to Neil.

He had six months' leave from his important job at the Smithsonian Institute, which Neil gathered was some sort of glorified museum. He had an avid interest in archaeology, and he had brought equipment, and was borrowing from the Army, via General Crook, shovels, axes, all necessary camp gear. His intention was to "dig" a prehistoric ruin of the Hohokam, who had lived farther south, actually, or the Anasazi, the Ancient Ones, or maybe the Sinagua culture which had flourished in a restricted area south of the Mogollon Rim. Upon Neil's questioning, he explained what an archaeologist meant by a "dig"—an ultracareful examination of the stratification of the floors of a ruin, to see which people had left what where, and who had come after them and left more artifacts on top of theirs, and so on, and drawings of all the artifacts uncovered, after their precise location had been charted on a diagram of the ruin or cave dwelling.

He had asked General Crook to find a man who could drive a team, set up camp, cook, handle stock, help with the dig under Whitman's orders. In other words, do all the work, Neil thought.

The general hadn't known anyone he would recommend until, day before yesterday, he had learned of Neil's discharge, whereupon he had told Whitman that Neil was the epitome (another new word to Neil) of all he required. General Crook had said that $150 a month wasn't excessive for Neil's all-around efficiency, and Whitman, a wealthy man, had agreed.

The project appealed strongly to Neil. His interest had always been captured by the many ruins in almost all parts of the territory, and his intention had always been to explore some of them, someday. The only thing was, already he didn't care a whole hell of a lot for Dr. J. Granville Whitman III.

He asked, "What about Miss Jennie? Where you gonna leave her?"

"Oh, she's coming along," Whitman said. "Where could I leave her?" There was a strong implication that she was like a stray kitten that he couldn't bring himself to drown. "Besides, we'll find her quite useful. Quite."

"It won't be a picnic," Neil said, and looked a question at General Crook.

Crook said, "Neil, she's very anxious to go. If you know of a good ruin that isn't too far from assistance in case of need, and not too rough to get to, someplace that could be reached by wagon, it should be all right. I'd never listen to any of it, if I weren't sure the Apache danger is over—I don't mean forever, I think they will be mismanaged into more trouble—but for a year, two years. Our Jennie's a good girl." He smiled at her and patted her hand. "She'll be a help to you, not a hindrance, Neil. I'll go bond for her."

Neil couldn't very well buck the general, but his skepticism must have been plain to all. He looked at her, studying her as though she were an inanimate object in her floor-sweeping skirt of wool and the long leg-of-mutton sleeves of her pinched-in blouse with all the rickrack braid on the tight collar that would have a corset under it laced to the point of cutting off circulation, and God knows what else in the way of corset covers and garters and stockings and petticoats—her brown hair a little disarranged, piled high on her small head, and all of her quivering with anxiety like a pointer aiming at a covey of grouse. The knuckles of her clasped hands were white, and her gaze was an appeal that he could almost feel physically, so great was its intensity. My God, he thought, she *is* like a dog! Like a mistreated pup crawling to you on its belly, craving nothing in the world more than an affectionate pat on the head, but certain only of a kick in the ribs. What in the world has been done to her! And how in the world could I turn her down?

He lied valiantly and said, "Why, it'll be my pleasure, Miss Jennie!"

The smile she turned on him was almost incandescent. He could feel its impact, too, like the anxiety of a moment ago. It made her almost beautiful. She said, almost inaudibly, "Thank you! Oh, *thank* you!" and gazed at him with the gratitude in her brimming gray eyes like the worship in the eyes of—well, there was that word again—a pup that has had the pat on the head instead of the kick in the ribs.

"Now!" Dr. Whitman had a habit of punctuating the progress of the discussion, like chapter headings in a book. "Now, Mr. Douglas, the general said you could find the place for us, you know, some undisturbed ruin not too far away, and there must be water, and some graze for the animals, and——"

General Crook intervened. "I think, Granville, that

Neil won't require explanations. I mean that, excepting your scientific gear, you'll do well to leave the rest to him. I'll requisition what you need from Army stores, for say a six-weeks' stay at your camp site. What's the use of being a brevet major general if you're of no use to your friends—and besides, you're government, too. I'm sure the august Smithsonian Institute rates all assistance from Fort Whipple. Well, Neil, about the ruin, what do you think? Tuzigoot, maybe, over by the entrance of Sycamore Canyon? It's on the Verde River, and there's a road of sorts."

"Sir, that road is awful. Tuzigoot would turn up a lot of stuff in the way of pottery and metates and such, but it's out in the open, sprawled all over that hill. All them covered mounds must be connected rooms, and there's a kind of a lookout tower. But it would mean a hell of —excuse me—a lot of digging out in the sun, and no shade trees except along the river a mile away. What would you think about the Citadel?"

"Perfect!" General Crook turned to Whitman. "It's the perfect place, Granville! Five stories high, maybe twenty rooms, sitting there in that great cave in the cliff. It's fantastic. And Beaver Creek not two hundred yards away, running strong all year, and the biggest cotton-woods and sycamores you ever saw. And only twenty miles from Camp Verde, for supplies, and help in case of need, and a pretty good road, too."

"There's a couple dry washes across the road that cou'd flash flood this time of year, come thunderstorm season." Neil said. "Might cut off the road for a few days. but no trouble if we don't get caught."

"What's the cliff?" Jennie asked. "Limestone, or sedimentary sandstone, or granite? Are there any signs of ancient marine life, such as trilobites or oyster beds?"

"Lady," he said, "you clean lost me, there, except for those oysters. Oysters in Beaver Creek? But then I guess you're just joking, huh?"

"Oh, no!" she said contritely, ashamed that she might have embarrassed him by calling attention to his ignorance. "I mean from the Cambrian age, or maybe——"

Dr. Whitman broke in, "That would be about five hundred million years ago, Douglas. You see, my little girl does know *something!* Few females have had the education I gave her, little good though it has ever done. But, my dear, we shall explore such esoteric matters ourselves, and leave the contemporary problems to our estimable Mr. Douglas. Now——" Neil smiled and said, "You're gonna have to talk English to me, the both of you." The smile was pasted on. Behind it, he was thinking, "The damn old bastard can't even say something nice about her without a slap on the end of it."

He said to General Crook, "What about transport, sir?"

"I've pulled rank again," the general said. "And after all, I outrank everyone in the Department of Arizona, don't I? At least till they send me off to the Department of the Platte. I've requisitioned a brand-new Dougherty wagon."

"What is a Dougherty wagon?" Jennie asked.

"Couldn't be better for our purpose," Neil said. "It's got four springs, rides like a rocking chair. Driver sits under an awning, out of the sun and rain, and there's two seats besides, with a door in the side to get at them. It packs a big load, and there's a luggage boot in the back like a stagecoach."

She gave him the dazzling smile again, and again he thought, she sure don't look it most of the time, but that smile makes her pretty. He turned to the general.

"Sir, what about the stock? Can you let me pick them out, myself?"

"I'll get you the requisition, but that's all I can do. You know our stable sergeant, Culhane? No? Well, the Chief of Staff could requisition the best mules in our stables, and he'd get exactly what Culhane would let him have. No better. He considers our mules his personal property, and he knows everyone will abuse them, especially a civilian like you. But he's not entirely unreasonable. You'll get something adequate, but that's all."

"Maybe I could kind of persuade him to loosen up a little. We're gonna need stock we can depend on."

"Absolutely not!" Crook was angry. "I'll not have Culhane stumbling around with one eye shut and his jaw wired together! You think I don't get the news, here?"

He waited, but Neil said nothing.

"All right, Neil. Sleep in the noncoms' quarters. I'll have my striker get you blankets. Eat at the troop mess. Talk over the plans with Dr. Whitman. Since you're going to the Citadel, you'd better stock up on supplies at Camp Verde. Save hauling them across the Black Hills from here."

"Sir," Neil said, "could we have another wagon for just one trip with supplies, from Camp Verde? We'll have all the camp gear and the tents in the Dougherty. And while there's pretty good graze across the creek from the ruin, if I have to picket the mules out, I'm sure to lose them. So I'll need grain and hay. And have to have a sack of potatoes and a half barrel of flour, at least, and a lot of canned stuff."

"Good idea. I'll fix it. And now, Granville, Jennie, thank you for a very fine meal and a pleasant evening. We'll say good night."

On the veranda, Dr. Whitman said, "Fine. See you in the morning, then."

Neil said he'd look forward to seeing Jennie tomorrow. She barely touched his hand and said, "Good night, sir," and hurried into the house.

As they walked toward General Crook's quarters to rout out his striker to find blankets for Neil, the general said, "They came by stage two weeks ago, a long, hard journey for Jennie. But she's stronger than she appears."

"She don't look so strong to me," Neil replied. "More like a whipped dog. What's chewing on him? Can't give her a decent word, orders her around like a slave. I don't know if I can stand him for six weeks."

"Well, Neil, it bothers me, too. He's changed. Always was a little overbearing, and now he seems to feel she's a burden, and doesn't know what to do with her. And she's so timid, so meek. I wish she'd show a little backbone."

"More like browbeat than timid, seems to me," Neil said.

"He raised her, you know, and I suppose it has hampered him. She was only twelve or thirteen when her mother died. And right after that, Granville ran into trouble that got into the courts, and the newspapers were pretty hard on them. Don't get the wrong idea. It was nothing criminal, and it's no business of yours—but it was an awfully rough road for the little girl."

They walked a few steps in silence, then the general said, "Don't back out, Neil. Give them a good time, and keep them out of trouble. She needs someone to cater to her and give her some companionship. But you watch out! There's a dozen men I could have recommended, but you're the only one that has any pretensions of being a gentleman."

"Pretensions, sir? What you think I'm pretending to be that I'm not?"

"No. you mistake me. It's just an expression, a figure of speech. But I'll tell you one thing, you treat that girl right! No monkey business, or I'll have your hide pegged out to dry!"

Neil seized his arm, turning him so that they faced each other. He said, "I'll tell *you* something. Don't tell me how to treat a lady!"

General Crook was not accustomed to being addressed in such terms. He glared at Neil, and Neil stared back, waiting.

It was a struggle for him, but the general managed to say quietly, "No offense, Neil. Tell the quartermaster, that's Lieutenant Lane, I'll give him the requisitions for whatever you need."

CHAPTER 7

Neil got up at 5:30 reveille, and shaved again. First time in his life he'd shaved on consecutive days. Immediately after breakfast, he walked to the Whitman house, anxious to get the plans settled, but there was no smoke from the kitchen chimney, blinds were down, no sign of life. He sat on the veranda through three cigarettes, then walked to the stables, to have it out with Sergeant Culhane about the mules.

Mules and violent profanity were inseparable and muleskinners were the acknowledged masters of profane invective. Troopers watering and grooming the horses were deriving great amusement from Culhane's vituperation directed at the mule polishers.

Neil stopped beside the sergeant, and although Culhane obviously knew he was there, he ignored Neil, and Neil forgot his determination to remain unruffled, no matter what. He jabbed his elbow, hard, into the sergeant's ribs.

Culhane turned on him, bawling an obscenity, then abruptly calmed down and said, "Oh, so it's you! The gineral sent word. Now lemme tell ya, me fancy fightin' man, that Culhane ain't scared of yer bloody reputation, an' furthermore, ye bloody Injun lover, irrespective and irregardless of whativer the gineral promised ye, ye'll get no beast that Culhane don't want ye to have."

Neil said, "Irrespective and irregardless of what General Crook told me, you call me Injun lover again, and I'll

78

break your bloody jaw. All you have to do is furnish me four mules in good condition, and no shavetails."

"*All* me mules is in good condition!" Culhane asserted.

"They're beautiful!" Neil said, sincerely. "But you're supposed to remember that Dr. Whitman and his daughter are special friends of the general, so don't saw off any man-killers on me, or loafers, or troublemakers. And all fresh shod."

"Douglas, I misdoubt ye can tie your own shoes, let alone tack a cold one on a mule, out in the brush somewheres, so Culhane himself will do the shoein'. Now, lemme see. I'll give ye Jennie and Maude an' Blackie an'——"

"Good God!" Neil said. "Couldn't somebody, sometime, just once, think up a name for a mule besides Jennie and Maude? Don't give me no Jennie, 'cause that's the name of Whitman's daughter."

"All right . . . Joe, then. An' if ye got t' have something fancy, what about Gotch Ear? That suit yez?"

"What happened to *him?*" Neil demanded. "Froze both ears up on the Rim, maybe? Maybe string-halted and splinted, too, huh?"

Culhane was affronted again. " 'Twas a 'Pache arrow! An' only one ear! Now just listen here——"

Neil patted his arm. "All right! All right! Simmer down! Just have four good ones ready, and the harness oiled, and the wagon washed and——"

"Quit tryin' t' *tell* me! An' Gotch Ear, she's a girl mule, ye ignorant black Injun!"

Neil walked away grinning, ignoring the profanity that followed him until he was out of earshot.

Dr. Whitman still had not arisen, but Jennie answered Neil's knock and led him to a seat at the dining table. She seemed flustered at being alone with him. In an effort to put her at ease, he said, "Is that coffee I smell?" and she hurried into the kitchen, to return with two steaming cups, and sat opposite him.

"I do miss cream for my coffee," she said.

Neither of them could think of any small talk, and they sat silent and constrained until she said, "Shall I wake Father, Mr. Douglas? I don't think he'll mind this morning, with all the planning to do."

She's scared to wake him up, Neil thought, but the risk is better than sitting here alone with me. Wonder if I smell bad!

"There's no hurry," he said. "How do you like Arizona Territory?"

"Well . . . I really don't know . . . we've only been here two weeks, and I haven't been off the post."

Again there was uneasy silence, and Neil sat, hoping for some sign of life upstairs. Jennie jumped up and hurried into the living room, stopped, turned to him and said, "Oh, yes . . . I found them in a drawer, and I wondered . . . maybe you could tell me . . ." and she went to the end table by the sofa and took an envelope from the drawer.

Returning, she stood by him and said, "Cup your hands, Mr. Douglas." From the envelope she poured into his hands a small handful of dull black ovoids, from the size of a pigeon egg down to a navy bean. Two or three had been polished, and were as shiny as jet beads.

"I'm sure they're obsidian, except that any obsidian I've seen, for instance in Aztec arrow points and sacrificial knives, has been sharp-edged, pieces split off from chunks, not rounded like this. Do you think perhaps these were melted by volcanic action, then fell into water when they cooled? Obsidian usually is related to volcanic action, you know."

"Miss Jennie, all I know is that these are what they call 'Apache Tears' and you can find 'em a lot of places in southeastern Arizona."

"Apache Tears," she said. "What a poetic name for them. Rather touching."

"Well, there's a story about 'em, Miss Jennie. I mean why they're called that. A long time ago, I mean before the war, there was a band of Apaches cornered with their backs to the edge of a high cliff, over at Dripping Springs on the middle Agua Fria River. A posse of ranchers and miners trapped 'em there. Apaches don't hardly ever travel, even on the war trail, without

the women and kids—so they were there, too. And the
bucks fought till their ammunition was gone . . . or
maybe they didn't have guns, just arrows and lances, I
don't know. But they wouldn't surrender. and they all
jumped over the cliff and got killed. Not the women and
kids. There's a lot of these Apache Tears at that place.
I've picked 'em up by the dozens. And folks say they're
the tears of those women and kids grieving for their men,
and that's why they call them that."

Jennie's eyes were brimming. "How sad!" she said.
"How very sad. Black and eternal symbols of grief. And
how symbolic of the way they've been treated. Father
gets mad at me when I say it, but I can't believe they
have to be exterminated like poisonous snakes. And
now, I suppose you'll think I'm foolish, too."

"Not me, Miss Jennie! I've had some lumps to prove
it."

She took the Apache Tears back into her hand and
studied them, poking them around with her finger.
"They'd make a lovely necklace, wouldn't they? To remind me of Arizona, and the sadness of the Apaches.
Only I couldn't ever wear it, because Father would find
out what they're called and say I was being very foolish
and sentimental. And I suppose there are a great many
very bad Apaches, aren't there?"

"There's bad and good, like everyone else," Neil said,
and to his surprise, found himself feeling a little sad
for *her*.

There were thumpings and movements upstairs, and
Jennie hurried to put the Apache Tears back in the
table drawer.

She was a funny one! Scared of him maybe, and certainly scared of her father, blushing even if you looked
into her eyes—some kind of woman notions that were a
waste of time for any man to try to figure out. But she
ought to stand up for herself more. Neil wondered what
sort of trouble the combination of the two of them
might stir up for him, camped there under the Citadel.

She stood fiddling with her hands, and he asked for
more coffee. Gratefully she hurried to bring it, and Dr.

Whitman came stumping down the stairs and into the room, in nightshirt and slippers and a striped silk robe. He was shaved and combed, and had some kind of stinkum on his face, lavender smell, or something.

He reared back like a shying horse at sight of Neil, cleared his throat, and said, *"Well!* You here? What time is it?"

"It's nine o'clock, Father," Jennie said.

Neil got to his feet. "Looks like I'm in the way. What time you wanta talk about the trip? I'll come back."

"No, no, man! Don't be foolish! I'm not accustomed to rising with the farmhands. Had your breakfast?"

"Three hours ago, with the farmhands," Neil said.

"No offense, man! Just a figure of speech!"

Someone was always using figures of speech on Neil, and he wished the hell they'd quit it. He said, "I'm easier to get along with if people just talk simple English I can understand. No offense."

Jennis was distressed by the undercurrents of the exchange. She said, hastily, "Why, you must be ready for lunch! I'll have eggs and biscuits in a jiffy. And prunes. How do you like your eggs, Mr. Douglas? Like Father's, three and a half minutes?"

Neil grinned at her. "I can eat, any time. But me, I'm a savage. I like 'em cooked. Could you manage 'em easy over?"

She smiled that smile that transformed her plainness, happy to please him.

Over breakfast and more coffee and cigars, they discussed the project and the supplies they would need. Dr. Whitman said Neil must prepare a list for his inspection.

"I did already," Neil said. "Last night, in the noncom quarters."

He got it from his shirt pocket and gave it to the doctor, who looked it over, ordered Jennie to bring him a pencil, and began to add notes, and strike out others. Neil reached across the table and took the list away from him.

"Huh-uh!" he said. "You can add on, if I agree, but you don't cut anything off my list."

Affronted, Whitman attempted to glare him down. Neil didn't react, and Whitman blurted, "Now see here, Douglas, I've canoe-camped in Michigan, and hunted moose in Maine, I've roughed it a good deal, I'll have you know! And I'll also have you know this is my expedition and you'll take my orders, like any hired hand."

"Like hell I will," Neil said, and got up from the table.

He turned to thank Jennie for the breakfast, but she was already retreating up the stairs, fleeing trouble and dissension.

Neil took his hat and started for the front door. Dr. Whitman bustled after him, red faced and angry, but ready to give a little. "Now wait!" he said. "Be reasonable. Perhaps I was hasty. Let's . . . let's hear your side of it."

Neil hesitated. He could perhaps make Dr. Whitman see reason, and he didn't want to go against the wishes of General Crook. And a hundred and fifty a month for six weeks was two hundred and twenty-five dollars.

The two stared at each other stubbornly. Neil said, "I haven't got any side. You take whatever you need to do what you want at the ruin. I put in what we need for a comfortable camp and a safe one. I'll take your orders, if it's connected with your work, and I'm helping. You'll take mine when it comes to the mules and the wagon and the camp, and believe me, if there's any kind of bad time, like say a flash flood, or a hydrophoby coyote in camp, or maybe some Apache runaways from the reservation, you'll take my orders, and you'll jump to it, and no questions. Now, if that ain't clear, get yourself another farmhand."

"Calm down, man!" Whitman didn't like it, but he was backed into a corner. "Why must you be so damn thorny? We'll go over that list of yours together, and——"

"No we won't," Neil said. "I'll make a copy for you, an' if you want some things I've left off, like say a case of wine or something tasty for Miss Jennie, why all right but the list don't get cut any."

Whitman made an effort to speak reasonably. "Well, for instance, Mr. Douglas——"

"Listen. Doctor. Make it 'Neil.' That 'Mister' makes me uncomfortable."

"All right," Dr. Whitman said. "But a block and tackle on your list! That's absurd! With two strong men to set up the tents——"

"We leave it if you say so," Neil said. "But suppose you find something up on the fifth floor of that ruin, a big olla or a hundred-pound metate. You gonna carry it down? 'Cause I'm sure not."

Dr. Whitman grinned ruefully, and for once genuinely. "I concede," he said. "You run your end, I'll run mine. Now suppose we seal the peace with a glass of port."

Neil hesitated. "It's kind of early——"

"Well, let's say a slug of bourbon. I've got a bottle I've been saving."

Neil grinned. "Just one," he said. "No, make that two!"

Dr. Whitman got the bottle and poured, and they both were laughing. Hearing the sounds of cessation of hostilities, Jennie came hesitantly down the stairs and when she saw the upraised glasses and the smiles, she, too, smiled in relief.

Dr. Whitman's equipment for exploring the ruin was not cumbersome. There had been little room for complicated gear, on the long stage coach journey, and as he said to Neil, "I'd have liked to bring a camera, but with all the accessories, dark tent, glass wet plates, tripods, flash powder, it was too much. And actually, this project is mostly just for my own edification, a long-deferred opportunity. Oh, I shall probably get a paper or two published in the *Archeology Review,* and some acclaim from my colleagues, but it is not an official project of the Institute. I'm hoping it will pave the way for one."

All he would carry would be tape measures, levels, cord for marking out grids, notebooks, bull's-eye lante.ns, a plumb bob, various brushes and hammers and a miner's pick, and a small quantity of plaster of Paris for molds, if such were available in Prescott.

"We'll be loaded, anyway," Neil said, "even though that Dougherty wagon will carry a lot. Listen to this, Miss Jennie." And he began to read the list of tools and supplies, got halfway through it, stopped, and began to laugh.

Whitman and his daughter were startled, and he explained: "It just came to my mind what Chalk Eye and Limpy would think of me. A couple of my Apache Scouts. You know how they set out to travel for overnight, or for six months? Makes no difference which. Probably not even a horse, to start with—just moccasins, a breechclout and one blanket, a knife, bow and arrows and a lance if they haven't got a rifle, a handful of jerky. They'd figure on stealing a horse, killing their meat . . . or the horse when they ran him to death, and making a water bottle out of his gut and new moccasins out of his hide."

Telling that to Jennie was a mistake. Whitman was mildly interested, but she was almost sick. She excused herself and went upstairs.

Whitman said, "Most interesting! When can we leave?"

"The wagon and mules will be ready whenever you say. I'll fix it with the quartermaster to load supplies and tools this afternoon, and we'll go tomorrow morning, if you like."

"Heavens, man! Impossible! Why, I have to pack, and check lists, and Jennie—why it will take her all of today and tomorrow washing and ironing and packing and unpacking suitcases and fussing with her hair, and making up her mind and changing it. No, Mr. Douglas, not till day after tomorrow, or better, the day after that. Let's say Saturday."

Saturday would suit Neil fine. He had business in Prescott which might take until Friday to complete.

On the way out he paused and said, "Dr. Whitman?"

The doctor stopped on the stairway. "Yes, Neil?"

"What about firearms? Now, I've got a Spencer carbine, and I'm gonna pick up one of those new Colt's Peacemakers. How are you fixed? And have you got plenty of ammunition?"

"Neil, I don't hold with firearms. I'm only sorry it's necessary for you to have them."

Neil was going to tell him about Gallo and his family just a few weeks ago, and a burned wagon and two teamsters tortured to death, but reconsidered. Whitman would probably think he was exaggerating or lying, and he certainly wasn't the one to pay attention to advice from his hired hand. But the eminent doctor was going to go armed, or the expedition was off.

He took the problem to General Crook in his quarters. Crook said, "He's a very learned man, Neil, but in some ways ignorant and bullheaded—which I guess is no news to you." He sat for a moment thinking, then went upstairs. He came down carrying a double shotgun, which he handed to Neil.

"Guess everybody knows my obsession with hunting," he said.

Crook was a noted hunter of big game, small game, anything that offered sport, and on all of his campaigns, the game he brought in—deer, elk, bear, turkey, grouse— was a considerable factor in supplementing the often scarce rations.

Neil admired the beautifully engraved metal, the ivory inlays in the walnut stock and forearm, the checkered pistol grip. It was a percussion gun, with two big curved hammers.

"I ain't much on scatterguns," Neil said, "but she's sure a winner. Ten gauge, ain't it?"

"Right. a gift from a wealthy friend. Now, Dr. Whitman considering himself a sportsman, perhaps we can persuade him, and not have to force him. Come on."

The doctor and his daughter were at the drawing room table. checking lists of one kind or another. Jennie squeaked in dismay when she saw the shotgun Crook carried.

Neil thought disgustedly, My God! She's scared of guns, too!

Crook said, "Look at this, Granville. Beautiful example of gunsmithing, isn't it?"

Dr. Whitman examined it carefully, rubbed his hand over the oiled walnut stock. "It's a beautiful piece all right, George."

He looked up at Crook, waiting, knowing there was more to come.

"Take it on the trip, Granville. Loaded with buckshot, it would stop an elephant."

"George, I don't expect to meet any elephants. And you know how I feel about firearms."

Crook stopped smiling. "If you don't take it, you don't go."

Whitman smiled. "You've got all the Apaches tamed or killed off, George, making the world safe for archaeologists, and I'll be too busy to hunt."

"All right, Granville—a few facts of life. Any man—and I include eminent brains from our great scientific institutions—any man who travels Arizona Territory unarmed is a fool. Did you ever hear of grizzlies? They attack. They don't run away. You never heard of sidewinders and desert diamondbacks? They don't always rattle. You ever hear of rabid skunks and coyotes? They don't run away either, Granville. And last, our Indians don't always stay on the reservations, as Neil can tell you. The old way of life still draws them. Their instinct, as natural as breathing, is to kill and plunder. No, Jennie, don't run away, now! You stay and hear this."

Granville Whitman said, "I, myself, was forced to kill a man. And nothing—*nothing on earth* could make me do it again! No! I'll leave the killing to you professionals, whose job it is."

Crook said patiently, "You're forgetting, Granville, our motives and circumstances have been vastly different. The Apaches are mostly under restraint, and you can depend on Neil, fully. But out here there's always the odd chance, and the man who isn't prepared for trouble invites it. I know you're not afraid, and I deplore the necessity of frightening Jennie. But you take the shotgun and keep it loaded and ready to hand, or you don't go. Not even if you should make other arrangements in Prescott. I'll stop you. Neil, take buckshot and powder, and a can of caps."

General Crook went out. Neil said, "He told you the possibilities, but he didn't tell you the odds. Believe me, they're a thousand to one against anything happening that would call for that scattergun. And Dr. Whitman, that place is crawling with wild turkey and quail. We'll take a sack of birdshot along with the buckshot."

Whitman wasn't mollified. In a surly tone, he said, "All right. Bring the shotgun."

"Father," Jennie said. "I've changed my mind. I think I won't go. I'll stay here with . . . with Mrs. Crook . . . or somebody."

"Nonsense! Jenny!" Having just backed down in the matter of the shotgun, Dr. Whitman was even more brusque toward her than usual. "Use your head! Mrs. Crook has gone to Tucson. Anyway, I wouldn't thrust the responsibility onto anyone else. No telling what kind of trouble you'd get yourself into, left to your own devices."

She wasn't crying when she hurried for the stairs, but Neil was ready to bet she would be before she got to her room.

Neil went to the quartermaster, and was assured that his list would be filled and the wagon loaded with all the camp gear, everything except the canned goods, potatoes, flour, hay and grain, that would be carried from Camp Verde in a supply wagon. He said, "Lieutenant, it's a long haul, and the driver's seat of that Dougherty wagon is none too wide, and Dr. Whitman is kind of broad in the quarters. Could you leave one of the other seats in, and still get the load packed?"

Reassured that this would be done, Neil went to see Sergeant Culhane at the stables. Culhane was quite affable. He said, "The boys tell me ye're the one that druv the escort wagon from Verde, when Maher got took drunk. Well, ye managed not to kill none of me mules, by some miracle, and for that I'm obliged to you." This was the equivalent of receiving the Medal of Honor from President Ulysses Simpson Grant, and Neil seized the opportunity:

"Sergeant Culhane, I need the loan of a horse this afternoon. Now you know I'm on special assignment from——"

"Quit yer yammerin! and see here, now! Don't ride no McClellan saddle, so's nobody'll notice you're ridin' gover'mint stock. There's a couple of them cowboy sad, dles in the stables, with them silly horns on the pommels. Find Corp'ral Schwartz. Tell him I told yez."

Neil rode first to Curry's Jewelry store, next to the Prescott Shaving and Bathing Parlors. Mr. Curry greeted him. "Something in a fine railroad watch, sir? or perhaps a stick pin for your cravat?" He was nearsighted, and upon inspecting Neil at closer range, sighed and said, "No, I expect not."

Neil said, "How are you fixed for Apache Tears?"

"They're a drug on the market. I've got a cigar box full; everybody brings me Apache Tears! You might as well toss them in the street, sir. They're just glass, you know, volcanic glass. They polish easily, but won't hold the polish. Good day, sir."

Neil laughed. "Hey, hold on! I'm buying, not selling!"

"What in the world for, if I may ask?"

"I want a necklace of them, for a lady friend. She's from the East and she thinks they're wonderful."

"Well," Curry said, "in the interests of romance . . . But it will be expensive, regardless. You have no idea how hard they are to drill. And there's the chain and the clasp. You want gold?"

"Yes. And I want it tomorrow afternoon. Not a long one, just enough to go around a lady's neck, and leave a little slack. How much?"

"Oh, dear! Tomorrow afternoon! Why, I'll be up half the night! I'd have to say twenty-five dollars, sir."

Neil said. "I'll be here around three."

He left Mr. Curry smiling and went to the Palace Bar for beer and the free lunch, consisting of hard boiled eggs, rye bread, pigs' knuckles, dill pickles, bologna and canned sardines.

After lunch, he rode to the Sportman's Emporium on Cortez Street and paid high for a Colt's Peacemaker, a holster and two boxes of those centerfire cartridges, and fifteen dollars for a wicked little Remington over-and-under .41 caliber derringer, a hide-out gun, a gambler's gun, that wouldn't shoot straight for thirty feet, but was deadly across a poker table. He bought a box of the stubby, rimfire cartridges for that, too, and was back at Fort Whipple by four-thirty, in time to pacify Sergeant Culhane, who had begun to fret about the horse.

Neil took the Peacemaker out to the target range, and took joy in its accuracy, and its smooth trigger pull but mostly in the speed and ease of loading, like magic after the awkwardness of the Army issue Remington 44.40 he had carried for four years, with all its appurtenances of bullet mold, percussion caps, nipple wrench, powder and shot flasks.

On Friday afternoon, with the wagon loaded and ready, needing only its passengers, and the last-minute luggage of the Whitmans, Neil borrowed the horse from Culhane again and rode to Prescott. The necklace was ready, the polished black glass picking up soft highlights, the thin gold chain and the clasp very elegant. He paid Curry, who warned him that the Apache Tears would get dull, and would scratch.

He rode to the Palace Bar and had two drinks, then bought a pint of good whiskey for Culhane, who received him with pleasure when he returned to Fort Whipple, but said only, "Ye're a rare one, Douglas, knowin' how to treat a mule an' stable sergeant both. Saints preserve yez."

In the evening, officers from Fort Whipple and Camp Verde and all the active posts in the territory who could get leave gave a banquet for Brevet Major General and Mrs. George Crook (who had returned from Tucson for the occasion) along with the prominent citizens of Prescott, Phoenix, Florence, and all the smaller towns. It was a gala affair to say farewell and Godspeed to a gallant man, leaving on the morrow for Omaha, Nebraska, to take command of the Department of the Platte.

Jennie Whitman was invited, with her father, but Whitman told General Crook, "She won't go. She's scared of crowds." And sure enough, it developed that she had a bad headache and could not be prevailed upon to enter any of the buggies and six-horse ambulances that left at dusk, even though General Crook had tried to entice her by offering the handsomest bachelor officer on the post as escort.

When Neil knocked on the Whitman door, it was about three minutes before she pushed aside the lace curtain of the window and peeked out at him. He had a bull's-eye lantern, and shone it on his face, and had to plead for another three minutes before she would let him in. Anger flashed through him as he realized how alarmed she seemed about his arrival; but anger changed suddenly to compassion, and he kept his distance, and sat stiffly on the horsehair sofa.

She was not only frightened to be alone with him, she was, for her, dressed exceedingly informally. She had, of course, the floor-sweeping, dust gathering skirt, with the small bustle that emphasized the roundness of her rump, and a white, long-sleeved shirtwaist, open at the throat, and tight-fitting, which disclosed to Neil for the first time, that she was slender waisted and big breasted —and he'd bet all he had that she didn't wear any deceiving pads and such, like Molly Killian, but was entirely her own woman. She apologized for being caught with her hair down, and clearly had no inkling of how attractive it was, that great mop of tawny chestnut gleaming in the warm lamplight, and falling to her waist. One thing gratified him: clearly she didn't realize it, but she trusted him to some degree, or she would never have let him come in.

She was prim and all business, wanting to know what brought him at this hour; was it something they had forgotten to load on the wagon? Some message for Father when he came home?

He grinned at her, and she dropped her gaze as she sat across the room, pleating folds in her skirt.

He said, "Not for Father. For you," and took the Apache Tears necklace from his shirt pocket and held it out, dangling from one finger.

She got up, hesitant and wary, and came around the table, staring at the jet gleam of the beads.

She said, "Oh!" softly, and put both hands to her face. "It's beautiful! Just beautiful! Where did you get it?"

"I had it made, in Prescott."

"For *me?*"

"Just for you, Jennie. Here, put it on."

She tried, but her hands were shaking and her hair got in the way.

"Let me," he said, and stood behind her and pushed her hair aside, letting it hang over his arm as he fastened the clasp. She was fragrant, and the back of her neck damp in the heat, and her hair like the touch of down across his wrist. And she was skittish as a boogered colt. He backed away, and returned to his chair.

She went into the hall and looked in the mirror, and when she returned, her eyes were misty. "I can't—" She choked up and had to start again— "I can't remember when anyone did such a nice thing for me."

He had brought the derringer, also, and had planned to tell her why she must always keep it loaded, in her pocket or within reach every hour of the day or night while they were camped at the Citadel—but that would purely scare the hell out of her. It could come later.

He got up and went to the door, opened it, and said, "Night, Jennie. See you in the morning."

She tried, but she couldn't speak.

CHAPTER 8

Immediately after 6 A.M. breakfast, Neil went to the quartermaster's supply shed. Lieutenant Lane had the wagon loaded and ready. The lieutenant said, "I rounded up a little wood stove and some stove pipe. The wall tent's got an insulated hole for the pipe. And Mrs. Crook sent along two quilts for the girl. There's a folding cot for her, too. You'll find your whole list there, and a few extras."

"Many thanks, sir! And I'd like a favor, if you will. Can I leave my fancy go-to-meetin' clothes with you?"

"Sure," Lane said, and Neil gave him the bundle, all but the new black hat, which was the only one he had. He wore Levi's and a cotton shirt, and had reverted to the knee-high rawhide-soled Apache moccasins, wrinkled and sloppy around his ankles.

Sergeant Culhane himself came along, walking behind the harnessed, four-mule team, and hooked them up. Neil noticed that he was pretty wary of the heels of Gotch Ear, the off wheeler, and mentioned it somewhat caustically.

"Aw, hell," Culhane said. "Ye know how touchy the beasts are about the ears an' her with that ruint one. She's a fine girl, ol' Gotch Ear. You just gotta be firm with her, that's all."

The load on the wagon was in perfect order, the gear they would need at tonight's Cherry Creek camp readily accessible.

Neil climbed to the driver's seat, released the brake,

and talked to the mules, but it was not until he flourished the ends of the reins and swore at them that they
moved. Once started, they went readily enough. Troopers
and dogfaces stopped to admire the smart rig as it
passed—the sparkling new Dougherty wagon with its dark-
blue wagon box, rust-red running gear, wheels and
tongue and doubletree bright varnished, white canvas
top stenciled with "U.S.A." and a regimental number,
white awning over the driver's seat, white canvas cover
strapped down over the luggage boot in back, the oiled
harness bright with brass fittings and the four fine mules
at a brisk trot. Neil halted it in front of Dr. Whitman's
quarters, where Jennie waited on the veranda in her
traveling costume topped with a linen duster, and a
straw boater tied onto her head with a veil. The luggage
piled beside her would fill the boot completely.

Neil got down, and she came down the steps and
shyly accepted his hand. She said, "Father's almost
ready, Mr. Douglas."

Two troopers, a private and a corporal, came riding
up, dismounted and bowed to Jennie. "Mornin', ma'am.
Corporal Jennings at your service. An' this here's Private Jones. We're comin' with you till you get to that
place. General's orders."

"Why—why—" Jennie turned to Neil. "Is this necessary? I mean, is there any danger?"

Neil would gladly have strangled Corporal Jennings,
who said cheerfully, "Oh, the 'Paches are whipped good.
But there's always a couple strays jumped the reservation. You know, no trouble."

Hastily Neil said, "That's a lot of"— he caught himself in time— "of foolishness! It's just a nice favor
from General Crook, Jennie. He sent word last night
—I s'pose he told you too—he's got too much to do, can't
be here to tell you goodbye."

She looked worried. Fool girl! Scared of her own
shadow!

She adjusted the loose knot of the veil tied under her
chin, and he was pleased to see that she was wearing the
necklace of Apache Tears. She'd said she was afraid

of what her father would say about her morbid senti-
mentality when he saw it, if he happened to know the
legend—but in this, at least, she would dare his sarcasm.

Dr. Granville Whitman came bustling out, quite sensi-
bly dressed. Canvas pants and stout shoes, a duck jacket, some kind of English shooting hat with a bill in front
and back.

He was hearty and full of enthusiasm. "Good morning! Ah, good lad! I see you've left a seat unoccupied,
for me. I was afraid the driver's seat would be a little
restricted for the three of us! Well, all ashore that's going
ashore, as the sailors put it! Let us be off."

"Sir," Neil said, "not without the shotgun."

"Well, Neil, I have stated my aversion to firearms
intended for use against humans, even the aborigines.
General Crook is far too busy this morning to check up
on me, so let's be off."

Well, we're off to a good start, Neil thought. "Sir,"
he said, "no shotgun, no expedition. I have the general's
orders."

Whitman flushed, glared, bit his lip, and at length
turned and stamped back into the house, flinging over his
shoulder, "Very well! You're a stubborn and aggravat-
ing man, Douglas. I must defer to General Crook's de-
mand. But you will find I'm just as stubborn as you!"

Corporal Jennings and Private Jones loaded the luggage.

The day's journey was made pleasant by the aggrieved
silence of Dr. Whitman and the lively interest of Jennie
in everything they passed, or that passed them—buzzards
wheeling in a sky where tremendous thunderheads
towered white against the faultless blue beyond Bill Wil-
liams Mountain; antelope grazing among the cattle, on
the long grade to the abrupt foothills of the Black Hills;
a badger which stopped mining for ground squirrels and
stared defiantly as the wagon passed.

The last steep haul to the crest, with its switchbacks
and hairpin turns, showed Gotch Ear up as a loafer who
leaned lightly into the collar while her teammates sweated

and pulled doggedly and hard. It required most of Neil's self-control not to use teamsters' language on her.

He really laid into her with the ends of the reins, and earned a scolding from Jennie; but Gotch Ear pulled the better for it.

The corporal and the private help set up the camp at Cherry Creek—a simple task of putting up the little two-man dog tent and the folding cot for Jennie, and finding relatively soft spots for their own blankets, and those of Neil and the doctor, who recovered his good spirits at the sight and smell of the steaks sizzling in two frying pans, and the dough-gods Neil baked by twisting biscuit dough around the ends of ramrods and sticking the ramrods into the ground close to the fire.

The troopers cleaned the tin plates and cups and the frying pans and buried the garbage and the fat from the frying well downstream, so it would not lure intruders such as skunks or ringtailed cats into camp. Soon those two rolled in their blankets, and Dr. Whitman, seeming to find the talk around the campfire boring, followed their example.

The small talk was all Neil's to fill a void of silence on the part of Jennie, who sat hugging her knees and staring into the coals as though hypnotized. He tried to draw her out, to learn a little about her, but she was unresponsive. She did, however, ask a few questions about Arizona and frontier life, and about Neil's background. He told her a little about his squaw-man grandfather, Bear Douglas, and that his mother had been probably the first schoolteacher in the territory.

"That accounts for it, then," she said.

"What's that?"

"Well, your grammar is a good deal better than that of your peers."

"She sure hammered away at it," Neil said, "but she never taught me that word."

He went on, as much to himself as to her, reminiscing about Indian scares and raids, and his mother's death when he was only fourteen, probably of typhoid, and how, soon after that, Indians killed his father. Abruptly,

Jennie got up and went to her tent, and he saw that he had upset her. Any reference to violence seemed to trouble her exceedingly.

He said, "Wait a minute, Jennie," and she turned, watched him approach as though she were afraid of him.

"I don't want to upset you," he said, "but I have to tell you. There is very little chance of it, but snakes run around at night. The boys put a lantern and matches under your cot. If you should get up during the night, put on your stockings and shoes, and take the lantern with you."

Her eyes went wide, and she put a hand to her mouth, probably as embarrassed by the reference to getting up in the night as she was scared by the warning. She mumbled something about thanking him, then surprised him by looking directly into his eyes and suddenly smiling at him. "I'll be careful. And I'll wear my beautiful necklace. I really love it, Mr. Douglas, and I'm going to think of it as my talisman, my good luck piece." She ducked into the tent.

He went to check the mules, now tied to a very soldierly picket line stretched between two trees.

That girl, he thought, she's a sight odder than any other I ever ran across, and God knows some of them were on the giddy side.

In the morning, anticipating trouble in hitching Gotch Ear, Neil showed her the six-foot chain attached to a halter, and shook it to make the links jingle. There probably was not a mule in the whole U.S.A. and territories not familiar with the use of halter chains for purposes other than confinement. Gotch Ear backed up to the doubletree almost eagerly.

The downhill drive to Camp Verde was uneventful, marked only by Jennie's bright interest in the flora and fauna, and by Dr. Whitman's reversion to fairly good humor. Quail and rabbits rambled through the brush, a red-tailed hawk flapped directly over the wagon with a twisting, four-foot rattler in its talons, at which sight Jennie cringed, pushed against Neil's side, and seized his shoulder. A while later, she actually seized his hand,

and pointed to the creamy glory of yucca blossoms, clusters a foot long, their long stems thrusting up from round masses of bayonet-shaped leaves.

About two hours before they would arrive, Neil sent the escort galloping ahead to report to Major Trumbull that the wagon would reach Camp Verde about four o'clock. Dr. Whitman, sprawled comfortably on his reserved seat, said, "Neil, let's compare watches. I've got two o'clock, but I let it run down a couple of days ago, and I'm not sure——"

"I haven't got one," Neil said.

"Then how can you say we'll be in at four?"

"Hell I don't know! You just get so you know what time it is."

"That I doubt," Whitman said. "And I'll thank you to watch your language in the presence of my daughter!"

Neil turned to Jennie. "Sorry," he said, but she didn't answer.

They pulled into Camp Verde precisely at four o'clock.

Major and Mrs. Trumbull and Captain and Mrs. Eastwood, apprised of the coming visit of the Whitmans, were waiting to greet them, as were Lieutenants Bingham and Underhill, and almost everyone else at Camp Verde, including Molly Killian, glowering at Neil from the back of the group as he handed Jennie down. Sergeant Eddie Burke, with Whitey at his elbow, stared at her from among a crowd of Indian Scouts and troopers in the background.

As the only young, non-dried-up, fairly attractive female to visit Camp Verde in many a month, Jennie was a sensation. Major and Mrs. Trumbull bore Dr. Whitman and his daughter off to their quarters, Mrs. Trumbull trailing remarks about a hot bath and a short rest before dinner with the other officers.

Neil drove the wagon to the stables and arranged with Lieutenant Underhill to have it guarded constantly. He went to dinner in the noncoms' mess, where, being now a civilian, and never popular because of living with his Indians, he was ignored. Even Sergeant Burke made no provocative remarks. Maybe he'd had some sense pounded into his skull by that left hook, on the Fourth of July.

Neil wondered where he would sleep. He had seen old Chalk Eye and Limpy in the crowd, but he had no intention of joining them in the tent. He'd had enough of that for one lifetime.

Major Trumbull hadn't forgotten Neil. His striker, waiting for Neil outside the noncoms' quarters, told him the major had assigned him a bed in Lieutenant Underhill's quarters. Neil grinned, and said, "Ten to one he didn't ask how Underhill liked it."

The soldier grinned, too. "I guess not, Sergeant. I kinda remember you an' the lieutenant havin' a little set-to, that time Eddie Burke brought back them Injun heads."

The major and the captain and their wives were having a stroll with the Trumbull's guests, as dusk approached. Neil leaned against the barracks idly watching as the group neared his position, noting the volubility with which Mrs. Trumbull drowned out all conversation as she pointed out things around the parade grounds. The troopers and infantrymen were all out, trying for a glimpse of the young lady. That they were respectfully keeping their distance did nothing to relieve her embarrassment at being the focus of attention. Neil felt sorry for her, knowing what an ordeal it must be for her to be thus on exhibition.

The Indian Scouts, Neil's old bunch and Eddie Burke's, were equally interested. Most likely, not one of them had ever seen a white woman dressed in the height of Eastern fashion, young, creamy-skinned, fresh and clean. They lacked the tact of the soldiers, and were boldly approaching, nearer and nearer to the strolling officers and women, and talking and gesticulating among themselves. Neil saw Mrs. Trumbull turn and look at them over her shoulder, then say something to the major, who glanced back at the Scouts, then took Jennie's arm and hurried her away.

Neil stared hard at the group of Scouts. They had begun to laugh, and in their midst was Whitey, outlining a woman in the air with exaggerated gestures, and thrusting forward with his hips.

The Eastwoods and Dr. Whitman turned at the sound of the Indians' laughter, and Jennie, being hustled away by the Trumbulls, looked back. A couple of troopers suddenly swore and began to run toward the Indians. Neil Douglas got there first. His headlong charge into the group knocked one sprawling and several staggering, and he got Whitey by the hair, began to back up, hauling Whitey off balance, and beat his face with the heel of his hand, swinging it in a full arc, hitting as hard as he could, again and again. Dazed and confused, Whitey groped for the knife at his hip, but Neil kept jerking his hair and slugging him, open-handed. Blood spurted from his nose. Men grabbed Neil and pulled him off Whitey, who, half-stunned, could barely stand. Neil jerked at the restraining arms, and strong hands seized his throat from behind. Gagging, Neil pried a finger loose and bent it back, jerking and twisting it, doing his best to break it.

The hands let go, and people let go of Neil, and he turned and crouched, and faced Eddie Burke. Burke was cursing and massaging the middle finger of his left hand. He snarled, "You sonabitch, you don't lay no hand on none of *my* Injuns!"

Neil, his right fist cocked, drove his left shoulder into Burke's chest, stepping on his feet, driving him stumbling backward. Men shoved between them and held Neil. Hoarse with rage, he yelled at Burke, "You keep that white-eyed slug away from her, you hear me? I'll break his back if he even *looks* at her! Get him outa here!"

Captain Eastwood yelled at Burke, "Get those Indians out of here, Sergeant," and waited, grim and quiet, until Burke had given the order in Apache, and the Indians moved away.

Captain Eastwood grabbed Neil's arm and said, furiously, "I'll spread-eagle you on a caisson wheel! I'll——"

Neil, quiet now, said, "Not *me*, Captain. *Not ever!* Get your hands off."

Captain Eastwood held on, and Neil's eyes slitted. He shifted his feet an inch, balled his right fist, and dropped his shoulder. Eastwood let his arm go.

Dr. Whitman, sputtering with rage, shoved his face close to Neil's and grated, "Douglas! I'll thank you never again to involve me and my daughter in a public spectacle! Of all the crude, bellicose——"

"Whitman, if you ain't man enough to enforce respect for her, I am." Neil stared into the suffused face of Whitman. "On second thought, *you* drive the wagon to the goddamn ruin! I'm through!"

He bumped Whitman aside with his shoulder, shoved Captain Eastwood out of his way, and stalked off to Lieutenant Underhill's quarters.

There was a cot made up across the room from the double bed. He hung his jacket and hat on a peg in the wall, and his gun belt on a nail above the cot. He was washing his face at the basin on the dresser, when Lieutenant Underhill came in.

Underhill had things to get off his mind. "*Well!* A more disgraceful exhibition I've *never* seen! And in the presence of the young lady! Violence! That's all you seem to know!"

"Wilbur——" Neil began, but was interrupted.

"*Not Wilbur!* Not from you! I'll hear you say 'Lieutenant Underhill,' or 'Sir,' when you address me, and make that as seldom as possible."

"Just this once more, Lieutenant Underhill, *sir*. Being I'm so violent, if I was you I'd keep my mouth clamped shut, because the next word you say to me, *I'm* gonna shut it! And that goes from now on out. Don't even talk in your sleep, else I'll come over and pop you on your flapping mouth."

He waited. Underhill, pale with the effort to restrain himself, finally turned his back and began to undress. Neil, slowly cooling down, sat on the cot and watched him.

Someone knocked on the door, and Underhill hastily

jumped into bed in his longjohns. Neil opened the door, and there was Dr. Whitman on the veranda, embarrassed, reluctant to speak. He blurted, "I owe you an apology. I'm very grateful for what you did. I really didn't see what that albino was doing. I heard you tell him not to look at Jennie, and I couldn't see any harm in their looking at her, even though it embarrasses her. She's too touchy, anyway. But Major Trumbull explained to me what that weird savage was doing, the obscene gestures and the filthy comments in Apache. Will you forget my outburst, and shake hands?"

Neil thought it over. For quite a while. Whitman stood anxiously waiting. Lieutenant Underhill raised up on his elbows, with his mouth hanging open.

"The project, the dig, means a great deal to me, Neil," Whitman said.

"Well, all right, sir, for just one reason. There's other troubles Miss Jennie can get into that won't be her fault, either, and you're gonna be busy. Somebody's gotta watch out for her."

The doctor seized Neil's hand in both of his and pumped it up and down. "Thank you, my boy! Thank you! And a bit of good news! Major Trumbull has ordered the young corporal and the private who escorted us to come to the ruin, and the driver and swamper of the supply wagon that will carry our flour and grain and forage, they, too, are to stay long enough to set up camp for us. And he says the driver knows of a narrow ravine—I guess you'd call it a box canyon—which can be closed off with a fence to corral our mules."

"I thought I remembered a place like that," Neil said. "All right, sir. See you tomorrow."

As he closed the door, Lieutenant Underhill said, "What obscene gestures? I didn't see any such——"

Neil advanced upon the bed, glowering. "Never see anything, and never hear anything, do you? Because not five minutes ago, I told you if you opened your mouth again—"

Second Lieutenant Underhill scuttled under the blankets and turned to the wall.

CHAPTER 9

As early as dawn, it was a sweaty day. Neil was up before reveille, and sitting on the veranda steps. Lieutenant Underhill, still in bed facing the wall, had betrayed his pretended sleep by a restrained cough. Sunlight slanted over the Mogollon Rim and painted the tops of Table Mountain and Pinto Mcsa red-orange. It would be another half-hour before it got down to Camp Verde. Late-hunting coyotes squalled in the chaparral, roosters crowed in Shanty Town, and a burro went through the prolonged gasping preparatory to a session of braying. The staccato notes of reveille shocked the camp awake.

Neil strolled to the noncoms' quarters and sat at one of the mess tables, while grumbling men crawled from the bunks, hauled on clothes and boots, and stumbled out to the privies, washed at the long trough, and came back to breakfast. Neil was alert for the appearance of Eddie Burke, but Burke had slept elsewhere, perhaps in the tent with his Indians.

Fifteen minutes after breakfast, Neil was looking the Dougherty wagon over, and the six-mule supply wagon, already loaded with canned goods, potatoes, a half-barrel of flour, hay, and six sacks of barley.

Surly troopers led out the six mules and hooked them up, then brought out Gotch Ear and her teammates and hitched them to the Dougherty wagon.

Major Trumbull arrived, escorting Jennie and the doctor. Jennie greeted Neil shyly. Major Trumbull said,

"I couldn't put Whitey in the guardhouse. It's against policy with the Scouts. I gave him and Burke a few days' leave to go hunting. Get 'em out of here before you tangle with 'em again. I think I'll transfer him to San Carlos."

Jennie walked away, distressed by the discussion. Dr. Whitman was walking around the supply wagon and team, very interested in the stringing of the jerkline from the bit ring of the nigh leader back through a ring on the collar of the nigh swing mule to the saddle on the nigh wheeler.

Whitman said, "Major, I'm still amazed that one man can handle all those animals with just that one rope. Never see anything like that back in Washington, of course, but out here I've seen as many as twenty mules in one team."

A sergeant and a private came up to them and saluted. "All hooked up and ready to go, sir," the sergeant said.

"My man," Dr. Whitman said, "tell me! How do you manage that team with just that single rope?"

"Well, you give her a steady pull an' holler 'Haw,' an' the nigh leader, he swings left. Jerk it two, three times an' holler 'Gee,' an' he goes right. An' the jockey stick, it's hooked to his collar an' across to the bit of the off leader, so's he hasta go along with his mate, an' of course, the swing team an' the wheelers, why they just naturally gotta follow."

"Major, this fascinates me," Whitman said. "I'd like the experience, and I need notes on it for an article I'm planning. Could I possibly go with the supply wagon?"

"There ain't no place to ride," the sergeant said hastily. "Hafta sit inside on them boxes and sacks."

"John " the major said, "I think we can accommodate Dr. Whitman. Put a saddle on the off wheeler for the doctor, and you can explain things to him as you go."

The sergeant turned to the private: "Git another saddle, Elmer!"

Neil said, "Sergeant, could I have a couple of cowhides? I'm gonna need some rawhide strips."

"Sure. There's some dryin' on the garden fence, if the coyotes ain't et 'em. Elmer, fetch three cowhides an' throw 'em on the load."

Neil said to Jennie, "Here, I'll give you a hand up. Looks like we'll have the wagon to ourselves."

She said nothing, but sat primly on the seat, waiting. He wondered if she were as pleased as he, or whether she was scared green at being alone with him again.

Corporal Jennings and Private Jones, yesterday's escorts, were ready and eager, and the sergeant driving the supply wagon called to Neil, "Take the lead. Keep the lady outa the dust."

Neil swatted Gotch Ear's rump with the reins, and reluctantly she leaned into the collar. As they rattled out of Camp Verde toward the juncture of the Verde River and Beaver Creek and the rough road leading to the ruin, Neil, who had been making a sidelong inspection of Jennie, said, "Lost the Apache Tears already? Or maybe you don't like them after all."

Startled, she turned to look into his eyes. "Oh, no! I love them! But Father asked about them, in fact he seemed to think it quite amusing that anyone would do such a nice thing for me. So I added a little silver chain, and now they hang out of sight, down—I mean, if he doesn't see them, he'll forget about them." She blushed, and turned away.

Neil grinned. She just realized where I'll be figuring they're hanging, right now.

The wagons clattered across the bridge that spanned the diminished river, and onto the road that ran for several miles along sparkling Beaver Creek, running thirty feet wide and almost bank full, probably from thunderstorm waters draining down the canyon all the way from Round Mountain and Hog Hill and seven-thousand-foot Apache Maid. The road got steeper and much rougher, and turned away from Beaver Creek through a maze of side canyons and across gravelly dry washes. The washes had Neil worried. Nobody with any sense ever camped in one, even in good weather. Because it might be good weather right there, bright and sunny and dry, and the thunder muttering so far away, you felt it rather than heard it—and without any warning, here would come a wall of water, mud-colored, brown-foamed, carrying along boulders and washed-out trees, and roll over man, beast, and wagon before you could jump off and scramble up the side of the wash. If the drowned were ever found, they'd likely be a mile downstream, hanging ten feet above the ground in a mesquite tree.

There was a hillside with a scattering of century plants coming into bloom. They'd sit there fifteen years doing nothing, then push out that great club of a stem six inches in a day, that put out horizontal little branches at the top with rows of green or cinnamon-colored pods on them, and these opened into the yellowest flowers you ever saw. The paloverdes were blooming again, too, after the rains—the green branches and trunks from which they got their name carrying clusters of bright yellow flowers, and the bees and the hummingbirds going crazy.

Jennie was so overcome with all the sudden, startling beauty that she forgot her shyness and began to chatter away, pointing everything out and saying, "Oh, I've studied them all in the books, but I wasn't prepared for this. Look, agave in bloom!"

"Agave? That's century plant. What the Mexicans call maguey. And them with the red flowers on the tips are ocotillo. Pretty, ain't they?"

"Ocotillo," she said. "Now I know why. 'Little torch.'"

"Now how would you know a Mexican word like that, Jennie? You talk Spanish?"

"Well, a little. But it's a Nahuatl word—Aztec, not Spanish. And—oh, Neil, look. Look there! Geococcyx Californianus! I never thought I'd actually see one!"

The big bird on a rock not far off the road had a large lizard half-swallowed, its tail and hind legs dangling from the heavy beak. The bird's crest kept raising and lowering as did its long tail, as if it couldn't make up its mind.

"What was that you said?" Neil gazed at her in wonder. "Why that's just a roadrunner. Mexicans call him

Paisano. They got a lots of stories about how smart he is. But you won't like him. He kills a lot of baby quail and other birds, and even baby rabbits. But they'll kill a rattler, too. Keep running around him and dodging and take a whack at his head every time he strikes. And after they finish him they eat him, if he ain't too big."

Well, he'd done it again. She was shocked or disgusted, or something. Talking with her was full of traps, and a man couldn't tell when he was going to stick his tongue in one.

The road wound among ravines and canyon floors and came out at Beaver Creek again. Neil pulled off under a huge sycamore, among the ash and cottonwoods and willow lining the stream.

"Noontime," he said. "Get down and stretch." He climbed down and hurried to give her a hand.

He unhitched the mules, but left the harnesses on, and slipped the bridles and put halters on them before leading them, two by two, to drink. As he brought the second pair back, Corporal Jennings and Private Jones, who had been ranging ahead, came back and built a coffee fire. Soon the supply wagon drove up and stopped on the road, and the sergeant driver and his swamper watered their stock and fed all the mules. Dr. Whitman almost fell out of the saddle and walked stiffly over to the fire, as though he had a boil on his behind. Neil saw the sergeant grinning as he watched the doctor's painful locomotion.

"Nice spot, here," Dr. Whitman said. "I think we should camp, rest the stock, and go on tomorrow."

The sergeant saved Neil the trouble of refusing. He said, "Sir, I got my orders. Major Trumbull says we got tomorrow to set up your camp, an' we come back Tuesday, an' we won't get there in time to do it all today."

"Oh, well," the doctor said, "doesn't matter to me. But, Neil, I think I've been graduated cum laude in my study of jerkline transportation. I'll join you for the rest of the journey."

"Certainly, sir." Neil kept a straight face, but Jennings and Jones were grinning, behind the doctor. Jennie saw them, and looked questioningly at Neil, but he gave her a barely perceptible shake of the head, and she asked no questions.

Mrs. Trumbull had provided a bountiful lunch. As soon as it was eaten, the teams were hitched and the wagons moved out. Dr. Whitman was heard to groan quietly as he settled himself on the seat behind Jennie and Neil.

After a mile, the lack of conversation began to bother Neil, and he began talk about his grandfather, the mountain man who had come down from Canada so long ago with his Piegan squaw, to trap the beaver so plentiful in this area. "The streams were all full of beaver . . . Live Oak Creek, the Verde, Clear Creek. They're still here, too. We'll see 'em, where we camp."

"It must have taken a lot of courage to marry an Indian squaw," Jennie said. "I admire that kind of courage more than, well, to stand up to an enemy or Indians with a gun."

He was beginning to get smart, so he didn't shock her by telling her that Grampa hadn't ever married her, or the others who preceded her—nor had any other mountain man married his Indian helpmeets. "He was one tough old boy," he said. "Got mauled by a grizzly once, broke his arm and a couple of ribs and clawed him up real bad. Left him for dead. Well, Grampa took a grudge against all bears, and he would drop his trapping, whatever he was doing, anytime he came across bear sign, an' go kill him a bear. Not just grizzlies, either. Black bears, little ones, big ones, anything bear shape. Folks got to calling him 'Bear' Douglas. He built a cabin not far from here. We'll pass there this afternoon. I mean where there used to be a kind of a road split off to the cabin. His old bear trap is still there. Must weigh fifty pounds. Everything anybody could use was taken long ago, but ranchers hunt stock-killing bears and wolves nowadays with dogs and rifles, or maybe set out poisoned carcasses."

"What became of him?" Jennie asked.

"Nobody ever found out. 'Paches raided a ranch over on Clear Creek, and him and some others took out after them, and none of them ever come back. Then my grandma, she disappeared, too. Guess she went back to Montana Territory."

"How sad," she said. "This is beautiful country, but it's terrible, too. All because of what men do to each other. So that makes you part Indian, doesn't it?"

"Yeah. I'm not ashamed of it."

"Oh, Mr. Douglas! I didn't mean that! I just——"

He grinned at her. "I don't think you ever meant anything mean about anybody in your whole life."

She didn't respond, but he thought she was pleased. Probably nobody ever paid her any compliments—certainly not her old man! And she wasn't bad-looking at all, not really plain, when you really looked at her. Not any beauty, for sure, but a long way from ugly. Specially when she smiled.

The road, rougher than ever, left the creek again and meandered through twisted canyons to emerge onto a fairly flat and sandy expanse. In another half mile, with the team swinging around a curve and the road hedged on both sides with thick chaparral, Neil ordered, "Hang on, everybody. There's a wash coming up, pretty steep, and I gotta hit it fast. Just pray there's no water or rocks in it."

He yelled at the mules and let the wheelers have it on the rump with the reins. Jennie squealed, Whitman swore, and the wagon tipped forward and went down with a rush across a dry bottom of sand and gravel, and up the other side with a rattle of gear and wheel hubs. Once topped out and on the level, Neil let the team stop for a blow.

Whitman was shaken up and angry. He had slid off the seat on the downgrade, and bumped his sore behind when the wagon tilted upward again. He growled, "Might give a man a little warning!"

Neil wanted to say, "Don't blame me for you being a fool and riding that mule all morning," but he only said, "I told you to hang on."

Behind them they heard the sergeant cursing his six mules and the rattle and crash of the supply wagon crossing the draw with a rush.

Shadows were lengthening when they came around a long bend, through trees and greenery, with the creek noisy beside the road, and a kind of park opened up—tall grass and a broad, flat area, a stretch of sand and cobbles where the creek ran in flood, and tall, spreading sycamores with their multicolored bark and ragged, golden leaves, and a stand of the biggest cottonwoods in the territory. Neil stopped the team and pointed ahead to the left, and Jennie couldn't say anything.

Whitman hunched down and looked between her and Neil, and for a moment, he, too, was speechless.

Then he said, "It's grand! It's magnificent!"

And there was the Citadel, five stories of it, tawny brown adobe and warm gray masonry, in the vast limestone cave whose floor was forty or more feet above the floor of the canyon, almost perfect, almost unchanged for five hundred years, a thousand, two thousand—Neil had no way of knowing.

Dr. Whitman almost fell off the wagon in his haste to get down and look at it, and Jennie sat staring as though entranced, until Neil set the brake and climbed down. He said, "Come on," and held up his arms to her. She seemed to be looking for a way to get down without falling into his arms, but finally put her hands on his shoulders and let him grasp her waist and lower her. He was surprised at how narrow waisted she was under the whalebone or whatever it was that stiffened her corset so that she felt like a wooden doll.

She stood enthralled while Dr. Whitman kept moving around for a better view, stumbling blindly over stones and roots.

The soldiers weren't interested. They'd seen many a ruin. The sergeant parked the Dougherty wagon where Neil directed, and Neil asked the private to put the three cowhides to soak in the creek, with stones to hold them down.

Neil glanced at Jennie to be sure she was out of earshot, then said, "Sergeant, will you sort of beat the brush for snakes without making a big fuss, because she spooks real easy."

"Sure, boy. But all you gotta do is toss a few stones. They get anxious about what's doing the thumping, and stick their heads up, an' you can spot 'em."

"Not in the brush, you can't," Neil said. "And for God sakes, don't shoot any. Use a shovel, and do it quiet."

Before dark, both tents were set up with flies stretched over them, on high ground close under the cliff, Jennie's about thirty feet from the wall tent, and ditches around them. The big tent sheltered supplies and beds for Dr. Whitman and Neil—piles of hay confined by small logs staked in place. The legs of Jennie's folding cot stood in cans of water in her two-man tent, to discourage ants and scorpions. Her luggage was neatly stacked in the back.

The soldiers dug a privy out of sight around an outcropping of the cliff; its post-supported sides and roof made of canvas from a big, worn tarp the quartermaster had thoughtfully sent along.

Late July was no time to be cooking inside a tent, so the small range was set up under a big sycamore near the creek, where the sergeant, expert with an ax, built a table and two benches of split and smoothed saplings, on sawbuck supports. Two coal oil lanterns hung to light the dining area.

Jennie was astounded at how much had been accomplished, and at the savory stew Corporal Jennings concocted with shredded dried meat, onions, beans, diced potatoes, and a lacing of hot red chile peppers to give it the international touch.

"They're professionals," Neil told her. "They've set up camp a hundred times. But I guarantee, never as neat as this one. This is all for the lady of the household."

The stew and the coffee made the sweat run, and Neil wondered how she could stand it, along with the radiation of the cast-iron range, plus her long-sleeved, long-skirted, tight-waisted armor of clothing. The sultry humidity of the night was enough in itself to keep you sweating.

Neil's dutch oven biscuits were acclaimed, and canned peaches ended the meal on a note of luxury. The troopers rolled cigarettes, and Neil and the sergeant were regaled with cigars from Dr. Whitman's lavish stock.

A yellow half moon hung low over the Mogollon Rim. Far away thunder grumbled. The sergeant checked the picket line. Corporal Jennings ordered Private Jones to scour the pots with sand, down at the creek. Dr. Whitman began to hold forth about ancient man in North America; a great deal of his dissertation went over the heads of the four soldiers, and a lot of it over Neil's.

"They all came from Siberia, over the land bridge that then existed, perhaps over a period of centuries . . . roving bands of hunters. They went all the way to Tierra del Fuego, and some started back. Now, wonderful as this ruin, the Citadel is, it is crude compared to those left by the Mayas in southern Mexico and the Toltecs at, for example, Teotihuacán. The Aztecs themselves, their religion probably the bloodiest in history, were master builders. Nonetheless, the Citadel is a remarkable achievement. For instance, those two-foot-diameter roof rafters and floor joists sticking out through the walls—how did they transport them from the Mogollon Rim, fifty miles away? How did they cut them, with no metal, only stone tools? How did they put them in place, a hundred and more feet above the canyon floor, without cranes, without block and tackle? Those things aren't known. We don't know either, exactly what people, what culture, built these structures in Arizona. First, of course, were the Basket Makers, very primitive, living in pit houses, half excavation and half thatched roof, or in caves, where they buried their dead in cists, and where later migrations built right on top of the old relics. There were the Anasazi, the Old Ones, and the later Hohokam. Up on the Moqui mesas, their descendants still live in their rock houses on the cliff. The Citadel here was probably built by the Hohokam, or a people, a small enclave, called the Sinagua."

"*Sin agua?*" Jennie said. "That's funny. It means 'without water' in Spanish."

"But there's always plenty of water around here," Neil said. "Oak Creek, Montezuma's Well, Clear Creek, the Verde—and Beaver Creek here never runs dry."

Whitman smiled condescendingly. "Ah, yes! Very astute of you both. But can you tell me what conditions were fifteen hundred years ago? Or, for instance, what made them go away, and all the surrounding populations, leaving all their valuable goods, huge pots, and metates, and sandals, and arrow shafts?"

"I couldn't say why they left," Neil answered, "but they didn't leave behind anything very valuable. The jewelry and such is always in a burial, and wouldn't be touched. And personally, I sure wouldn't want to lug away a fifty-pound metate or a forty-gallon olla, or a couple of worn-out fiber sandals or a bundle of cane arrow shafts I could cut by the dozen someplace else."

Whitman ignored that. "Of course, there was the great explosion of Sunset Crater a hundred miles north of here. But the lava flow and the fires never got this far. At any rate, I expect to find much of interest when I go into the ruin tomorrow. Maybe even a mummy, or a burial."

"I never saw any mummies, like in some other ruins," Neil said, "but there's parrot skulls and parrot feathers, and bracelets cut from clam shells. Never could figure that. Clam shells and red and blue parrot feathers in Arizona."

The doctor was excited. "Bully! First thing in the morning I want a ladder made."

"Sorry," Neil said. "First thing is a fence across that box canyon, or ravine or whatever. Your ladder will have to wait. And when we make it, I go in first and look the place over. Those floors could be pretty weak, and the ground's too hard to dig for burying you."

Dr. Whitman conceded. "Did you ever see any evidence that there was a natural ramp, or footsteps in the cliff up to the plaza or patio or front yard—whatever you call it?"

"Maybe there was once, but the creek wore it away a long time ago. I'll show you a high water mark, tomorrow, twenty feet up the cliff wall. You can keep busy poking around them storage bins, and there's a couple of ground level rooms over there."

The soldiers went to their blankets. Dr. Whitman stood for a few minutes before he went to the tent, gazing up at the ancient structure in its tremendous, shallow cave, ghostly in the faint moonlight.

When he had gone, Neil said, "Wait a minute, Jennie," and went to the tent and brought back a lantern.

He lit it, and said, "If you leave the tent in the night, take this with you. You can leave it turned low till you need it. If you need anything else, I'm only thirty feet away."

She said, meekly, "Yes, Mr. Douglas."

Neil caught her arm and stopped her. "Please forget the 'Mr. Douglas.' Nobody ever calls me that. I'm Neil."

By dusk of the next day, the camp was in perfect order. To Neil's relief, Dr. Whitman had been totally absorbed in exploring several storage cists and the ancient rooms that were small, walled-in caves at the level of the canyon floor, and had thus kept himself from underfoot. The troopers put the sacks of barley in the storage cists—very small caves, walled in with dry masonry, each with its low, T-shaped doorway designed to allow a man to enter with a load on his shoulders. That the grain storage rooms were once more being used for their original purpose was indicated by a half dozen corn cobs not three inches long caught in cracks of the masonry.

Jennie, deeply interested in the ruin, was equally fascinated by the camp setup, which was entirely outside her experience. Reassured by the deference of the troopers, she so far forgot her shyness as to ask questions, and lend a hand where she could.

Neil and the troopers closed off the narrow, winding

ravine with a fence of trimmed saplings which had a
gate of removable poles. The structure was lashed together with wet strips of rawhide cut from the soaked
cowhides, which would shrink to make connections as
firm as bolted planks. Corporal Jennings had explored
the ravine, and reported that it narrowed down to nothing, was too steep-sided for mules to climb, and had
some grass, and considerable browse which horses would
ignore, but mules would relish.

Two light ladders were constructed in the same way,
one long enough to reach the lower end of a natural ramp
—or perhaps one improved centuries ago with stone axes
—which led up to the patio of the ruin. The second ladder was for getting from floor to floor inside the ruin,
where the ancient ladder poles were still in place, but
frail and shaky, their rungs long gone.

With Jennie tagging along, Neil put the washtub inside the corral gate. When he took two buckets to the
creek, Jennie said, "That's one job I can do; Father
won't let us in the ruin while he's working, and I have
to have something to do."

Neil spent half an hour whittling a yoke for her and
padding it with canvas. When she went to work hauling
water to fill the tub with a bucket hung on each end of
the yoke, it was clear that she was happy to be of prac-
tical use. It was a rather long haul over uneven ground,
not easy, and Neil patted her shoulder and said, "You
know, you're a good kid!" at which she beamed like a
child on Christmas morning. He left her hard at work,
and got his four mules from the picket line, led them to
the corral, leaving their halters on. The halter chains he
hung on the fence.

The two privates and the corporal cleared away brush
for a fifty-yard stretch along the creek, where lay a huge
cottonwood log. While they dug a garbage pit, Neil and
the sergeant attacked the last task, which was to use the
new ladder to reach the rough ramp that led to the patio
in front of the ruin, hand up a twenty-foot length of
slender tree trunk, lash the block and tackle to one end,
push that end out three feet past the patio edge, prop

the pole up at a steep angle, and weight the inboard end with rocks, achieving something like a gin pole or crane boom for the block and tackle.

Dr. Whitman came carefully up the ladder. "Neil, you really think we'll find artifacts heavy enough to require a block and fall?"

"I really don't know, sir. You can see, there's only four, five windows in the whole building. It's plenty dark in there, just a ladder hole in the floor and a smoke hole in the ceiling in each room . . . and I never did explore the whole thing. There's some big ollas, all right. But the main idea is, I think we oughta put most of the supplies in the ruin. We don't want a storm washing us out. Matter of fact, it wouldn't be a bad idea to move camp up here, except for the trouble coming and going on the ladder."

"Why that's a remote possibility, surely," Dr. Whitman said. "Lots of trouble. Waste of time. The supplies are dry in the tent, and the drainage is good."

Corporal Jennings produced another fine dinner. All were tired, and the relaxing around the table after supper was brief.

Before the morning sun struck down into the canyon, the air was already sultry, and Neil and Jennie were standing by the table, waving goodbye to the troopers and the supply wagon.

"More coffee?" he asked.

"No, thank you."

Quail called. A brown thrasher chased another in the brush. A half-grown cottontail came hesitantly into the open.

Jennie's abundant hair, hastily put up, was straggly around her face, which was shiny clean as was her fresh costume—a white cotton blouse and a linen skirt. The slender silver chain that held the necklace of Apache Tears barely showed at her collar.

Neil wasn't sure but what he could still hear Dr. Whitman snoring, even above the noise of the creek.

Jennie said, "How quiet! How very peaceful!"

She looked pretty happy yesterday, and she looks more so, today, Neil thought . . . and now I've got to spoil it.

"Come over here and sit down," he said. "I've got something for you, and I've got to tell you something. You ain't gonna like it."

She came hesitantly and sat beside him at the table, her eyes frightened.

"This is important, and if you don't promise you'll do as I say, we'll break camp and go back. I thought maybe if I told you before you left, you wouldn't come at all."

She said nothing, but her eyes looked enormous. He hadn't noticed until now that they were so dark brown as to appear black.

He said, "If you let this scare you, you'll spoil all the fun. Now you know there are dangerous animals, and we have to be careful, so I got you this." He took the derringer from his pocket and laid it on the table. "Last night, I took the bullets from half a dozen cartridges and replaced them with bird shot, so you couldn't miss a rattler, within six feet. They don't always rattle, so don't step over a rock, or pick anything up, without looking first. Also, there are rabid skunks and coyotes. Skunks, you can't tell. They're not scared of you, anyway. Any skunk you see, get away from him. If you see a coyote that don't run from you, *you* run, and yell for me. If he's close to you, shoot him. Any of 'em, snake, rabid animal, you shoot both barrels, 'cause with a double derringer, you don't know which barrel's gonna fire first, the upper or lower."

She swallowed painfully and said, "I'll be scared, but I'll try. But I never fired any kind of gun."

"I'll show you. Nothing complicated about this one."

She smiled shakily. "I think I could do it."

He put his arm lightly around her shoulders, and she tried to pull away. He held her, and said, "Now, this is the worst, and I hate to say it. But there's men around worse than rattlers. Saddle tramps, prospectors, men on the dodge all over the territory. Somebody might camp close to here, or just come riding up the road. If anybody like that comes into camp, I'll run 'em off. Them kind always back off fast if you show 'em a gun." He held her tighter. "But now comes the real hard part."

He had thought long and hard before deciding, with extreme reluctance, to give her this last order. The possibility was so remote, the chance so very unlikely. But still, it was there—and he had seen women after Apaches had got through with them.

She turned her face away. "What—what is it?" He could hardly hear her.

"Jennie, once in a while 'Paches run away from the reservation. They make tulapai and get drunk, or they knife a soldier, or they just get bored. There's still some wild ones, too—but they're many miles from here. Now you *must* keep the derringer with you, or within reach, every minute, day or night. Sew a pocket on your skirts if you haven't got one. And Jennie, if the one in a million thing should happen—if you should wander away out of sight, maybe in the corral or wading in the creek, or I might be helping your father up in the ruin and couldn't hear you yell—and some renegade Apaches should get hold of you, you have to kill yourself."

Spoken aloud, the words were terrible, even to him. He watched the shock hit her, the incredulity, the slow realization as she stiffened. She looked terror-stricken, as if *he* were a drunken Apache holding her.

"That's the hardest thing I ever had to say," he told her. "And now I've spoiled it all for you, haven't I?"

He waited. Then, slowly, she faced up to the implication, and the reality, of what he had said. Finally she drew a deep breath, and said, "All right, Neil. Father would never forgive me if I insisted on going back to Fort Whipple. In fact, he wouldn't let me. The ruin is more important to him. I know the chance of such a thing happening is, well, it almost doesn't exist. Anyway, I promise, Neil. I'll keep it with me. I'll be scared from now on, but I know I have to carry it."

He could hardly bring himself to emphasize it, but she

had to realize. . . . "And the rest of it, Jennie, remember? If I was off having a swim, or chasing a loose mule, and your father was up in the ruin? . . ."

"Don't explain," she said. "I understand why I would have to kill myself. You might be surprised how easily I could do it."

He looked down at her still, white face, wondering what she meant by her last remark, but decided he'd better not ask. He showed her how to load the derringer, a simple matter of moving a latch, tipping up the double barrels hinged to the butt, pushing in the two stubby cartridges, and snapping the weapon closed.

She put the deadly little pistol into the pocket of her skirt, and Neil gave her the five other shot-loaded cartridges and a dozen of the solids.

Dr. Whitman came from the tent in a striped nightshirt, unshaven, hair on end, yawning, scratching his pot belly. "They gone *already?*" he asked incredulously.

CHAPTER 10

Jennie had been subdued and depressed all the day before, ever since she accepted the derringer and its implications. Neil had tried without success to cheer her up, but her manner still had not changed this morning. Dr. Whitman hadn't noticed, but he seldom spoke to her in any case, except to complain of something trivial. Neil was getting a little disgusted with her. She ought to realize that an isolated camp in Arizona Territory wasn't that Smithsonian Institute, or whatever, back in Washington, and that the risks were real, not stuffed in glass

cases, and that the humans were human—and some inhuman—not plaster dummies dressed in cowboy and
Indian suits. If they were going to stay here, she'd better
face up to the facts, and not go around suffering, so long
as nothing serious happened. He supposed it was really
beyond her to understand that the odds against any real
disaster occurring were too high to have any meaning.
In fact, she had said that she understood, but she sure
wasn't acting like it.

Jennie and her father and Neil were standing together,
gazing up at the Citadel. The sun had just cleared the
Mogollon Rim and painted the lower portion of the ancient structure red. The upper third, set back in against
the cave wall, was warm gray, in the perpetual shadow
of the overhang of the cave.

Neil said, "This one's different from a lot of them.
The kind of rock in this cliff doesn't break off and shat-
ter, but in some places, where the rocks broke up almost like cut stone, cliff ruins are laid-up masonry, some
of it mortared with adobe mud, and the walls so true and
the corners so square you'd think they had plumb bobs
and levels. This here's just good old adobe with a lot of
stones mixed in, and the walls maybe four feet thick.
How high you reckon it is, Doctor?"

"Well, from the platform, or patio, to the top of the
parapet of that setback right up against the cave roof,
it must be seventy or eighty feet. It's ingenious how
they made use of the natural form, sort of amalgamated
the structure to it, you might say, and look there, that
natural outcrop under the main floor, see? Where the
long shallow cave runs under the supporting shelf, they
built it up with masonry and made a big buttress, a kind
of huge pilaster."

The front facade of the Citadel was flat and plumb,
part of it quite smooth, as though it had been plastered.
It was probably eighty feet long and had a square tower
at the north end, projecting eight or ten feet above the
rest of the flat roof, and pierced with one opening four
feet square. At the other end of the front face was a similar opening, and a smaller one centrally located.

"There's four or five rooms in the first part there," Neil said. "The little opening was for ventilation. You get into the thing from the tower end. There's a low doorway, behind that section of wall. The roof of the front, and the tower too, makes a kind of big veranda for the higher part that's set back."

The larger face of the building, perhaps twenty feet back from the front facade, was slightly concave, following the contour of the cave, and extending thirty feet beyond the front section at the right, and was built right onto the end of the cave. The only one way to get into it was through a doorway opening off the roof of the front section. In the whole rear section, approximately eighty feet long, there was only one small, square opening, just below the roof line. Across the face were three rows of projecting beams, the great logs that upheld the floor.

"Is it safe to walk around in there, Neil?" Dr. Whitman asked.

"Well, it is, and it ain't," Neil said. "I think the floors are safe. There's a row of small logs laid crosswise of the big vigas, maybe six inches in diameter. Then brush laid crosswise of them, two feet thick, packed down and covered with a foot-thick layer of packed dirt. You have to watch out for the hole in the floor where your ladder will stick through. You could easy step into it, it's so dark in those closed rooms. You'll need a lantern with you all the time. I'm going up first and look the whole place over."

"Neil, I don't want anything disturbed till I get a chance to study it, its position and condition, measure distances, and make sketches."

"No dice, Doctor. I'm going first."

Immediately Whitman was angry. "We had this out, Neil. You're boss of the camp, agreed. But the ruin is my business, and I won't have you tramping around disturbing artifacts and making it impossible for me to know where things lay in relation to each other. Not only that——"

"Hold up, Doctor! Where'd you get the idea you're

gonna be the first man ever went in there? You'll find artifacts all right, the real old ones mixed in with tin cans and Bull Durham sacks and beef bones that weren't left there by your old Hohokams. Lots of people have camped in there one time or another. Only ones haven't been in are the Indians. They're scared to death of the spirits hanging around. Now I'm telling you—stay down here while I fetch a lantern."

"You're quite right," the doctor said, grudgingly. "But surely there's no objection to my going with you up to the veranda."

"Not even there," Neil said, and went for the lantern, knowing the last order sounded senseless and mulish, but if there were a couple of rattlers taking the morning sun—he'd never been in a ruin that wasn't homesteaded by a few—he didn't want Jennie to hear the uproar Dr. Whitman would certainly make, which would scare the hell out of her. She had been frightened badly enough yesterday, of necessity. And actually seeing one of those devils coiled, head pulled back, tail a blur as it sounded its dry warning was a lot worse than just talking about them.

When he carried the lantern and a shovel up the ladder and ramp, Dr. Whitman asked what the shovel was for.

Neil was ready for that one. "Stuff keeps falling down from the doorways in these places. Those old log lintels are exposed to the weather, and they rot away. Thought I'd clear it out a little. You'll be going in and out a lot."

There were two of them. One outside about three feet long, and one in the first room, a granddaddy of a diamondback. One thing about rattlers, they'd almost always get away if they could. But they didn't like to get out of their defensive position, stretched out with their guard down, you might say, instead of coiled like a spring, and if cover wasn't near enough, they'd fight every time.

He killed them both with the shovel, with a minimum of fuss, saving the need to shoot and scare Jennie clean out of her wits. Sure enough, Dr. Whitman called up to ask what all the thumping was about, and he just mumbled some meaningless reply and dropped the two carcasses, which were still writhing, into a deep crack in the rocks, where he hoped the ants would clean them up before they began to stink.

He went back into the first room, holding the lantern high to be sure there weren't any relatives of the big diamondback scared out of hiding by the noise, and that was when Jennie screamed, and Dr. Whitman squalled, "Neil!"

He set the lantern down and skidded going out the door and made it across the patio in four strides.

At first, all he saw was Dr. Whitman and Jennie hanging on to each other and staring into the weeds at the base of the cliff. Then he saw the deadly weaving of the spade-shaped head and heard the locustlike buzz of the twin brother of the granddaddy diamondback he'd killed in the ruin. Jennie and Whitman were ten feet from it, and in no danger.

The rattler uncoiled and began to move, keeping close to the rock.

Neil tossed the shovel down and yelled, "Here. Kill it! Don't let it get away!"

Whitman glanced hastily at him, then back at the snake. Jennie clung to her father, her face against his shoulder.

Neil, hurrying down the ladder, yelled again. "Throw stones! Do something!" and jumped the last eight feet to the ground.

Whitman said, "Let it go! It's only trying to get away."

"God sake, Whitman! What's the matter with you! You want that thing roaming around camp, and you never know where it's gonna show up?"

Dr. Whitman pushed Jennie away and picked up the shovel, but stood rooted. Neil tossed a stone, and the rattler immediately coiled. He drew his revolver, approached the snake from an angle that wouldn't throw a ricochet off the rocks at Jennie, cocked the revolver and aimed. Then he lowered it, and picked up a handful of small stones.

"Jennie," he said, "you got that derringer, like I told you?"

She nodded, continuing to stare at the snake.

"All right, shoot it!" he ordered.

She shook her head. "I can't!"

"You're going to." he said, and went to her.

The rattler straightened out, and he tossed a stone at it, and it snapped back into the coil, never stopping that dry buzzing that, once heard, is never forgotten.

"Get it out of your pocket," he ordered, but she shook her head.

"Then I'll get it out for you. You ain't gonna like that."

The hammer of the derringer caught on her pocket, but she freed it, and held the weapon out to him.

"Don't get rough with her, Neil," Dr. Whitman said. "I don't like this, her having that weapon!"

"Hell. you're rougher with her every day of her life! You rather we'd be treating her for snake bite? Or you?" He took Jennie's shoulders and turned her toward the snake.

"You forgot everything I showed you yesterday?"

She shook her head, cocked the derringer, and raised it in both hands. It wobbled, and he said, "Steady down, now. Take it easy."

She jerked the trigger, flinched, and the derringer kicked out of her hand with the recoil. Neil's ears rang, and he blinked through the white smoke. Apparently the fired cartridge was the solid slug, and she had missed, of course. by several feet.

He picked up the derringer and handed it to her. The rattler was still coiled. He said, "Now just hold it steady, and for heaven sakes, aim. Hold it out at arm's length and look right down the barrel. No, wait! You have to cock it again!"

She was shaking, but she managed to cock the hammer. She raised it, aimed, made an effort to control the shak-

ing of her arm, bit her lower lip and fired. The derringer
kicked up, but she held it.

Some of the spray of the birdshot hit the snake. It
uncoiled, moved a foot, coiled again, and struck at nothing several times. Its movements were sluggish.

Jennie turned away.

Neil said, "You did fine. Load the derringer again,
remember, one shot load and one solid. Tonight I'll
show you how to clean it."

He finished off the snake with the shovel, and tossed
it out into the open.

Dr. Whitman said, "Neil, I object to the way you
talked to me concerning my daughter. And you did not
consult me about that derringer. You know my feelings."

"I apologize for what I said, Doctor, but not for the
derringer. And here's something else. I killed two more
up there. You'd have blundered right onto them. I
take it I'm responsible for her, but not for you. You do
what you damn well please. But if you don't carry a
stick with you at all times, and watch where you're going, you're a bigger fool than I think you are already,
for not carrying a gun. You got that shotgun loaded?"

"Young man, you watch your language, and don't
presume to instruct me about loading a shotgun. It's in
the tent. Should it be needed, it will be ready."

"Listen," Neil said. "We might as well learn to get
along, or we'll go back, so let's quit fighting. I'll admit
ten times over that you're a lot smarter than me; you're
educated and I'm not, you're a famous man and I'm
nobody. But don't think you know it all. You just
proved you don't. Stood there yelling for help. I know
my job. If you've got any real sense, you'll let me do it,
and we'll all get along fine."

Dr. Whitman smiled, and held out his hand. "I
must confess you get the job done, Neil. And I know
I'm a little—well, difficult at times. And you're right
about Jennie's having that derringer. Now, does that
do it? And, please, don't try to force one on me. I hate
firearms, even when they're necessary."

Neil took his hand and grinned. "We'll get along."

Whitman said, "Fine. But let me ask—are we just going to leave that repulsive thing," he pointed at the dead rattler, "right out in plain view? Can't you bury it?"

"I'll take it around the bend there. Ravens and vultures'll have it all cleaned up 'fore sundown."

He carried the snake dangling from the shovel and dropped it behind a cluster of rocks. Dr. Whitman climbed the ladder to the ruin.

Jennie waited for Neil at the table by the creek. When he came, she said, "I have to thank you, Neil. I would never have believed I could do it. I'm so used to following orders, I just did what you said, yesterday, but I knew I would never be able to use the gun. But now I can. But it isn't only that. It was ugly, and I hated it, but now maybe I can do some of the other hard things, things I always avoid. That's worth a lot, Neil. It's worth the whole trip out here."

She looked away, faintly pink, then hurriedly walked to her tent, her long skirt dragging in the dry grass, raising a small dust.

Each day, Jennie's extreme shyness and reserve, which seemed to Neil to be almost abnormal, subsided—or perhaps retreated to some inner recess of her being, ready to reappear under the stress of embarrassment, the wrong word spoken, some thoughtless and natural act on his part. Several times, he deliberately brought about situations that would upset her, in the hope that he could make her see how inconsequential they really were. For example, the matter of her laundry:

She was scrupulously clean, a difficult habit for her to live with in camp, considering the intricacy and excessive modesty of her dress. On a hot afternoon, with thunder rumbling somewhere in the distance and the white, white cumulus clouds stacked miles high to the east, she started for the creek with a bundle of soiled clothing under her arm, and a bucket with a bar of yellow soap in it. Neil, idling in the shade, noticed that she didn't stop by the big cottonwood log in front of the campsite, but turned upstream and disappeared behind the brush screening the creek.

He got up and followed unhurriedly, and did not come upon her until he was a quarter of a mile from camp. She had shirtwaists and a couple of skirts draped on a bush, other clothing soaking in the creek, held down by stones, and was vigorously scrubbing a pair of drawers or underpants or whatever, long loose ones of cotton with lace around the bottom of the legs. He said, "You sure this is Monday?"

She jumped as though he had pinched her rump, and with frantic haste wadded up the underpants and snatched up some kind of breast band with shoulder straps, and thrust them behind her, her face scarlet.

"Go away!" she screeched. "Get out of here!"

He sat on a rock and leisurely rolled a smoke while she stared at him defiantly, breathing hard through nostrils distended like those of a boogered bronc. He studied her, wondering how to handle the situation, unwilling to back away from it.

Then he said, "Put those underpants down and listen to me. Where'd you get the notion I never saw any women's underwear before? What's to be ashamed about underwear? Everybody I know wears it, 'cept when it's too hot. And if they're clean people, they have to wash it. I even wash mine! Every ten days or so."

Her stiffness slackened a little. She dropped the garments in the bucket and stood facing him, still angry, still upset, her hands clenched at her sides.

"And another thing," he said. "How many baths have you had since we been here?"

"How dare you! How *dare* you talk to me like that!"

He grinned at her. "Oh, cut it out," he said. "I've seen you lugging buckets of water into that little dog tent, and the tent bulging and jumping like a couple catamounts were fighting inside. Why don't you show a little sense? The creek is wonderful, these hot afternoons! You could go in naked, like me! Feels great! Wash your clothes at the same time."

She was so mad she was sputtering, and deeply embarrassed at the same time.

"You dirty-minded . . . you *awful* man! And I was starting to trust you! Is that the kind of woman you think I am? *Is it?*" She stooped and began blindly to grope for the rest of her garments. She was crying again.

He had known many good women as well as bad ones—pioneers, rugged and matter-of-fact, but not immodest, women who were careful not to show too much ankle when they climbed into a buggy, and women who wore riding skirts that were like two skirts sewed together—but he'd never run into anyone like this, so damn priggish it hurt. He got mad at her, not for the first time.

"Listen, you little fool! What did you expect, camped out in the brush? A gold bathtub and a polar bear skin on the floor and a couple of padlocks on the door? You've been pretty good about a lot of things. You're a good campmate—but let's get it straight. If you wanta have a wrestling match with yourself every time you take a bath in that tent, that's your affair . . . but you don't know what you're missing. If you wanta wash your clothes right under my nose, I don't give a damn. I don't get steamed up over a pair of drawers with lace on 'em."

She gasped and got even redder.

"Now this is how it's going to be. You don't go anywhere without me. And if you sneak off, by God I'll turn you over my knee and paddle your behind!"

She stumbled back a step as though he had slapped her.

"I'll never try to sneak a look at you, I won't go prying and peeking through the bushes, but I'll be within call."

She relaxed, but not much.

"You showed you've got good horse sense when you shot that snake," he went on. He had almost said, "guts," but that was a prohibited word. "You're brave enough, so why do you have to be foolish about anything as natural as bathing and washing your clothes?"

She looked at the ground and to both sides, and finally straight at him. At last she said, "You're right. I know you are, in my mind. And you're good to me. So I . . . I'll trust you. I could hardly stand it when you'd take a towel and go up the creek and I could hear you splashing and blowing like a porpoise. And you *won't* look, will you?"

"I promise, Jennie! And here's something else. Why do you wear those kind of clothes, those high collars and long sleeves and skirts that just drug up the dust? They're fine for town, but out here, who's going to see you? Now look, I've got an extra pair of Levi's. We'll cut 'em short for you, an' cinch 'em in at the middle. And I've got two cotton shirts. Sure, you'd get lost in 'em, but you can take a couple of tucks, and roll up the sleeves."

"Trousers? You're telling me to wear *trousers?* No decent women *ever* wore trousers, Neil!"

"Well, I know you're right on that," he said. "Even the girls on Whiskey Row wouldn't be caught dead in trousers. Maybe out of 'em, but not in 'em."

"That is *not* funny, Neil. And I'll thank you not to talk like that to me ever again."

"Don't be so damn touchy!" he said, and she replied, "Don't say 'damn' to me!"

He swallowed a hot retort, but thought, well, she's got some spunk, and that I wouldn't have believed. And when she gets mad, she looks handsome, not scared like most times.

"Well," he said, "while we're on the subject, there's one thing you do that's just plain stupid. In this weather and all."

Instantly she bristled. "I am *not* stupid! I was graduated from college! In anthropology! The only woman I know that ever did! And I work with scientists at the Institute."

"You're still stupid. Why don't you take off that damn contraption of whalebone and canvas? That corset, and all that other stuff that don't show! You're torturing yourself! Who cares out here? Your father? Me? *I* sure don't! You think how a woman's put together is some kind of secret that nobody knows about? I know what kind of conformation you got under there, and it's pretty nice far as a man can tell."

Once more she was furious. For just a moment. Then she gave him that shining smile that always transformed her.

"To tell the truth," she said, "the damn thing *is* killing me! I'll store it in the suitcase. Will you put up a clothesline for me, by my tent?"

"Sure thing!" he said, trying to hide *his* shock at that word she had used.

He stretched out in the tall grass, and soon went to sleep.

The sun stood at about three o'clock when she woke him. Her bucket was piled high with clean, damp clothes, and she had a couple of damp linen skirts and two blouses over her arm.

"I brought an iron," she said, "one of these you fill with hot charcoal. But I don't know what I could use for an ironing board."

"We can pad the table with canvas," Neil said. He picked up the bucket. "Come on, I'll walk you home."

All the way back to camp, she held his hand, lightly— the touch of a feather, of a butterfly's wing. She would look anywhere but into his face, and when he squeezed her hand, she pulled it free—but for once, she wasn't skittish or scared.

CHAPTER 11

The days passed serenely insofar as the human re-lationships were concerned; but at this season, almost every afternoon the clouds that had been only a white hump on the horizon at daybreak grew and swelled until by midafternoon they could no longer withstand their own weight and inner pressures, and exploded into a fury of jagged lightning and appalling noise, and the rain came driving, the wild wind thrashing the trees, roiling the creek, overturning the table, sending buckets and even firewood tumbling. The tents would have gone the way of the buckets if Neil and Jennie had not taken heroic measures with extra ropes and stakes.

Sometimes Dr. Whitman helped, but usually he was oblivious to storm or sunshine, squirreling around in the rabbit warren of the Citadel. He found many a treasure—great ollas, fired clay pots three feet in diameter still half filled with three-inch ears of corn, and some with grass seeds, if the pack rats and mice had been unable to climb the smooth sides. There were many small pots, nearly all broken, but a few intact, some just red or gray fired clay, strictly utilitarian, but others elaborately and beautifully decorated with weird animals, stylized birds and geometrical designs, mostly in glossy black or yellow ochre or rust red.

The artifacts Dr. Whitman intended to keep were stored in a ground-floor room. Frequently he called up-on Neil to help carry down some special treasure, per-haps a delicate bowl with sides no more than an eighth of an inch thick; perhaps a big olla, which had stored water. There were metates so worn with use that their cross section was a U eight or ten inches deep. There were arrow heads and spear points of flint, chert and agate, along with drills, awls, scrapers, and knives of the same material. Hand hammers and axes of stone, along with hammer heads grooved for the attachment of wooden handles. To his great disappointment, Dr. Whitman found no burials, but he planned to probe for them after collecting the surface artifacts. Burials were treasure troves for archaeologists, because the corpses were accompanied by weapons, jewelry of turquoise, shell necklaces and wampum beads, and two to three bowls turned over the face of the skull. Burials were frequently in the living quarters, just below floor level, or perhaps in refuse heaps, where the digging had been easier.

"Of course," Dr. Whitman told Neil, "these things will go to the Smithsonian, except perhaps two or three small items. I am hopeful that they will induce the Institute to finance a thoroughgoing scientific dig. There is much to be learned here, despite the surface intrusion and pot hunting that has gone on."

The doctor seemingly didn't care what Jennie might be doing with her time—certainly he never inquired. He accepted the clean, ironed clothing, the well-prepared meals, as though they were natural phenomena like the air he breathed. Occasionally he would sit chatting after supper in the sultry heat, or the clean coolness after a thunderstorm, but usually he went early to bed, leaving Jennie and Neil to talk—with Neil doing most of the talking because of her deep-rooted reticence, as well as her interest in him and Arizona Territory, which prompted questions rather than discussion.

He was beginning to get tired of never being alone, himself, because she tagged along wherever he went, and wanted to help with everything he did. She did help too—feeding the mules, carrying water to them, keeping the camp clean, burying the garbage, as well as her daily stints of pot washing. They divided the cooking chores.

Actually, his duties were light, there was lots of time to kill, and it certainly was not unpleasant being with her.

Almost everything delighted Jennie except snakes. She recoiled in horror from the first horned toad Neil showed her, until he demonstrated that its fearsome appearance was deceiving, that it was as timid as she, and had no teeth. Birds were myriad along the creek— Gambel's quail, big gray cranes, brilliant yellow and black orioles, blackbirds by the thousand, and once, a strayed cardinal, probably from Ouk Creek—brilliant, scarlet red, with black trimming around its eyes.

She had become much freer with Neil, her obsessive prudery almost gone, along with her somberness of mood. Her nervous deference toward her father, which had amounted almost to slavishness, was subsiding. On occasion, she went so far as to argue with him, and even to defy him in small matters.

All of which was great, Neil thought as he sat watching her one afternoon. She was sprawled almost indecorously, leaning back against the big cottonwood log after a bath and a change of clothes. Her eyes were half closed and there was a slight smile on her lips. Her long, thick hair, still damp, clung to her brown forehead and fell in a mass around her shoulders. Yeah, it's fine. She laughs and jokes with me, and has a lot of fun, now. It really is fine . . . for her. But for me, I don't know. She's getting pretty careless whether I get a look at her legs or not. I'd bet a thousand dollars she's a virgin, that she hasn't even ever had a crush on anybody . . . until now, maybe.

Quite often, now, she put a hand on his shoulder or leaned on him as he helped her across a rock or a windfall, and today, returning from her bath, coming to him where he had been sitting on a rock out of sight, she had taken his hand and hung onto it all the way back. And several times, at supper, while he was talking with the doctor, he had looked across at her and found her eyes on him, and seen her blush faintly and turn away.

Added all together, it was making him uncomfortable.

She's the age, and past, he thought, where she needs a man. And she don't know it, but it don't matter much who, so long as he ain't too ugly and don't eat with his fingers and chew tobacco. And here's me, and nobody else. And that ain't all. She's getting damn good-looking, brown like that and laughing a lot, not all tied in knots and worried somebody's gonna look at her shape. I got an idea she's maybe even a little proud of her shape, and she's got a right to be. One of these days, when she's splashing around out there in the creek, I'm liable to forget what I promised. No, it ain't only *her* that might get foolish! God! Her old man would shoot me!

He got up, and a beaver cruising in the creek slapped its tail down like a pistol shot, warning its kin, and woke her. She looked up at him and flashed that dazzling smile, and his heart did a little flop in his chest. She reached her hand up, and he pulled her to her feet. She went a little off balance, and fell against him. Without intending it, his arms went around her, and she pushed against his chest with both hands, shoving him back, and said, "I'll start the fire," and went to the wood pile. almost running.

Neil followed slowly, his mind pulled several ways. It was pretty clear that she "had a crush on him," the way people would say, and he hoped it wasn't more than that. He sure hadn't made any moves at her, hadn't tried to put his hands on her with one excuse or another, had observed the rules when she went to bathe, and hadn't tried to look at her naked, which would have been very easy to do, now that she had come to trust him. But the physical contacts, though meaningless and brief, had been many—her round hip against his where a path narrowed, his reaching up to take her under the arms to help her down from a rock and feeling the warmth of her, her habit of catching his arm, even hugging it lightly, at some sight that delighted her: a yucca in full bloom with its cluster of creamy blossoms a foot and more long; a parade of baby skunks in file behind their heedless mother; the swirling dance of a thousand sulfur-colored butterflies over a muddy place after rain. The

feel of her in his arms a few moments ago, and the soft-
ness of her breasts against his chest, the yielding of her
slender waist as he pulled her against him. No, she wasn't
the only one with a problem! And his was getting harder
to control, day by day. He had to be more careful than
he had warned Dr. Whitman to be about snakes. If he
didn't, it was going to be very hard on two people—
Jennie Whitman and Neil Douglas.

She was kneeling, putting twigs into the firebox of the
range. The afternoon was stifling, the temperature had
to be well over a hundred degrees, and the air so satu-
rated you could have wrung water out of it. Her cotton
shirtwaist clung to her as though she had been swim-
ming in it, making it plain that she wore nothing under
it. Maybe that was why she was so careful not to look
up at him—knowing he couldn't help looking at her—and
maybe she was still embarrassed at that little accident
when she had fallen into his arms.

He said, "Let it go, Jennie. Stove'd be too hot, near
the table. We can have cold canned vegetables and fruit,
and there's biscuits left from breakfast."

"Father likes his coffee," she said, still not looking at
him.

"Father can make his own," he said. "Why should
you fry for it?"

She turned and grinned at him. "Why, I do believe
you're right! It's a kind of new thought, for me."

She got up, hugging her arms across her breasts, then
laughed, perhaps at her own modesty, and let her arms
drop. Her face was pink, and he looked away too obviously from the round breasts so cleanly displayed by the
clinging garment.

"It's going to storm, isn't it?" she asked.

Clouds to the south were moving as though boiling
inside, and had turned from purest white to ugly, purple
gray. Lavender lightning flashed from cloud to cloud and
stabbed at the earth.

"Won't get here for a while," he said. "Maybe miss us
entirely. I kind of hope it gets here, the way it would
cool things off."

Dr. Whitman was querulous rather than indignant over the absence of coffee. Lately, Jennie had refused a couple of his imperious demands rather sharply and answered some of his sarcastic complaints flippantly, and he seemed at a loss to cope with her changing attitude. Tonight, however, he was happy, having found an infant burial in the wall of one of the upper rooms of the Citadel. He had recovered a piece of twilled cotton wrapping, and another of a most intricate woven design, three tiny wrist bracelets made from slices of clam shell, and a small clam shell pendant covered with a mosaic of bits of turquoise. He said that nothing could dampen his enthusiasm tonight, not even the lack of coffee.

He was wrong. Much more than his enthusiasm was dampened that night.

It was nine o'clock, and no one sleeping, what with the heat and the racket of approaching thunder and the first gusty stirrings of wind flapping the tent door. Neil wondered just how scared Jennie was thirty feet away in her tent.

There was a sudden rattle of hail, then the storm hit like a huge bomb. Even above the shouting wind, Neil could hear branches thrashing, and something went bounding across the clearing. Dust invaded the tent like heavy fog. He lit the lantern, to be ready. Thunder had been rumbling and rolling all around, since dinner. Now there was a tearing, ripping sound, and with it the stunning blast of a near strike, and another and another.

Neil pulled on a pair of Levi's and yelled, "*Doc!* Get your clothes on! This is a bad one!"

He couldn't hear an answer. Most likely Whitman hadn't heard him, in the stupefying bombardment of sound. The closed tent was lit brilliantly, again and again—every object in sharp relief, the momentary pauses black as a mine stope. He yelled, "I'm going for Jennie!"

The tent swayed and rocked, and he felt the tearing away of the fly. ripped loose from its guy ropes and kiting off into the night.

He was groping for his moccasins when the wind began to let up and the rain came driving, hammering

down. It was as though there were no tent. He grabbed
a rubber poncho, and ignored whatever it was that Dr.
Whitman was bawling at him. He thought of snakes
washed out of their crevices and gopher holes, but shoved
the thought away and stopped groping for his moccasins.
He turned up the lantern and set it on a case of canned
fruit, and saw the stream of muddy water running between his bed and Dr. Whitman's. The ditch behind the
tent couldn't handle the water flooding down the cliff.
Water was filtering through the tent. He got a folded
blanket from the middle of a stack of them, wrapped the
poncho around it, and went out.

The wind had almost died and the rain came down
solid, heavy, as though he were standing in a waterfall.
Jennie's tent was flattened, showing the hump at the back
where her two suitcases were, and another that had to
be Jennie, huddled under clinging, soaked canvas. He
grabbed a handful of tent and pulled it away from her
and picked her up with one arm around her waist, and
somehow got the blanket and the poncho pulled around
both of them.

For a moment he thought she was naked, so flimsy
was the nightgown she wore, and so molded to her body.
She clung to him, pressed as close as she could force her
body, and he was more aware of her, sharply and won-
derfully aware, than he was of the mud squelching be-
ween his toes, the rain that poured straight down and almost blinded him running into his eyes, in the intermittent
glare of the retreating lightning. What he was going to
do he knew with only a part of his comprehension; the
rest concentrated on the feel of her body in his arms,
warm and alive and intensely exciting, of her hugging
him tight, her wet face pushed against his throat.

The creek was a dark, roaring torrent threatening to
tear loose the old cottonwood log that was now almost
submerged. Neil could hear the rumble of boulders grinding their way downstream. The rain stopped as though
someone had put the lid on, and suddenly the air was
fresh and clean and light and so cold he began to shiver.

He carried her to the Dougherty wagon, whose roll-down canvas sides were buckled in place. He wanted to keep her in his arms, but made himself lift her up to the driver's seat and tuck the blanket and poncho around her.

He said, "I'll get the side door open and take the other seat out and fix some kind of bed for you. Don't be scared. It's all over, now."

He could smell something scorching before he got back to the tent. The rear tent pole had fallen and wet canvas lay partly across the lantern, beginning to smoke. He propped the tent pole up and uncovered Dr. Whitman sitting in a huddle of sodden blankets on a flattened sponge of hay that had served as his mattress. Runnels of water still coursed through the tent. Dr. Whitman looked dazed and didn't respond when Neil asked, "You all right?"

He found his moccasins and pulled them on, rolling the thigh-length leg part down to his knees. He buckled on his shell belt, found two more blankets in the middle of the stack that were only a little damp. From a carpet bag in which he kept his few possessions, he got a dry cotton shirt. As he picked up the lantern and went out, Dr. Whitman hoisted himself from his soaked nest and stood up, his flannel nightshirt clinging to him like the skin of a snake.

Jennie was huddled on the front wagon seat, as he had left her. He handed her the dry shirt and said, "I'll put the lantern in back for you. Get the wet nightgown off and put the shirt on."

Dazedly, she pushed the blanket and poncho off her shoulders, and he said, "Hey, wait till I go round in back! You don't want me staring at you."

She blinked at him as though coming out of deep sleep, and hastily pulled the blanket around herself. He said, "Holler when you're ready," and walked behind the wagon.

Soon she called, and he unbuckled the side canvas, opened the low door in the wagon box, and removed the second seat. She wasn't very big, and there was ample room for her to stretch out. He remembered the folded tarpaulin in the luggage boot in back, and got it, and folded it to about the size of her cot bed in the tent, and spread the blankets on it, folded lengthwise.

"Come on," he said, "climb over the seat, your bed's ready," and held the lantern up for her.

She tried to keep the blanket around her as she climbed over the back rest, but didn't succeed in hiding her slim legs. He was too cold and wet and discouraged now to let them bother him, and in a moment she was snuggled into the blankets.

"Don't be afraid," he said. "I have to take the lantern and go check the mules. I'll be back."

She didn't answer. She hadn't said a word since he carried her through the deluge.

Alert for snakes, he went warily to the corral and could see nothing behind the fence. He lowered one gate bar and went in. There was a rivulet running down the middle of the arroyo, and a few hundred yards along it, he caught the shine of eyes, like little moons in the lantern light, and found the four of them. Maybe they had been wild with panic when the storm struck, but like all of their kind, once a crisis was past it was past, and out of mind.

When he returned and looked in on Dr. Whitman, he found him fairly comfortable, swathed in a big, cut-up piece of canvas remaining from the old tarp. Neil spent the rest of the night in his damp blanket-lined coat, awkwardly hunched on the driver's seat of the wagon under a brilliant moon and a hundred million stars spilled across a cloudless sky. One thing about Arizona Territory, it never got into a rut as far as weather was concerned.

It took three days of hard work to put the camp back in order. Dr. Whitman grudgingly worked with Jennie and Neil, and worked the harder for his driving desire to get back to poking around in the Citadel. The storm seemed to have wrung the air dry, and although the weather continued hot, it was pleasant. Clothing hung drying from lines strung from tree to tree, Jennie's em-

broidered and enlaced undergarments unblushingly flapping in the breeze beside Neil's butt-sprung woolen
drawers.

The tents were up again, taut and tidy. Neil found the
fly for the big tent a quarter mile upstream in the wreck-
age of a huge cottonwood that had taken that first hor-
rendous shock of lightning. Some of the grommets were
ripped out, but it was otherwise intact. He repaired a
broken table leg, and cleaned the caked ashes from the
range.

The only important loss and damage—not counting all
but three sacks of Neil's Bull Durham—was to the food
supply for both humans and mules. What was left of the
hay was blown to hell and gone, only a couple of hundred pounds of it recoverable from where it had been
caught in the brush. Jennie took it upon herself to collect what she could, packing it on her back in a blanket
and helping Neil to hoist it to the patio of the ruin,
where it was spread to dry. The sacks of barley, of which
only three were left at the time of the storm, had been
soaked in their prehistoric storage bin, and one of them
had burst already from the pressure of the swelling grain,
its contents irretrievable.

"We'll haul the other two up and spread it to dry,"
Neil told Dr. Whitman. "But if any mildew shows up,
or it starts to sprout, we throw it out. Mules wouldn't eat
it. But we've got a good substitute, if we can collect
enough of it. That wind and rain knocked all the mesquite beans off the trees. And the water washed them
down a lot of little gullies it cut to the creek. There was
branches and twigs washed down, too, and some places
it made a kind of screen, and the mesquite beans piled
up there. We can pick up a half dozen bushels. Watch
the mules go for them! Like candy. You know, there was
emigrant trains through Arizona in the early days that
got stranded when their stock ran out of feed crossing the
desert. Stock starved to death and wagons couldn't move,
and people died of thirst. And all the time, here was all
the stock feed they could use growing on the mesquites."

Dr. Whitman said, "You've demonstrated pretty thoroughly that not all knowledge comes from books. I'm not ashamed to confess you have taught me a great deal. I'm properly grateful."

"You've worked hard getting the camp back in shape," Neil said. "How much longer do you have to stay to finish up what you're studying?"

"Why, I don't know, Neil. I'm in no hurry. Are you getting restive for the fleshpots and the bibulous joys of Whiskey Row?"

Neil grinned. "It ain't that, but we do have a problem. Our flour got ruined, and that sack of beans broke open, and I could only save about five pounds. We've got maybe ten pounds of potatoes, and a small sack of onions, but they're sprouting, going soft in the middle. Canned goods, we're in fair shape. Maybe I can get some turkeys and quail, but it takes a lot of quail to make a meal, and we didn't bring much birdshot along with the buckshot for the scattergun. . . . And I won't leave camp for bigger game, even if there was any around."

Whitman was concerned. "I *must* continue my work, Neil. I know it seems inconsequential to you, but take my word, it is of great importance. I . . . I'll try to eat less, to stretch the food out. How long do you think we can hold out?"

"I don't know, Doctor. We'll stick it out as long as we can, as long as the stock don't go hungry. That's more important than food for us. Anything happens to those mules, we're stranded. And anybody but a 'Pache that tries to walk twenty miles in August is going to die of heat and thirst. There's a lot of miles between here and Camp Verde where you can't follow along the creek in those canyons—and you couldn't pack enough water."

"Well, couldn't you drive in for supplies?"

"Sure I could, Doctor. But maybe I wouldn't leave you here. I'll have to study on it. Well, Jennie and me can do what else needs to be done. You go on back to your pots and arrow points."

It was three days before the creek was running clear, and back in its normal channel.

Dr. Whitman snored. Like a swarm of bees humming in his nose. Like somebody gargling a sore throat. Sometimes he mumbled unintelligibly, and thrashed around. Sometimes Neil could reach across and kick him lightly, and turn him off. Other times Whitman would be awakened and was very indignant. But tonight, nothing worked. He buzzed and garbled and snorted, and Neil pulled on his moccasins and Levi's, buckled on the gun, and stepped outside into moonlight so bright it delineated every pebble, every blade of grass, and threw impenetrable, inky-black shadows. It also delineated Jennie sitting on the big cottonwood log by the creek, entranced by the silver path on the moving water.

When he had approached within fifty feet of her, he whistled a tune, softly, so as not to startle her. She turned and he could plainly see the smile on her face. Her hair was a dark cloud frosted with a silver halo. She was bundled in some sort of voluminous robe. When he sat beside her, she took his hand.

"I bet you haven't got the derringer," he said, and she patted the pocket of her robe. "Right there, boss."

Without thought, as naturally as breathing, he slid his arm around her and gently pulled her close. She tilted her head, laying it on his shoulder, and said, "Did you ever see anything so beautiful? It's magic. It isn't real."

When he saw the gleam of the silver chain on the necklace of Apache Tears, the extension she had added so the necklace would be out of sight below her neckline, he hooked his finger under it and pulled the necklace into view.

"I could never tell you," she said, "what it means to me. The sad symbolism, the story about the Apaches . . . but mostly that someone was kind to me, someone thought about me enough to do a friendly thing . . . to give me a gift just because he thought I'd be happy with it."

He slid his hand inside the neck of her nightgown, gently and softly, and laid it on her warm breast, and could feel the beat of her pulse.

Jennie gasped, sat as still as death for a moment, then

shoved at him with hands and elbows, her face twisted, tears squeezing from her tightly closed eyes. Shocked at himself, because he truly had intended no lechery, he let her go, and she ran and tripped on her long robe and fell sprawling.

He picked her up with an arm under her knees and the other around her waist. She didn't try to fight him, but lay against him as rigid as a clothing store dummy, except that she was racked with silent weeping.

He carried her to the log, and sat with her in his lap, and said, "My God, Jennie! I never meant . . . I wasn't really trying to . . . " He couldn't put it into words.

She yielded not at all, still stiff and awkwardly bent. He tried to pull her head onto his shoulder, but she wouldn't relax, and he began to smooth her hair back from her forehead.

He said, "I wasn't following you, I just happened to come out here and found you. You hate me now, don't you! You'll never trust me again. Jennie," he made the age-old, specious excuse which right now, between him and her, was the plain truth— "Jennie, it just happened. I'm a full-grown man, and my feelings with a woman in my arms are no different from anybody else. I'd be lying if I told you I don't get excited just looking at you, watching you move. To you, that's dirty. Something to be ashamed of, but I don't understand why. If I'd've tried to force you, I'd've done it long before now."

He knew she was deeply hurt, deeply disillusioned with him, but he wasn't going to say any more. He wasn't going to crawl and beg her to forgive him, because he didn't figure he'd done anything wrong.

She said, "It isn't you, Neil. I don't think it was dirty. It's me. Something wrong inside me. I just can't bear to have anyone touch me. You could never understand how hard it's been just to make myself be free and easy with you, to hold your hand and be friends with you—but at least, I got that far. You mustn't blame yourself."

He began to get a little mad. So she knows she's odd! Why the hell don't she do something about it! Why the hell didn't she keep on shoving me off, the way she started out!

She put her warm palm against his face and kissed his cheek, which confused him more than ever. Then she began to talk, and her voice was hardly audible. He leaned his head against hers, to hear better.

"It began a long time ago. If you knew how hard it is to tell you, maybe you'd understand how much I love you."

This shocked him. Who said anything about love? He had been sorry for her and her unknown troubles from the first—but love?

"Please don't talk or ask any questions. Just hold me and let me tell you now, or I never can."

She drew a long, shuddering breath. "My mother died ten years ago, when I was thirteen. I loved her very much, and her death almost killed me. We were living in Cambridge, Massachusetts, and Father was at the Peabody Museum. He was an important man. And my Aunt Julia—she's my mother's sister—came to help with the things that had to be done, she and her husband, Uncle Harry. Their name was Everly. I didn't like Uncle Harry, because when I was little, he was forever pulling me onto his lap and kissing me. Anyway, they were good to me, then. And one day before the funeral, Father and Aunt Julia had to go in to Boston for some of the arrangements, and I wanted to go, but Father told me to stay and keep Uncle Harry company, because he had a headache.

"And after they left in the buggy, he went into their bedroom and lay down, and in a little while he told me to bring him a headache powder and a glass of water, and I did. And when I handed him the water, he put it on the stand, and I saw he didn't have any clothes on. He grabbed me and pulled me onto the bed, and he kept talking to me, so soft and nasty and putting his hands on me, and I was about out of my mind. I screamed and screamed, and tried to get away, and he swore at me terribly and said he'd kill me if I ever told anybody.

And he hit me when I wouldn't stop screaming and fighting.

"I don't remember much more of it. But Father and Aunt Julia had forgotten something and come back. And I think I was screaming so loud Uncle Harry didn't hear them come in. He was trying to pull my clothes off, and my skirt and shirtwaist were torn. And all I remember is Aunt Julia screaming 'No, Granville, no!' and the awful noise when Father shot him with the pistol he always carried. And . . . and he was dead, lying on top of me, and his blood all over me."

She told it all calmly enough, but he could feel her getting more and more rigid, and the trembling beginning. He said, "Easy, Jennie! Easy now. It's all over!" and pulled her close, cradling her in his arms.

"It won't ever be over," she said. "They put me in some kind of a nursing home for a while, and Father had to go on trial. The newspapers were awful. And some reporters got into the nursing home and tried to ask me horrid questions. And when I felt better and the trial was on, I had to be there. They didn't make me testify in court, but they asked me questions in the judge's chambers—about whether I had . . . had tried to provoke Uncle Harry, or did anything to make him think I wanted him to . . . to . . . and when each day was over, we had to make our way through the people outside, reporters yelling at us and people calling me awful names. The newspaper headlines were terrible."

She paused, quiet and relaxed now, and Neil tried to think of something comforting to say—but what was there to say? Something cheery, like "Everything always turns out for the best, I always say"?

"But that wasn't the worst," she said. "They acquitted Father, and said it was justifiable homicide, and we moved to Washington to get away from the people, and Father had this good job at the Institute. But the whole thing followed us there, and people would look at me in a funny way, and nobody would be friends with me. I know I was a burden on Father, and he was glad when he could send me away to college for four years. But then, of course, I came back, and what could he do with me? He had a lot of social obligations, and entertaining to do in his job, and I wasn't good at it, I was so shy and scared of everybody, by then. I was no good to him at all, just a bother to him. I don't know how many nice young men he had out to dinner, and for the theater and iceskating parties and buggy rides, but I was just in a shell, and I hated and feared every man—every one until you, Neil."

The poor kid! The poor little kid! was all he could think of and his heart ached for her.

"None of them ever came around a second time. Who could blame them? And I think it was Aunt Julia put the idea in Father's head. She hated me. But, anyway, Father, himself, began to wonder if I hadn't led Uncle Harry on that day, if maybe I hadn't tempted him and . . . and teased him."

She began to cry, her warm tears running down his neck. She said, "He never actually said so, but I knew by the way he acted, and some of the clever questions he asked, that weren't clever enough. He still thinks so, Neil."

"The son of a bitch!" Neil said. "I'll damn well set him straight!"

She put a warm palm over his mouth. "No, you mustn't! But you do understand now, Neil? Do you? Why I can't bear to have anyone touch me, not even you . . . not for a while. I'll try. I'll learn, Neil, because I love you very much. But you have to be patient. And, I know, after we're married it will be fine. If you'll just give me time."

Married!

He almost dropped her. Who the hell said anything about getting married! Good God Almighty! Where did she get the idea I . . . But shocked as he was, he did understand. Jennie simply couldn't imagine intimacies before marriage, just for the fun of it. That was the way good women were, and nowhere was it better understood than on the frontier, where they were too scarce— the bad ones for fun and frolic, the good ones untouch-

able, almost sacred. And if you told one of the good ones
you loved her, or tried to fool around with her, and she
happened to love you, why then marriage followed as the
night the day. Yes, he understood well enough what she
had taken for granted, and why—and the trap had
snapped shut on him.

But he simply could not bring himself to hurt her.
She'd been hurt too much, and somehow had kept her
sanity, if not her balance. Warped and damaged, she was
still wise enough to see the flaw in herself, and somehow
he had given her the courage, the reason to try to heal
it. How could he destroy her with one sentence?

So he said, "I love you, too, Jennie. We'll work it out.
Come on, now. I'll carry you back. You shouldn't have
come out here in just those slippers."

CHAPTER 12

Dr. Whitman, having finished his study of the ground
floor of the Citadel, now made no objection to Jennie
and Neil looking around in there. Heretofore, he had
insisted that they stay out so as not to disturb his archae-
ological detective work, and Neil hadn't cared much.
Now Neil was pleased at Jennie's pleasure in the col-
lection of artifacts gathered in a ground-floor room—tiny
ceremonial arrow points of obsidian which Arizonans
called "bird points," worn sandals woven of yucca fiber,
bundles of moth-eaten turkey and eagle feathers, beautifully woven, conical baskets with tumplines for back packing. Neil told her the Apache women and others still
used identical baskets for gathering grass seeds. There

was the remnant of a blanket woven of strips of rabbit fur, and many other fine relics in addition to the pots and metates and the great ollas.

Neil managed to step on a couple of scorpions without Jennie noticing, and brushed away the ragged web of a black widow spider, and wondered how the doctor had so far escaped kneeling on the one or putting his hand on the other. He would have to warn him.

Back in Fort Whipple, planning the expedition, the prospect of exploring the ruin had been of great interest to Jennie, but now, when he suggested they climb to the second floor, she grabbed his hand and pulled him outside. "Come on," she urged, "I've seen enough. The things are beautiful, but everything is old and dark and a thousand years dead. Let's go wade in the creek or walk up the canyon, get out in the sun."

He was glad to see the new mood, because for two days now, since the night she had told him of the shock of her mother's death and the accumulation of horrors heaped upon her thereafter, she had again been subdued, depressed, hesitant, sometimes avoiding him, probably regretting that she had not kept her secret. His sympathy for her was deep, as was his regret for these long-ago but still terrible blows to her pride and self-assurance. His sadness for the dark loneliness of her life, for the injustice, for the suspicions of her pompous father, grew deeper the more he realized what cruelties she had endured.

He wanted to comfort her, to tell her it was all right, that vicious as it had been, it was over, and that him, at least, she could trust; but he hadn't dared to make the approach, speak the affectionate and compassionate words, reach out and take her hand, for fear she would sink again into her private hell, scared of everything, deeply distrusting him again. Now he had to go easy, like talking quietly to a horse you were trying to halter, letting it recognize you before you got too close.

There was another angle to it, too, that his mind sort of slid away from ever since she had told him she loved him, and he had found himself incapable of saying other-

wise in reply; any advance by him, intended only to re-
assure her and restore her shaky new-found confidence,
could well mean that her allusion to marriage had been
joyfully accepted by him, also. My God! *He* didn't want
to get married! *He* hadn't said anything about marriage,
hadn't meant to arouse any such prospect any more than
he had intended to seduce her that night. And he really
hadn't. Slipping his hand down the neck of her nightgown, putting it gently on her breast, had been as auto-
matic and undeliberate as breathing. A warm woman
on your lap, in a light nightgown, and all that moonlight—why, your hand just naturally, all by itself—his
thoughts skidded away from that, too.

For three days, he devoted himself almost entirely to
her, acceding to her whims, rambling up the canyon, exploring the side ravines, wading in the creek, or sitting
hand in hand on the big cottonwood log, which was again
high and dry. The heat was intense, the humidity very
high, and late each afternoon there was a thunderstorm, but only weak imitations of the gullywasher that
had hit them. Now Jennie seemed to need to be in
physical touch with him, leaning against him on the log,
holding his hand as they walked, even daring to sit with
her head on his shoulder after Whitman's day's work
was done and supper over, and the doctor devoted himself to port wine and learning to roll cigarettes, his pre-
cious cigars having gone the way of the flour and the
beans, in the storm.

Well, she was in love with Neil, no doubt about that,
and his tenderness for her grew deeper, considering all
that had been done to her, and what he, himself, would
inevitably have to do to her, when she must be made to
understand that he didn't love her. But he could not
bring himself to smash her illusion, not yet, and convert
her joy in these weeks at the Citadel into permanent
heartbreak.

She kept arousing him, physically, too, which he knew
was the last thing she intended. She was now a gay,
pleasant, quick-witted companion with whom he passed
the days most pleasantly. But if she had to love him, he

wished to God she didn't have to be so girlish about it, gazing adoringly at him in a half trance as they sat at meals, even daring to kiss him on the cheek when they said good night, then scuttling into her tent as though the devil himself were clutching at her.

She was by turns coy and flirtatious, and much more provocative than she realized—"smitten" was the way people would have described her—but it was more as if she had been hit between the eyes with LOVE and knocked a little loopy.

Then there was the doctor. Whatever else he might be, he was neither stupid nor unobserving, and he would have to be both, not to see what was going on. During the days, he immured himself in the Citadel like a mole in its labyrinth; but the evenings were getting cooler, and now most times after supper, they sat around a small fire while he cross-questioned Neil about the living and eating and dying and religious habits of Apaches, and she clung to Neil's hand and gazed lovingly up into his face.

The thought got into Neil's mind and rapidly hardened into conviction, that Dr. Whitman would gladly marry her off to any white man at all, just to be rid of her—even to a scarcely educated ex-sergeant of Apache Scouts, and that he simply wasn't going to make an issue of Jennie's open infatuation. Neil's respect for Dr. Granville Whitman III, never very high, dropped to near zero.

The coals burned low, the moon rode high, the air was soft, and Dr. Whitman pursued his catechism, with half-filled notebook handy.

"It appears," he said, "that you harbor an inordinate respect for these aborigines. Maybe admiration is the better word. And I find that unique among Caucasians. Would you explain?"

"Guess you never talked to General Crook about them," Neil said. "Or maybe he ain't Caucasian, whatever that is. But anyway, he knows them better'n anybody, and he's tried real hard to keep them from being robbed and cheated, and to get them settled onto farms.

They trust him, because he never once lied to them. And he beat them at their own game, fighting on their own ground, summer and winter, never giving them a chance to rest. Only them that surrendered, that came in to the reservations, why he treated them right. And the BIA and the contractors and the government and the Tucson Gang broke all his promises to them and spoiled everything he did."

"But Neil, you've fought them, you've come near being killed by them many times, and you've helped defeat them. Why, then, the admiration for them?"

"Exactly because I have done those things, and I know them. Now you take the cavalry. There's a lot of tough, brave men in the cavalry, but some of the generals sent out here took the notion the Apaches ain't much, and mostly they've tried to catch up with 'em and kill 'em, or corner 'em . . . and nobody could do it till Crook came. Now, sir, you just might as well not write this down, because you ain't gonna believe it, like other things that don't tie in with what you got out of all those books."

"Never mind the personalities, Neil. What I write down is my business."

"All right. A 'Pache buck will start out on the war trail with maybe three ponies, and carry hardly anything but his weapons and a little jerky, and about a dozen holy charms to keep him bulletproof . . . rosaries that like as not came off a priest he killed down in Sonora. or a piece of petrified wood, things like that. He knows every water hole from Mormon Lake to Hermosillo down in Sonora, and from Prescott to the Staked Plains. And if he thinks the water holes are guarded, he'll go forty-eight hours without water across country so rough you wouldn't believe it. That'll kill a cavalry horse and a trooper in twenty-five miles, and twenty-five miles was a standard day's travel for the cavalry, before Crook got here. The 'Pache, he'll go seventy miles a day, day in day out for a week. And if by dumb luck and cussedness, some detachment stumbles onto him, why he'll go one way and the rest of his bunch about fourteen other directions, and get together again someplace they've agreed on."

The doctor said, "Well, you're right, Neil. I can't quite believe all that." Nevertheless, he wrote it down.

"Why don't you write General Crook and ask him?" Neil said. "Are you by any chance a betting man?"

"No. No, I'm not," Dr. Whitman said. "But if it's true, how did General Crook defeat them so utterly?"

"Because he's smart. And he's tougher and a better shot and a better trail reader than anybody in his command, and he really knows Indians. Not only that, he left behind all the heavy gear—the wagons and forage and camp gear and draft horses, when we were on a hot trail, and he had his mule trains that could keep up with the cavalry. Every mule fitted with his own aparejos and pack saddle, and every mule could pack three hundred pounds, after Crook trained his packers how to condition 'em. And once on a trail, he never let us quit. Not even if our horses laid down an' died, we kept on, even in Mexico. And summer and winter, the 'Paches got no rest—no more of that spending the winter resting and getting fat up in the White Mountains. Because some cavalry outfit might cut loose at 'em any time, night or day. No sir, they were kept on the run, and they starved and got shot, and finally saw the light."

"Well, all right, Neil. Let's grant for the moment that the Apaches are tough . . . but they're not intelligent; they just act through instinct like animals."

"Well then, Doctor, their instincts are maybe as good as brains. One time, Limpy—he's a Mojave named Doka that pulled me out from under a dead horse one time, and got himself shot through the knee when he could've got away—Limpy got himself cut off by a band of broncos down in a canyon. You bet he was riding for his life, and he got ahead, around a couple bends, and dropped off his horse onto some hardpan that wouldn't show tracks, and climbed up a ledge about ten feet off the canyon floor, and his horse kept going. He laid down and got a couple handfuls of dust and wet it good and smeared it on himself so he was colored like the rocks and dirt, and didn't move and almost didn't breathe. Now those broncos, they knew by the horse's tracks, where it ran off the hardpan and into the dirt again, that Limpy had dropped off somewhere in the last mile, and they studied the ground and looked at very inch of canyon wall, and they never spotted him."

"Most resourceful. Most ingenious," Dr. Whitman said.

"But," Jennie said, "where did he get any water to make that mud, lying up on the ledge?"

Whitman roared with laughter, and Neil came close to slugging him, as Jennie, her face flaming, beat a retreat to her tent.

"Oh, that's capital!" the doctor said, when his snorts of laughter had subsided. "Where did he get the water! My poor stupid little Jennie!"

Neil said, "No she's not, Dr. Whitman. Not stupid. Can't say the same for you." He got up and went to bed.

About ten the next morning, Jennie was doing something in her tent—maybe still embarrassed, and hiding—and Dr. Whitman came down from the Citadel for coffee. He and Neil sat at the table smoking, and heard the shots, way off to the north somewhere, so far that Whitman wasn't sure he'd heard anything, but Neil knew. There was one rifle shot, then four or five almost together, then one more.

Neil said, "Get the washtub from the corral, Whitman. I'll get the food together. We'll haul about everything but the tents up to the ruin . . . plenty of water. and all the food and blankets and firewood, then pull the ladder up after us."

"But Neil! Even if it was shots we heard . . . you heard, really . . . why get excited? Probably just somebody hunting."

"I think you're right, Doctor. But don't argue. Jump to it!"

"But, Neil!" Dr. Whitman wasn't going to comply meekly with what he considered supercaution on Neil's part.

"*Don't argue! Get going!*" Neil yelled, and Whitman

jumped as though Neil had kicked him, and trotted off toward the corral.

"Just a minute!" Neil yelled, and Whitman skidded to a stop.

"When you bring the tub, I'll help you haul it up, with the tackle. Then you can start bringing water in the buckets, with the neck yoke, and Jennie can take them off the hook when you haul them up to the ruin. And take the shotgun and all the powder shot and caps up there."

Whitman looked away from him, hesitating, then said, "It broke, Neil. After the storm, when we were hammering in the tent stakes. It broke off at the stock. The stock was cross-grained, and——"

Neil was so jolted by such suicidal carelessness, so choked with obscenities to shout at the man, that he could find no adequate words. He flapped his hand at the doctor and said hoarsely, "Hurry it up, will you?" and walked to Jennie's tent, trying to dampen down his outrage so she wouldn't take fright from the mere tone of his voice.

Jennie came out.

He started to give her instructions, but she said, "I heard you, but I don't know what it's about."

She was scared already, and he had to scare her worse. "It's nothing, Jennie. Your father thinks I'm foolish, and he's probably right. It's just the way I've been trained. We heard some shots, way off over there. Somebody hunting. But there are a few wild Apaches still loose. They're way southeast of here, in the Dragoon Mountains, but I won't take a one-in-a-thousand gamble, that's how stubborn I am."

CHAPTER 13

Food, blankets, clothing, ammunition, and water were stored in the entrance room of the Citadel. Firewood had been hauled up and stacked on the patio, with much sweating and grumbling on the part of Dr. Whitman, who said the whole thing was foolish, and he wasn't used to pulling on the fall of a block and tackle. Neil ignored his complaining, and showed him how to load the carbine and change the tubular magazine in the butt. He told the doctor he might be gone an hour, and that the doctor should haul up the ladder as soon as Neil got down. If anyone showed up, he was to fire one shot as a signal to Neil, and keep out of sight in the ruin—even anyone in uniform, because Army deserters were apt to be desperate, and could well be vicious.

He took his lariat and went to the corral. The mules, fat and fractious from easy living, didn't want to be caught, but he cornered them at the far end of the arroyo. They were rope broke, and stood like statuary the moment a rope fell across their necks, whether the loop caught them or not. He had brought two halters from the fence, and two by two, he led the jugheads to water. Gotch Ear, lazy as she was, was the easiest to catch and the hardest to lead, and he laid it into her good with the end of the halter chain. He carried about half of the mesquite beans he and Jennie had gathered into the corral, which left only a couple of bushels. The mules had already cleaned up all of the scanty browse, including the berries on the junipers, as high as they could reach.

Returning, he approached the ruin warily. Dr. Whitman was sitting on the lip of the patio with the Spencer across his lap. The Bull Durham cigarette he was trying to roll was a worse disaster than usual. Jennie had a small fire going, and something cooking. She saw Neil and waved to him.

Whitman lowered the ladder and Neil ascended. He said, "Leave it in place. We'll have time to haul it up if we need to. You see anything while I was gone?"

"You can't see what's not there," Whitman said petulantly.

"You can't see Apaches that *are* there, and if you think they're around, that's the time to start worrying."

The wisdom of this wasn't obvious to Whitman. "Neil, come on, now. This is a lot of foolishness. We're short of supplies, and that's going to cut my work short if you continue to be stubborn about getting more. We've lost the day, already, and for what? Because your ears fooled you into thinking you hear shooting."

"Who's stopping you?" Neil said. "Go ahead. Go find some arrowheads."

"Just like that, eh?" Whitman's sarcasm was undisguised. "The great Scout returns, so the settlers are safe, and may return peacefully to their humble tasks. Well, let me tell you——"

"*Shut up!*" Neil yelled. "I oughta take Jennie outa here and leave you with that shotgun!"

Jennie said, "Please, Neil! Please, Father! Come and eat. I've got beans and stewed jerky and biscuits. Neil, the flour we saved is a little moldy. Is it safe?"

"Sure is." Neil patted her hand. "Long as it's cooked I could eat a raw skunk!"

"Must you be so crude?" she demanded, and he almost told *her* to shut up, but only said, "Sorry, Jennie."

Everyone's feelings were wounded and the meal was a silent one, until Neil, his fork halfway to his mouth, put it on his tin plate and set the plate on the scrap of canvas Jennie had laid down for a table cloth. He stood and said, "Keep quiet so I can listen."

"So you can hear what's not there?" Dr. Whitman asked.

Neil turned on him, jaw clamped shut, eyes slitted, and Whitman hastily got up and backed away, saying, "All right, Neil! All right, now!"

Two riders topped the hill across the creek a quarter mile away, and rode carelessly toward the camp.

Whitman said, "Surely you didn't hear them, at that distance!"

"Are you deaf?" Neil asked. "They're from Camp Verde."

"Well, then! Let's lower the ladder! Is there plenty of coffee, Jennie?

"Just hold on, Doctor. Don't you recognize them?"

"Why, they're Indians! Apaches! Members of the Scouts, Neil?"

"You're blind as well as deaf," Neil told him, no longer caring a plugged peso whether the doctor liked the way he was talked to or not. "That's Eddie Burke and his lap dog, Whitey."

"Eddie Burke? Oh, look, it's that albino Apache! I want a close look at him. He's a weird one, isn't he! Is albinism frequent among these savages, Neil? Jennie, find my notebook!"

"You're gonna talk to them, after what happened at Camp Verde?"

"Why not, Neil? After all, you subdued him most effectively, in fact, somewhat brutally. That other one hardly looks Indian. What in the world is he? The costume, I believe, completely Apache. But the short hair? Why would an Indian wear his hair short like a Caucasian? You think they'll let me sketch them? Particularly that weird albino?"

"He ain't albino, and he ain't 'Pache, Doctor. And the other's half 'Pache, but he won't admit it."

"Now Neil! Don't mislead me! I want no misconceptions or warped humor in the paper I'll write for the Smithsonian."

First Sergeant Eddie Burke on a saddle horse and Whitey riding bareback splashed across the creek and dismounted. They tied their mounts to a young sycamore by the big cottonwood log. Burke was packing his service revolver. He left his Spencer carbine in the saddle boot. Whitey was armed with a big knife in a beaded sheath, and a Springfield Long Tom which he carried as they walked past the tents. His sunburned and hairy chest was encircled by a catridge belt slung over his left shoulder.

Jennie stood behind Neil, clutching his arms. He shook her hand off his right arm.

As usual, Whitey was sunburned and peeling, greased with bacon fat or cosmoline or whatever he used. His straggly, colorless hair was bound with a strip of red cloth, his breechclout filthy, his moccasins with the turned-up toes badly worn. He raised a hand to shade his eyes and blinked up at the three on the ruin's patio.

Eddie Burke, somewhat of a dandy, wore the full Apache regalia he affected for the war trail, or when hunting with Apaches whom he disowned as blood brothers. His clout was buckskin in the old style, and his short-legged moccasins beautifully made, his hair, ragged around his ears but not down to his shoulders, tied with a yellow scarf. There was a band of yellow painted across his nose and a circle of white on each cheek.

Whitey squatted on his haunches, his left arm extended, holding the long rifle erect for support. Burke came to the foot of the cliff, studied the ramp which was ten feet beyond his reach, and said, "S'matter of you, Douglas? We been huntin'. We're hungry. You ain't gonna let us go hungry, are you compañero?"

Whitey said, "C'mon, Duggles! Eat!" He bunched his fingers together and jabbed them several times at his open mouth. "Today no eat nothin'."

"Just a minute. We'll lower the ladder," Dr. Whitman said. "Jennie, get two more bowls!" He stooped to seize the ladder, and Neil grabbed his shoulder.

"Drop it! They ain't coming up here!"

Whitman was furious. "*They certainly are!* Turn hungry men away? Not from *my* camp! You forget yourself, Douglas! And not only that, I wouldn't miss this chance to get firsthand notes for anything! That albino is a real oddity, and my colleagues——"

"You forgot what they did to Jennie, Doctor? Or you just don't give a damn about her, is that it? And I'm telling you, they're poison, those two!"

The doctor said, "Neil, you lower that ladder! That white one—why you can control him easily, primitive as he is. And I never saw the other in my life!"

"You what? You didn't see him grab me by the neck, right after—" Then he remembered that Burke had been in uniform that evening. No one would recognize him as the same man. "Listen," he went on, "they're not coming up here! That's flat! If you want to go down there, you can damn well go. And I'll go with you to see nothing happens. If you wanta feed 'em, I guess it's your business. Me, I'd poison 'em!"

He turned to Jennie. "Maybe you oughta sort of disappear, go inside. I'll get rid of them soon as they eat."

She appeared not to hear him, but stood, mouth slightly open, eyes wide, as though both repelled and fascinated. He thought, then, that maybe she hadn't seen Whitey's obscene gestures and mockery of her, that evening at Camp Verde, and that maybe the major and Mrs. Trumbull hadn't explained to her, to spare her feelings. Maybe she hadn't seen Whitey at all, in the group of Scouts. And certainly, she wouldn't recognize Eddie Burke in that get-up, any more than her father had.

Whitman started to lower the ladder, and Neil said, "Jennie, you're not thinking of going down there?"

She started as though coming out of a trance. "What? Oh, no! I don't want to go anywhere near them!"

"Well," he said, "I can't buck your father. Take some food out for yourself, and put the rest in the big pot, will you? And wrap some biscuits in one of those grain sacks you washed. I'll lower it down with the tackle."

"And the coffee?" Whitman asked, as he hooked the fall onto the ladder and started to slide it over the edge.

"The hell with coffee," Neil said. "Let 'em go dry, or drink out of the creek like the other animals."

"For a man that professes to like Apaches," Whitman

said, "I find your attitude contradictory, to say the least."

"Just hope your own attitude don't get us in trouble. If you had any sense you'd run 'em outa here!"

When the ladders were in place and the food lowered, Whitey squatted by the pot, laid his rifle on the ground and dipped the beans out with his hand. Eddie Burke, smirking up at Jennie where she stared down from the patio, said, "You fergot the spoons, sweetheart. Just drop me down one. An' what about coffee?"

She went out of sight, and Neil said, "No coffee."

Eddie Burke grinned at him. "You kinda not friendly with your o'd friends, Douglas. What you scared of? You figger maybe she likes my looks better'n you?" He walked over to stand by the ladder, and Jennie reappeared and dropped a spoon, which he caught deftly. He bobbed his head and said, "Yer a good kid, sweetheart."

She didn't answer, but she didn't go away either, standing there staring down at him as he walked back to the pot and squatted beside Whitey.

Dr. Whitman, muttering to himself, was hurriedly trying to make a sketch of Whitey. This made Whitey nervous, and he said to Burke, "What that sonabitch do?"

"He's takin' your picture, mud brain."

Whitey threw his handful of biscuit and beans at Whitman, yelling *"No good! No good!"*

Grinning, Burke said to the affronted doctor, "Very bad medicine mister. You take their picture, they think you got a piece of their soul. Me, I don't believe nothin' like that."

"Well, I'll get *you* down on paper, then," Dr. Whitman said. Burke's grin disappeared. "Uh . . . not this time. Mebbe some time you come to Camp Verde or somethin'. Me, I ain't no real 'Pache, mister. I'm Irish. First Sergeant Eddie Burke. I dress this way when we're on a campaign 'cause my Indians, they take orders better from their own kind, even if I ain't the real thing. Now you take Douglas, there, he never could handle his Indians right. That's why they give him just the riffraff, that Mojave and them Mescaleros."

"I handled *you* a couple times, Eddie," Neil said.

"How'd you get the hump on your nose?" That was when he fell on his face in the ring, Fourth of July, Neil thought. It was the pleasantest sight he'd seen all day.

"You ain't always gonna get lucky, Neil," Burke said. "One of these days we'll have it out fair and square!"

Burke was glaring at Neil, and Dr. Whitman, to break the tension, said, "Well, Sergeant, you aren't on campaign, now."

Burke grinned and looked sidewise at Neil, and shifted his gaze to Whitman. "Oh, me an' Whitey just out huntin'. Yeah, we just out on little hunt. Maybe you heard the shootin'."

Whitey, full of beans and biscuits, stood up, belched, patted his stomach, and looked up at Jennie, who still stared down, from the lip of the patio, with what seemed a combination of repugnance and morbid attraction.

Whitey grinned, a grimace intended to be ingratiating, and called to her, "Hey, Pooty womans! Me Whitey!"

"What's that?" Dr. Whitman asked Burke. "What's he saying?"

"He thinks she's pretty," Burke answered. "She is too. Right pretty woman."

"Eddie," Neil grated, "you get that son of a bitch out of here, right now!"

"Neil!" Dr. Whitman was angry. "You quiet down! Don't spoil it for me. I'm gathering valuable notes."

"You forgot what this goddamn slug did at Camp Verde, Doctor? Or don't you give a damn?"

"Oh, that didn't hurt her!" Whitman said. "She's been too protected. Anyway, I fail to see any insult in telling a girl she's pretty."

Neil looked up. Jennie hadn't moved. He was about to tell her to get out of sight, and Burke sensed his intention.

Burke said, "What's eatin' on you, pal? She wants to look at me, an' you're scared to let her get any closer?"

Hastily, Dr. Whitman changed the subject again. "We heard the shooting, but I gather you were unsuccessful."

"Huh? Oh, we got it all right." Burke was amused. He gabbled a spate of Apache at Whitey, who trotted off to his horse, and Burke squatted and reached into the pot for another biscuit.

The doctor began asking him questions on some phase of Apache culture, and Neil was thinking, If I don't break this up, there's gonna be trouble. Whitey came trotting back, behind him.

"Show this fellah what we got," Burke said, and Neil and Whitman turned.

Whitey was untying the cord that fastened the neck of a bloody sack. With sudden horror, Neil jumped for him, hit him with his shoulder, and sent him sprawling. The sack fell, and a bloody head rolled out, an old Apache head, the tangled hair matted with blood and the open eyes filmed with dust.

Dr. Whitman gasped and shied sideways. Jennie screamed. Whitey was scrambling to his feet, and Neil kicked him in the face, dropping him again.

Eddie Burke said, "Jeezchrist, Neil! What you sore about? You done the same thing youself! Just 'nother runaway, got drunk, killed the clerk."

Neil wheeled toward him and, too late, Burke saw his face. Rising, Burke frantically grabbed his pistol and Neil caught him full in the face with his knee. Burke's head snapped back and he fell on his side and lay there, twisting, his hands to his face.

Whitey, mumbling through mashed lips, was on his feet, lurching toward his rifle where it lay by the pot. Neil jerked his pistol from the holster and said, *"Vámos, Whitey, Voy a matarte!"* (Go away, Whitey! I'm going to kill you!)

Whitey staggered toward his horse, but Neil yelled at him again in Spanish, and he looked back. Neil motioned toward the head with his pistol, and Whitey came back and put it in the sack. The only sound as he carried it to his horse, tied the sack to the tie rope around its neck, mounted, and rode through the creek, was Eddie Burke's groaning and swearing as he recovered from the heavy blow of Neil's knee.

On his knees, Burke looked sideways at the pistol he

had dropped. He looked up at Neil, back at the pistol, then got to his feet. Staggering a little, he walked toward his horse. Halfway there, he stopped and turned, his face a mask of hatred. He started to say something, and Neil fired a shot that struck between his feet. Burke sprinted to his plunging horse, loosened the tie rope, jerked savagely at the reins, and managed to get his foot in the stirrup and swing up.

Neil yelled, "Hold it, Eddie! Let's have the carbine!"

Burke pulled it from the saddle boot, the horse bucked, and he dropped the carbine. It struck the ground butt first and exploded—a shocking blast of sound, a cloud of white smoke, and flying fragments of the stock.

Burke landed hard on his left shoulder, and the stampeding horse plunged through the creek in great, spasmodic leaps and went charging up the hill. Whitey had stopped up there, and he went after the runaway.

Eddie Burke picked himself up and limped to the creek, waded it, and went lamely up the hill and out of sight, without looking back.

Neil punched the empty from his pistol and reloaded the chamber. Dr. Whitman gibbered something at him, but he shoved the man aside and climbed to the ruin. There was a place where Jennie had vomited. He found her stretched out, face down, in the entry room.

She said nothing, and kept her eyes closed as he gently turned her over and pulled her hands from her face. He squatted on his heels beside her, and she reached groping for his hand and clutched it to her breast.

He said, "For God sake, let yourself go! Cry! Talk to me!"

She still said nothing, and he freed his hand and got up. He soaked his bandanna in water and came back and cleaned her face and hands, then sat holding her in his arms for a long time, until he knew she was asleep. He managed to get up without waking her, and got one of the grain sacks she had washed, folded it, and slid it under her head for a pillow.

On the patio, Whitman was walking back and forth

in the dusk. He said, "My God, Neil! Why didn't you tell me! Those inhuman beasts!"

"Did you pull the ladder up?" Neil asked.

"Why, no. No, I didn't. I didn't think——"

"Go do it! And start thinking! And don't talk to me!"

CHAPTER 14

Two days later, Dr. Whitman wanted to move back to the tents. He argued that water was easier to get, cooking was more convenient on the range, and he wanted room to stretch his legs after a day in the dust and darkness of the Citadel. For once, Jennie stubbornly opposed him, because she now felt safe only with the ladder pulled up. Neil told him flatly that they would stay put for a while. He had humiliated Eddie Burke and Whitey, and not for the first time. And for all Dr. Whitman knew, they were out in the brush across the creek right now.

Dr. Whitman said, "You are a violent man. There was no need to do more than send them packing."

"Who wanted to run them off when they showed up?" Neil demanded. "Not you, Whitman."

The doctor ignored that, and turned to Jennie. "And as for you, it's time you got over this absurd squeamishness. Decapitation is no new thing in the world. What are you trying to do? Impress Neil with your great delicacy of feeling? If so, you're wasting your time, because our Mr. Douglas is devoid of such feelings. The American frontier breeds roughnecks, my dear."

Jennie retreated hastily into the entrance room of the ruin.

"So *she's* delicate!" Neil said, grinning at the doctor. "You about threw up your lunch when Whitey rolled that head out, and you were scared pea green when I dropped that shot between Eddie's feet!"

Jennie had been so shaken by the events of day before yesterday that she had lain all the following day, silent and half sick, on her cot. Neil had coaxed her to eat, without success. He wasn't sure how he felt about her, now. There was affection, and real sadness for what had happened to her back there ten years ago through no fault of her own, and not entirely because of her uncle's assault. Whitman carried a big share of the guilt for her present condition, for his utter lack of understanding of the effect upon her, and of compassion, and more for his dirty suspicion that she, herself, had invited the attack— the suspicion never quite stated, but obvious enough to a girl as oversensitive as Jennie.

On the other hand, she should have got back some confidence in ten years, and she ought to understand that life wasn't all sweetness and light, even for girls who hadn't gone through what she had. She should realize that bloody-minded Apaches and rattlesnakes and violence and deceit and death existed in her world, as in everyone's.

Whitman broke into his thoughts: "Neil, let's quit quarreling. You're right about staying up here for a while . . . and I guess you know by now, admitting I'm wrong comes hard for me."

Neil grinned ruefully. "You ain't alone there, Doctor. All right. We've got to get along. So I'm not going to tell you flat out that the wisest move is to pack up and leave, today. I think we ought to. But the general told me to do what you want. How much more time do you need here?"

"I'd like another month, but I'll say, well, ten days. Maybe two weeks."

"All right," Neil said. "We'll keep on living up here. We can cook down by the tent, but if I say 'Get up here!' don't ask questions; you get up here fast, you and her. At night we pull up the ladder. You don't rightly understand about those two, Doctor. Renegades, runaways from the reservation like that old man they shot, they could be bad enough . . . but Eddie and Whitey are something else again. I've had trouble with both of them before now, and," he lowered his voice, "there's her."

"I think I've learned my lesson," the doctor said. "By the way, you said something about that white one not being an albino, or Apache either. And the other, that Eddie, being half Apache."

"It's true. Eddie's mother was a Tonto 'Pache. She told him his father was a trooper. He told me all about it, one night when he was real drunk and feeling sorry for himself. He's always been ashamed of her and his 'Pache blood. What makes him maddest is calling him 'Pache. She got killed in a cavalry raid on a ranchería, and some troopers caught Eddie. He was about eight. Troop B of the Sixth Cavalry sort of adopted him, and he just grew up in the Army. He don't quite know which he is, 'cause whenever he gets a chance, he dresses 'Pache. He's a damn good Scout, and I hated his guts even before they came here."

"Oh, something else," Whitman said. "What made his rifle blow up when he dropped it?"

"Well, you know the Spencer, Doctor. Damn good carbine, but some call it 'the fool killer.' That magazine tube in the stock, there's seven cartridges in there, nose to tail, with the primer of every one sitting right on the point of the bullet behind it. And if you drop it on the butt, they'll all go off at once."

"I just about jumped out of my skin," Whitman said, "with that on top of everything else. What about Whitey?"

"Well, it happened with him almost the same as Eddie. Nobody knows for sure, but it had to be that way. 'Paches must have killed his folks and adopted him, real young. He's gotta be a Swede or a Dutchie. There's a lot of German farmers and miners."

"You mean," Whitman asked, "they'd actually kill his parents, and spare him, and then raise him as an Apache? A white child?"

"Sure. Indians don't care if you're white, black, red,

or purple. They really don't. People are just people, to them. And they love kids. Many a fighting 'Pache buck is pure Mexican, kidnapped down in Sonora when he was little. Didn't you ever hear about the Oatman massacre, how they killed most of the family and took away the two girls and the little boy? One of the girls died, but the other had 'Pache kids and a tattooed chin, when they traded her back. Some say she wasn't too anxious to come back. It was in all the papers. Anyway, Whitey don't even know he ain't 'Pache. Sounds funny, don't it? But it's true. And he ain't albino. I've seen a couple of them, and animals, too, and their eyes are always pink and they're half blind. Whitey's got blue eyes, and believe me, he'll see things you and me wouldn't know was there till it r'ared up and bit us."

"What a weird pair! Neanderthals!" Dr. Whitman said.

"Well, Doctor, call 'em what you want, but you better understand, they're dangerous!"

"Oh, yes, I know that now, Neil. Why, I believe that halfbreed would have shot you if you hadn't—what is the term?—'beat him to the draw.' Oh yes, I'm convinced! I'll be 'ware and waitin',' as the Scots put it. By the way, I think we shall be returning east as soon as we can, after we get back to Fort Whipple. I'm most anxious to start organizing my notes and cataloging the artifacts. Will it suit you if I pay you then, a lump sum?"

"Why, sure, Doctor!"

Neil hoped his vast relief didn't show on his face. Not because of the money, which would be substantial, but because of their departure, soon. Now he could get through the next ten days or two weeks, be as nice and brotherly and friendly to Jennie as he could, let her hold his hand and moon around after him all she wanted . . . then get them back to Fort Whipple and say goodbye forever and never see her again, and all her half-sick troubles. Already he felt lighter on his feet, eager, rarin' to go. He shoved out of his mind the realization of what the parting would mean to her. There was not any doubt whatsoever, now, that it would be a heartbreaking blow to her, and the thought hurt him, somewhere inside—the picture of her returning to the empty, joyless life with this puffed-up, sarcastic fool of a father who didn't want her.

Dr. Whitman said, roguishly, "But it seems I might be returning alone, judging by some little things I've noticed, eh, Neil? Little signs of propinquity? Little signs of mutual regard, shall we say?"

Neil almost slugged him. With great difficulty he refrained from explaining his full and uncensored opinion of the doctor and adding that none of the little signs was mutual, and that no one could help feeling sorry for Jennie with such a horse's ass of a father, but that wasn't the signal for wedding bells.

In a moment, he was thanking God that he hadn't blown off, because he had forgotten that she was just inside the door of the entrance room, lying there depressed and scared. Such words as he contemplated would probably have been as damaging to her as anything she had yet gone through.

He pretended the doctor hadn't said anything. He'd ease her onto the stagecoach when the time came, with all the gentleness and display of affection he could manage—part genuine, part pretense—and that would be the end of it.

He said, "Let's say two more weeks here, then. We're out of nearly everything, and I'll have to drive to Camp Verde tomorrow. Time we check in with Major Trumbull, anyway. And I'll make sure he keeps Eddie and Whitey away from here. I'll tell him straight, I'll shoot them if they show up here again."

"My God, man! *Shoot* them?"

"I don't know," Neil said. "It would depend. But Major Trumbull, *he'll* believe me, because he knows me. And we won't have any more trouble with them two."

"Would you, actually, Neil?"

"Doctor, you mean you really don't know how close I came to it, when they rolled that head out in front of her? Now, speaking of shooting, I'll leave you my Spencer and Eddie's Colt. And if you go hammering stakes with that carbine, you'll blow your own head off."

Jennie came out of the entrance room. She hadn't washed or changed clothes or combed her hair. *Those son-of-a-bitches!* Neil thought. *When I get to Camp Verde, maybe I'll go find Eddie before I report to the major.*

In his pity for her and her weakness and defenselessness, her deep loneliness, he wanted to hold her and tell her again that it was all over—everything that had gone before, including the horror of two days ago—but there wasn't going to be any more of *that!* No more hugging her and playing big brother and getting himself all steamed up physically in the bargain. And her mistaking it for something else—for love, for the answer to all her hopeless dreams.

She came up to him and hugged his arm, and said, "Can I go with you, Neil? Could I stay with Mrs. Trumbull until Father gets through here? Please?"

"Not unless we all go, Jennie. Not till we break camp and get out. I've got to tell you straight, I'm scared of those two. Easiest thing in the world would be for them to bushwhack me, and I don't dare take you along."

She turned toward the doorway of the ruin, but he caught her shoulders and gently turned her to face him. "We can't pretend, Jennie. We're not playing games. If your father would come and handle the carbine, sort of ride shotgun, we'd make it fast, with the wagon empty like it is. But he won't do it, you know that."

He looked expectantly at Dr. Whitman, who stubbornly said nothing, and Neil went on, "I'm not trying to scare you. You're scared enough, and your father, he's not. I don't think they'll be back, and I don't think they'll drygulch me on the road. But you both get this straight. I'll take no chances. And you won't either! Doctor, while I'm gone, you stay up here! Don't lower the ladder, don't go down for *anybody*! Only for Army officers in uniform, nobody else. You swear it, or we start packing right now."

"I promise," Dr. Whitman said meekly.

"All right. I'll leave tomorrow, at daylight. Ought to be back late the third day, but maybe it will take four."

He spent the day getting ready for the drive to Camp

Verde. Dr. Whitman spent the day in the upper floors of the Citadel. Jennie spent the day getting in Neil's way. She held his hand when she could, on trips to the corral and the creek, trotted at his side wherever he went, but said almost nothing. Unsmiling and depressed, she seemed to feel secure only with him, and he knew she dreaded his coming absence. He would gladly have taken her along and left her with the Trumbulls, but there were twenty miles of winding, rough road, dry washes, canyons, and chaparral between the Citadel and Camp Verde, and Sergeant Eddie Burke and that white Apache on the loose almost whenever they wanted to be, if indeed they had returned to Camp Verde.

He greased the wagon, oiled the harness, cut firewood and hoisted it to the patio of the ruin. Toward evening, he caught the mules and watered and fed them amply with mesquite beans, then tied them to the fence with their halters. Into the wagon he put an ax and a shovel, a tarp, the last of the mesquite beans, the four nosebags, and two two-quart canteens of water.

After supper, he asked Jennie to bake biscuits in the dutch oven, and grind a handful of coffee. He put two cans of tomatoes and one of peaches beside his bed roll on the patio so he wouldn't forget to take them, along with the Colt's Peacemaker and a shell belt with every loop full. He and Dr. Whitman pulled the ladder up. Jennie ignored her father's presence and put her arms around Neil's neck and pulled his head down to kiss him on the mouth.

"Please, can't I go?" she pleaded.

"Jennie, you can't," he said.

Faraway thunder grumbled during the night, but the Citadel and the sleeper on the patio were washed in moonlight.

He had set the clock in his head for dawn, and when he got up and pulled on his pants and moccasins and buckled on his gun belt, the sky over the Rim was faintly washed with lemon yellow, and quail were beginning to call. Dr. Granville Whitmann III was continuing to snore, where he had chosen to make his bed in the second room of the ruin. Neil let the ladder down.

By the time he had taken the mules two by two to water and fed them well with mesquite beans and got them hooked up to the wagon, spears of light were lancing from behind the Rim. The tents and the trees by the creek were grayly visible, and Jennie had a small fire going on the patio. He could smell the coffee and hear the bacon sizzling—slices from the last side in camp.

Underlit by the coals, Jennie's face looked gaunt. She was unsmiling, sad, unkempt, her hair tangled, her big robe getting in her way. Neil felt a sudden twinge, like a knife stab in the guts—pity, tenderness, regret, love—he didn't know. Maybe all of them together. His mood matched hers, including the uneasiness at his leaving, which he knew approached panic on her part. For a moment he thought he would tell her to hurry and dress, that he would take her with him, but he suppressed the impulse. The twenty miles he had to travel might not be achieved—and here she was safe if trouble should come and if Dr. Whitman would for once do what Neil had told him to do. Nothing could get to her, so long as the ladder was raised and the doctor held firm.

Neither spoke during the meager breakfast. When Neil got to his feet, she rose from her squat by the fire and faced him, watching him without expression. He thought she would reach up and kiss him, but she stood quiet, arms at her sides.

He said, "Thanks, Jennie. And Jennie, you mustn't worry. With any luck I'll be back tomorrow, but it'll be late. I'd take you with me if I thought—" He cut that off, not wanting to steer her thought onto such words as "unsafe" and "dangerous."

"Just be my good girl, and don't worry." He hugged her to his chest and kissed her cheek, and tasted the salt tears.

He almost whispered, "I love you, Jennie"—almost, but not quite. And he meant it—almost, but not quite.

She hugged him then, her wet cheek against his unshaven face, and said, " 'Bye, Neil."

He patted her shoulder and stopped to pick up the Springfield Long Tom Whitey had dropped in his frantic haste to get to his horse, with that bloody sack bumping his knee as he ran. There was only one cartridge for it, the one in the chamber, but it would reach out three times as far as his Peacemaker.

Jennie went into the ruin and came back with a clean handkerchief in which she wrapped a few biscuits. She put them with the canned tomatoes and peaches and wrapped them in his two blankets. He took the bundle and the rifle under his arm and went carefully down the ladder. When he had stowed the bundle and climbed to the wagon seat and laid the rifle within reach behind it, he watched her heave on the tackle and haul the ladder up to the patio.

The mules were pretty hot after six weeks' vacation, and only the threat of the halter chain had kept Gotch Ear on her good behavior when he hitched them. Now, with no word from him, they broke into a smart trot as soon as he released the brake.

With only one stop to rest and let them drink, and for Neil to eat a hurried lunch, he kept them at a trot, except on the few long, uphill hauls and the crossing of a number of washes, some running a foot deep in chocolate brown water.

He enjoyed the run, enjoyed being alone, with such a lightening of spirits, such a feeling of release and freedom as surprised him, in spite of the need for vigilance, and the nagging worry.

The wagon pulled into Camp Verde about one in the afternoon, rattled past the parade ground and pulled up at the wagon sheds. Troops drilling turned their heads to watch, and Lieutenant Underhill stepped out on the veranda of the administration building to have a look, and Whitey stood leaning against a veranda post at the enlisted men's barracks. He grinned at Neil as the wagon went past, and with both hands made the shape of a woman in the air, then walked away, moving fast. Looking back, Neil thought he must be heading for the noncoms' barracks.

The stable sergeant was profanely upset because the

mules were pretty well sweated, but Neil shoved him aside and walked rapidly the quarter mile to the noncoms' quarters, thinking, If that goddamn ghost tells Burke I'm here, and if that means trouble, I better hit it head on instead of waiting for it to catch up with me. Burke's my trouble, not Whitey. He just does what Eddie tells him, or puts in his mind.

They weren't in the noncoms' barracks. Corporal Muller, malingering in his bunk with fake sickness— probably a real enough hangover—said he thought Sergeant Burke was away somewhere.

Neil went to see the quartermaster, Captain Eastwood, with his request for supplies and grain for two more weeks. Eastwood said, "We've been expecting you, sort of. Major Trumbull said you were supposed to stay at the ruin about six weeks, and it's over seven. Sure we'll fix you up . . . but not tonight, or tomorrow either. We've got a wagon load of canned goods and flour and some fresh bacon due in from Fort Whipple tomorrow. Too bad about the incident with Whitey. At the time, I thought you were pretty rough on him, but I didn't actually see what he did. Major Trumbull told me."

There was no help for it, he couldn't start back tonight, so Neil spent a while with Captain Eastwood, describing the camp and what Whitman was doing.

Eastwood grinned. "Pretty soft life for a bummer like you, hey, Douglas? Lollygagging around in the idyllic wild with the daughter of the illustrious windbag from the Smithsonian!"

Neil looked at him sharply, but the captain was smiling, evidently envious, not malicious.

Neil said, "With her, it ain't as romantic as you might figure. I planned on getting back tonight, if it took all night. Them two are tucked away nice and cozy, but I can't depend on Whitman to use his head, and it nags at me."

"Right after noontime dinner Thursday, Douglas. Bring the wagon to the supply shed around eleven, and we'll load up. Maybe I can find a few special treats for the lady."

"Thanks, sir! You know where Major Trumbull is?"

"In his quarters, I expect. Not much doing for any of us here, now. Eddie Burke and Whitey brought in another renegade, or part of one, that is. He shot the agent's clerk. First excitement around here since they brought in Gallo and his family."

"Haven't you ever figured out Eddie Burke is a liar?" Neil asked. "It wasn't him that got Gallo."

Mrs. Trumbull's striker answered Neil's knock, and went to get the major. When Major Trumbull came to the door, he said, "Let's go sit in the shade, out in the back yard. Good to see you. How are things going out there?"

Neil hadn't expected to be invited into the house. Mrs. Trumbull lumped Indian Scout noncoms with the Scouts themselves as equally savage and crude, and had never yet given Neil the time of day.

After a short account by Neil of activities at the Citadel, the major said, "Well, it all seems to be going fine. You want anything else, just holler."

"Most of it went fine, sir, till Eddie Burke and his ghost showed up with the head of that renegade in a sack."

He gave the major the details of that event, and the major said, "I wondered! They claimed they lost their weapons in a flash flood. But Eddie was purple and yellow round the eyes, and his nose swelled up to twice its size. Well, the whole thing was just Eddie's idea of a joke, Neil. They're both savages. I'll talk to him when he gets back with the supply wagons tomorrow. I sent him to Fort Whipple with a personal message to General Kautz. You knew he arrived to take over from General Crook?"

"No, I didn't. I hope he's a good one. Major, that Whitey don't bother me much, it's Eddie Burke. What with one thing and another, he hates my guts, and——"

The major cut in, "Well, Whitey won't be any more trouble to you anyway. One of the Scouts, that Mexican, was just here. Said Whitey just left to go visit his people down in the Dragoons."

"Sir," Neil said, "couldn't you restrict Burke to the post, just till I get Jennie and Whitman back to Whipple. We came near shooting one another that day, and Jennie's scared half to death. I don't trust those son-of-a-bitches out of sight, either of 'em."

"You know I can't, Neil. You were a Sergeant of Scouts yourself. You had a lot of leeway. And all he did, far as I can see, was scare her. I agree, it was anything but funny—but it wasn't a punishable offense, and he got a good kick in the face for it. I'll give him a stiff lecture, but no more. Anyway, you've got no worries about Whitey, he's headed just the opposite direction from the Citadel."

"With all due respect," Neil said, "how does the major know what direction Whitey's really headed?"

Neil slept in the noncoms' quarters, and hung around the next day, bored and impatient, until the supply wagons came in from Fort Whipple about five in the afternoon.

Eddie Burke got down from the big freight wagon and went to Major Trumbull's quarters, probably with an answer to the message he had carried. Neil waited for him, out of sight behind Captain Eastwood's quarters. When he came out and walked past, Neil stepped out to confront him.

"Eddie, you come out to the Citadel again, and I'm gonna let you have it. Far as I can see, you'll just be another renegade sneaking around in the chaparral, when I cut you down."

For a moment, it looked as if they would tangle again, but Burke muttered something and pushed past. At supper, they sat at the same table, but ignored each other, and to avoid trouble, Neil slept in the barn on a pile of hay. Lightning glared and thunder rumbled, and he got little sleep.

Somehow he got through Wednesday, though he was increasingly on edge. He kept an eye on Eddie Burke, making sure he came to meals and didn't just disappear, as Whitey seemed to have done. He asked Chalk Eye and Limpy, now under the command of an old cavalry sergeant who spent as little time with the Indians as he could manage—but all they could tell him was that Whitey had ridden over to the reservation the evening before.

His wagon was loaded and ready by eleven in the morning, and Neil was on his way, pushing the mules hard. Rain sluiced down most of the afternoon, and when he came to the big wash, about four-thirty, it was running half full. No wagon could cross for another day, at least. Cursing, he swung the wagon around, lashing the rumps of the wheelers, forcing the team to crash through catclaw and manzanita, circling back to the road. On a sunny day, it would have been easy, but in the gloom of the downpour he had to look sharp to find the faint track that led to the long-abandoned cabin of his grandfather, Bear Douglas, mountain man. The mules didn't like the overgrown, rock-strewn trace of road, but he was merciless, and the wagon rocked and jolted the two miles in about an hour.

Someone had used the place not long since. Repairs had been made to the corner of the ten-by-twelve structure, where adobe bricks mixed in with the rock of the walls had melted and let the sod roof crumble in one corner. Inside, where boot tracks were printed in the dust among ten thousand pack rat droppings, the fireplace and chimney had fallen apart.

In the corral were lumps of quite fresh horse manure, disintegrating in the slackening rain, and the recent sojourner had cut some new poles to reinforce the fence. Neil took some of the old, frail poles inside and broke them up for firewood, although they wouldn't burn until dry, or perhaps if he used them to reinforce a fire made from the broken-down bunk in the corner.

In the corral, Neil fed the mules, then put the halters on them and the sideline on Gotch Ear. There was no way to water them. They looked miserable, but all members of the horse family, even the smartest of them, the burros, had been standing in the rain for centuries, maybe millions of years, and would stand like martyrs in snow or rain, with good shelter not twenty feet away.

With a piece of board from the bunk, he scraped an area on the earth floor free of rat droppings, then built a fire with the last pieces from that source. Smoke drove him out into the drizzle until the cabin heated a little, and a draft from the doorless doorway cleared it. With a flaming splinter, he burned out a tangle of black widow spider webs in one corner.

Biscuits and bacon and canned tomatoes and coffee made supper, and he lay with his head propped on a rolled-up tarp from the wagon, remembering the times he visited Grampa and his silent, wrinkled old Piegan squaw who never learned a word of English; but there had been good food, and laughter, and a lot of love for a small boy—and a range glowing in the corner, and a table and four chairs, and a real door with hinges, and real glass in the one small window that opened outward, hinged at the top.

All that was long gone—the door, the window, the beaver traps hung in a corner, the old Plains rifle with its powder horn, the wolf skin blanket, the stove. Whatever anyone could find use for had been taken, including the two big C-clamps Bear Douglas had used to set the springs of the monstrous bear trap. Since his day, men hunted bears and wolves with dogs and rifles, or killed them with poisoned carcasses, and no one in all the years had been able to think of any use for such a deadly mechanism. It still lay in a corner, fifty pounds of spring steel and murderous, toothed jaws, half buried in dust and debris.

For a while, Neil considered trying to cross the wash in the morning, riding the gentlest of the mules; but that would mean the temporary abandonment of three fine government mules and a new wagon, for which he was responsible, and very likely, their loss to some wandering prospector or cowboy. Not only that, but the supplies in the wagon were urgently needed at the Citadel. Dr. Whitman and Jennie would just have to sit alone tonight in their dry cave and worry it out.

Just one more example, Neil thought, of the many he had seen and experienced—the white man with all his gear and wagons and tools and teams of two to twenty draft animals and harness and food and forage, stuck tighter than a cow in a mudhole, stopped by weather, or rough country, or lack of feed or a broken wagon wheel, while the Indian could live off the country and go where he pleased when he pleased, and not be stopped by a normally dry wash running full, if his business was urgent enough.

The thought was not just a general comparison of the relative intelligence and efficiency of white and Indian fighting men, but a nagging worry in Neil's mind, even while he slept.

He slept badly. There was intermittent rain all night, sudden heavy downpours, then a slackening, a stop and silence, dead, wet air, then another smashing onslaught. The local rain didn't worry him. It would run off downstream. But if it was raining hard, way upstream, he might not be able to move for several days. It was about five A.M., and he got up and managed to kindle a small fire with the last of the ax-hewn boards from the demolished bunk.

A sudden, short deluge was the dying gasp of the rain.

Coffee and biscuits lifted his spirits somewhat, and as soon as daylight crept slowly in, he hung his blankets on a peg and went out. A short search discovered several small pools of rain water. He took the mules to drink, two by two, hung on their nose bags with their barley breakfast, and when they finished, took the Long Tom rifle and walked the two miles back to the road, and on to the wash.

The rain upstream must have stopped, because the water was lower, but not yet enough. He sat for an hour watching the stick he had stuck in the ground at the edge of the water, and saw the band of wet earth widening slowly between it and the water. Maybe he could cross before noon, if there were no more surges from upstream. He went back to the cabin and cleaned the cup and the tin can he had used for making coffee, and rolled his blankets and stowed them in the wagon. About ten o'clock, he hitched the team. Gotch Ear decided she wasn't going to go, and he laid into her hard, with a halter chain, peeling hide from her rump, before she backed into place.

He drove slowly to the wash, taking the wagon over the rocks and newly cut miniature arroyos with care. At the road, he whipped the team into a trot.

The water was lower, but still too high, and he sat until two o'clock, then got down, pulled off his moccasins, and waded across.

The muddy water came to his knees, and the bottom was sound—gravel and scoured rock. He couldn't see into the muddy water, but he found no boulders in the crossing. With moccasins on again, he climbed to the seat and pondered his problem.

At length, he decided it would take too much out of the team to turn back two hundred yards, turn around again, lash them into a gallop, plunge down the steep side of the arroyo, and hit the water running. Maybe, too, there were small boulders or cobbles in there that he had missed, and a broken wheel or a stove-up mule was the last thing he needed.

He said, "Easy, now!" and shook the reins, and the mules pulled to the edge and went cautiously down, ears aimed forward, nostrils extended, Gotch Ear and her wheelmate sitting back in the breeching. The rear wheels locked and slid as he stood on the brake. He knew that if the mules were too nervous, no amount of swearing and beating would make them cross—no mule would go into a situation it considered dangerous to itself, no matter what you might do to it.

They were a good team. At the bottom, they put their shoulders into the collars and pulled steadily together with no plunging, and moved the wagon across. The real struggle was the haul up the far side, and if they stopped they'd never make it on a second try. He shouted and lashed them with the reins and kept yelling at them, and they made it, barely made it, with breath rasping, heads down, small hooves digging in, and great muscles jumping out on their haunches. When the wagon tipped level again onto the road, they stopped, and Neil didn't start them for a half hour.

He didn't try to make them run. The nigh leader was limping badly, and all four were exhausted from the pull out of the wash. It took three hours to reach the Citadel —after five o'clock. He yelled, a quarter mile before he pulled up in front of the ruin, and the ladder was lowered from the ramp and Jennie was there to greet him, and Dr. Whitman shouting angrily down at him, "What kept you? We've been hungry here! Have you no consideration for——"

Neil yelled back, "Get the hell down here and help unload this stuff. Then you haul it up, because I'm tired. I'll tie it on, down here."

He got down, and Jennie took his hand in both of hers.

She said, "Oh, thank God! Thank God! I've been so frightened!"

"I was held up at Camp Verde," he said, "and the big wash was full of water. I stayed in Grampa's cabin. Tell you about it later."

Her face seemed thinner. It was a little dirty, as was her long dress. Her hair was untidy. Her eyes looked haunted, as though she'd been having nightmares. And maybe she had, like the real one, when Whitey rolled that bloody head out of the sack. And probably that swell-headed, pot-bellied bastard coming down the ladder, who didn't give a damn about her, had been giving her a bad time. The neck of her shirtwaist was open, and she nervously fingered the necklace of Apache Tears.

Suddenly swept with rage, he yelled, "I said get down here! Hurry it up!" and Dr. Whitman said, "Douglas, don't take that tone of voice with me! What's wrong with you!"

At his yell, Jennie had jumped like a startled rabbit, and he put his arm around her shoulders and hugged her to him and said, "I'm sorry, Jennie. I'm tired out, and sometimes your father gets under my hide. Well, I'll get this stuff up to the patio, and put the mules to bed."

She said, "You're exhausted, aren't you? I can tie the boxes and sacks onto the tackle, down here, and Father can go up and haul them up. You unload, then take the mules to the corral. If you will unhitch them, I can feed them."

"What's that?" Whitman demanded. *"Me* pull that stuff up there by myself?"

"Why not?" Neil said. "If you ain't man enough to handle it, say so. First, we unload."

"I'll handle it!" Whitman replied, and began to roll up a side curtain of the wagon. "I don't care much for your attitude!"

Dr. Whitman worked grimly silent, and Jennie worked too hard in an effort to spare Neil, and the three of them had the supplies unloaded quickly, except the opened sack of barley, which Neil left in the wagon. It was growing dark when he drove to the corral, unhooked the team and haltered them. The nigh leader's limp was worse, and his mate had a skinned knee and cannon which Neil couldn't account for.

As he waited for them to finish drinking before he fed them, he caught a flicker of movement back in the brush in the arroyo. The mules flung up their heads, and he dropped flat and got the pistol out almost before he hit the ground. Back there in the gloom a horse whinnied, and the back of Neil's neck prickled. Then three horses walked out and came up to the mules, grunting deep in their throats, asking for feed. Nothing else moved. Neil lay for three or four minutes listening, straining to see into the deep dusk of the arroyo, before he concluded there was nothing else there.

There was a goose-rumped, cow-hocked calico horse that looked to be thirty years old, a runty little buckskin with its ribs showing and its hip joints jutting out so you could have hung your hat on them, and a bay mare that didn't look too bad in the semidarkness.

Neil got up and put the nose bags on his mules. He studied the newcomers, felt sorry for them, and poured some barley on the ground. As soon as his mules were finished, he hung the halter chains on the corral fence. Disturbed and worried, he walked back to the camp.

Jennie finished tying the fall of the hoist around a sack of grain and straightened slowly, her hands on the small of her back. Neil said, "You shouldn't be doing this. Why don't you go up and start a fire? Put on a pot of coffee, will you? I'll finish up, down here. But I want to talk to your father first. Come on, up you go!"

She smiled, and said, "All right Neil," and slowly climbed the ladder. He followed.

Grunting, Dr. Whitman hauled the sack up and swung it in and lowered it to the patio floor, beside the cases of canned goods. Jennie got kindling from the pile Neil had cut before he went to Camp Verde.

Neil put his fists on his hips and stared at Whitman's back until the man seemed to feel it, and turned to face him.

"How'd those horses get in the corral?" Neil demanded.

Whitman was still sore, like a child reprimanded unjustly. He said, "None of your damn business. They're mine!"

Neil said, "If you put 'em in the corral, you had to lower the ladder and go down on the ground. And I not only told you to stay up here, but you gave your word you wouldn't go down."

"You listen to me, Douglas! You don't know the circumstances, so don't go off half-cocked! Your judgment isn't infallible and your word isn't law around here!"

"I asked you—how'd you get the horses?" Neil was finding it hard to keep his temper.

"They're a gift!" Whitman said, and before Neil could question him further, Jennie said, "It was that white Apache, the one that was here with the other one that day, the day they——" She wouldn't pursue that, but went on, "He came yesterday morning and tied them beside the big cottonwood log."

Neil was so appalled he couldn't speak.

She went on, "He gestured at them, and to us, so we knew he meant them for us, then he rode away. Obviously, he was trying to make amends for what he did the other day, a tangible thing to show he was sorry, and I was very surprised, really touched by it."

Whitman took up the account. "That's a costly gift for a man in his circumstances, a most generous one. Goes to show you that there are *some* good Indians. But then, maybe it was the white blood—because you don't expect that kind of generosity as recompense for a great error such as he committed, not from a full-blood. Why, think of the trouble he went to, to make up for his blunder. Didn't even wait until it quit raining. It must have been *very* difficult to swim them across that wash, tied nose to tail, as he had them. How could we insult him by rejecting his peace offering? I don't want the miserable horses, but I couldn't spit in his face, now could I? And if you still think that didn't constitute sufficient cause to lower the ladder and go down and lead those horses to the corral, why——"

"Shut up!" Neil yelled. *"Stop babbling!"*

Jennie squawked and dropped the coffeepot. Dr. Whitman stepped back as though Neil had slapped him. His face went white, then red, and, hugely affronted, he gasped, for once unable to find words.

Neil fought for control, while the two stared at him, Jennie with both hands to her face, the doctor half turned, as though petrified in one split second.

Neil said, *"Gift!* You fat-headed fool! Those horses are a bride price! They're for buying Jennie! If you just let them alone, or went down and turned them loose, it would've been all finished. But you took them! You led them away! You son of a bitch, you've married your daughter to that animal!"

Jennie backed slowly against the wall of the Citadel, her palms still against her face as though to hold her head together.

Whitman said, loftily, "You're a fool! I agreed to nothing! I wasn't asked anything, and I didn't answer anything. Whitey made no proposal, there was no discussion, and I never heard anything so absurd! You're jumping to a stupid and unwarranted conclusion, which I reject categorically!"

But there was no conviction in his bluster, and after a silence, he said, "Well, if his benighted mind is so stupid as to mean what you say, to infer what you claim, why I'll just give the horses back."

"Just like that, huh? You'll give them back. Doctor, when they make an offer for a woman, and you accept, it's a deal. He did it in good faith, and both you and her, if you back out, you're in bad trouble. He won't lack for help to get her. Every damn 'Pache in his clan is related to him, and it's a big insult to every one of 'em. They won't let it pass."

Jennie was whimpering, and he went to her and put his hand on her shoulder. "Don't think I like telling you this. You've had way too much trouble, already, and it sure ain't your fault. Maybe it ain't your father's fault, altogether, but he swore he'd stay up here. Anyway, I can't keep from you how serious it is. You've got to realize it. And I've got to figure what I can do, and I have to do it fast. Now you go in and lay down. I'll talk to your father."

He led her in to her bed, and hugged her briefly and said, "We'll get out of this. Want some coffee?"

She shook her head and lay down, and he went out and beckoned Whitman to come out of her hearing.

He said, "If you promise again not to let the ladder down for anybody, how can I trust you to keep your word? You got any idea at all how important it is?"

Whitman nodded. He was scared. Really scared for once. Neil could almost smell the fear on him.

He said, "I haven't got much time to think. This could build up into something real bad. People could get killed. I mean *you* could get killed, Whitman. If Whitey don't get his woman. You've got to realize, this thing could build into an outbreak. Whitey's clan are broncos, wild ones, and nobody really knows how many of them there are. Outbreaks have started on less than this, because the goddamn white men don't ever keep their promises. And whether you know it or not, you made a

promise when you took them horses. I couldn't stand off
any bunch for very long, alone. If we knew when Whitey
was coming for her, maybe with a whole wedding party,
I could stay. If the bridegroom's shot through the guts,
there can't be any wedding, huh? But I can't hang
around waiting for him. I'm going back to Camp Verde
in the morning and put a stop to this foolishness. When
I tell Major Trumbull, believe me, he'll know it's serious,
and they'll pick Whitey up if they can get him. And he'll
send an escort to get you and her out of here."

He lowered his voice, and put his face close to Whitman's, "And you son of a bitch, if I get back here and
you've let the ladder down for *anyone*, or *anything*, I
swear I'll shoot *you* in the guts!"

Whitman was beyond speaking. Neil said, "I'll leave
you the carbine and Eddie's pistol. You shoot at anything that moves, unless it's me or troopers in uniform!"

Rolled in his blankets on a folded tarp, on the patio
of the Citadel, Neil slept as though drugged, and woke
at dawn, aroused by slight noises Jennie made as she
started a small fire. He pulled on pants and moccasins
and walked around the far end of the ruin and relieved
himself.

Such undisguised response to a bodily need would
have shocked her, ten days ago—but Jennie had changed.
No longer was she meticulous about cleanliness or dress,
or even careful about letting her shirtwaist hang open at
the neck, and she scarcely bothered to hide her legs
when she squatted to tend the cooking. No more
laughter, no more gaiety, no more interest in little animals and strange plants. The thinner she got, the bigger her eyes seemed. That stab of pity, of half-guilt because he wasn't able to love her took him in the guts
again.

"You shouldn't have got up," he said. "All I need is
a drink of water and a couple of pieces of bacon."

"You need a good breakfast," she said. "I couldn't
sleep, and I heard you cough, and I could tell it was
morning."

He washed his face and raked his fingers through his

hair. He hadn't changed his clothes in a week, and he smelled. He'd have to shave one of these days, too.

She brought coffee in a tin cup, and set it on the ground so he could take it by the handle. He drank it slowly, and ate the bacon and a couple of biscuits, then rolled a smoke, and squatted on his heels, looking across the fire at her, trying to think of something comforting to say. Nothing came to mind, and he stood, and said, "I'll be back tonight. Have to ride one of the mules, but I'll get a good horse at Camp Verde. I'll bring some troopers, and we'll get you out of here."

He held his arms out, and she came to him eagerly, hugging his waist, pushing her face against his throat, and he could feel the hard lump of the derringer in the pocket of her robe. He laid his cheek against her uncombed hair. She wasn't crying this time, just acting like the worst possible was going to happen, and she was only waiting to submit.

"I've gotta go," he said, and she stepped back. He patted her cheek lightly, and turned to the ramp leading down to the ladder.

He cut about ten feet from the end of the tackle fall to use as reins, and got his lariat and a full two-quart canteen from the wagon. As he approached the corral, he talked to the mules so as not to spook them. They snuffled at him, hoping for grain, when he took down two gate bars and went into the corral. It was barely light enough to see their shapes. He wished he had time to check the bay mare, but the driving bridle would never fit her, anyhow. When he hung the bridle on the fence and shook out the loop of his lariat, the mules began to edge away, and when he swung the loop once to open it out, they snorted and ran into each other in their haste to get out of reach. His throw stopped one of them, the loop falling across its neck. He wasn't sure he had looped it, so he went hand over hand up the rope, very easy, so as not to pull it off. Somebody had sure taught them about a rope, and what happened to a running mule roped by the neck, when it hit the end of the line.

Already his luck was bad. The one he got was Gotch

Ear. He grabbed the ring of her halter, snapped the china on, and led her to the creek to drink, then back to the corral for a good feed from the nose bag. When she finished, he slipped the bridle on over the halter and tied on the rope reins. He put the loop of his lariat around her neck, and stuffed the rest of it, coiled, under his belt in back, like a horsebreaker, so that if she dumped him, he might grab it before she got away. He had no spurs, and the snaffle bit wasn't severe enough to bother her cast-iron mouth, and he knew he had trouble.

Outside the corral, he tried to mount, and she lunged sideways. When he led her to the fence and tied her short, with a slip-knot in the lariat, she tried to bite him. He hit her across the face with the doubled rope reins. She brayed and pulled back, and he let her have it again, hard, and she stood trembling and let him mount. He pulled the slip-knot free, but when he tried to start her past the Citadel and onto the road, she circled and balked. It was almost impossible to separate a single cavalry horse from its mates, and mules were worse.

He yanked on the rein, but the bit might as well have been rubber, for all the good it did. "By God," he told her, "if I had a pair of Mex spurs, I'd gut you!"

Well, there was one way to make a good mule out of her, considering that mules were touchier about their ears than even Jennie was about her breast—and Gotch Ear had a bad one to start with. With the doubled loop of the rein, he slashed sideways across her ears, left and right, and she straightened out and went into a trot. As he passed under the Citadel, he looked up and waved at Jennie, who stood motionless at the edge of the patio. She raised her right hand about six inches and let it fall slack at her side.

Gotch Ear was no easy-gaited riding mule, like General Crook's "Apache." Her trotting jarred his spine, and the canteen bounced, pounding his hip, and he got sweaty in the crotch from the heat of her back, and called himself stupid for forgetting to strap a folded blanket onto her, and maybe rig a couple of loops of rope for stirrups. She hadn't given up, but from time to time, without warning, would try to head back, which rebellions he put down with a cut across her ears with the rein.

He expected trouble with her when they reached the big wash, but she surprised him by pausing only to drink from the six-inch deep remnant of flood waters in the bottom, then climbing steadily up the far side. The farther she got from her teammates, the more she settled down, because now she was heading for Camp Verde.

It was about ten in the morning and four or five miles past the arroyo when he saw the fresh hoof prints in the road, heading toward the Citadel. Two shod horses. They were so fresh that as he looked at them, a little lump of sand fell from the sharp-cut edge of one of them. The horses had stopped abruptly, right there, turned back toward Camp Verde, and suddenly swung east into the chaparral.

A spasm of fear shook him, and it took him only a moment to make his decision. That the horses were shod meant nothing in particular—most horses ridden by wild Apaches, acquired by theft or murder, were shod. These tracks could have been left by the mounts of prospectors or cowpunchers, but anyone at all might mean danger for Jennie, specially a pair of bummers who had to hide in the chaparral when they heard a lone rider coming— road agents, escaping criminals, Army deserters, any of the many territorial citizens without roots or scruples or morals. Any man who couldn't afford to be seen was a menace. And if they were Whitey and some Apache cousin, or even Whitey and Eddie Burke again, the danger was trebled, quadrupled. What Neil had refused to think about now demanded attention—and that was the ease with which anyone at all could lie in the brush across the creek, or in the trees at the edge, and simply gun down Jennie's father. There would be no great problem getting up to the ruin, even if she couldn't be frightened into lowering the ladder. He had to get back there fast!

He looked around, trying to penetrate the tangle of mesquite and manzanita and buck brush and a dozen varieties of cactus, but knew he was wasting time. Off to his left, to the east about two hundred yards, was a small

hill that rose a little higher than its neighbors, and even as
he studied it, he saw the blossom of white smoke and
heard the crack of the rifle.

A handful of gravel burst upward into Gotch Ear's face,
and she went crazy, bucking and sunfishing. Neil hugged
her neck grimly, his legs clamped around her ribs, the
canteen flailing at his shoulders. He got a short grip on
the rope reins, and jerked and wrenched at her jaw. This
pulled her head up a little, and she stampeded into a flat
out, pounding run down the road, the way they had come.
Neil could only hang on. There would be no slowing her
until she ran herself out. At a sharp bend in the road, she
made no attempt to turn, but crashed blindly into the
brush and went plowing straight through it, her crazy
speed scarcely diminished.

Everything but the rocks had thorns, and everything
tore at Neil, battered him as they swept by, hammered his
legs, tried to tear him off her back, and all he could do
was hang on with his eyes shut, and wonder what kept her
on her feet.

He didn't see the six-foot-deep, straight-sided arroyo
that was too wide for her spasmodic leap. She crashed to
the bottom, her neck snapped like a rotten branch, and
she rolled once, throwing him clear. He brought up
against the far side, stunned and battered.

He came to like a man coming out of a prolonged
drunk, the realization of what had happened slow to
crystallize in his mind. Shakily, he stood and leaned
against the bank.

His hat was gone, his shirt ripped, face and hands
bloody from thorn cuts and scrapes on rocks. The canteen
was under the mule, or torn loose in that crazy stampede.

Next to the loss of his mule, the worst disaster was his
empty holster. All he had left was his skinning knife. When
he had gathered a little strength, he searched fifty yards
back on the track, but couldn't find the pistol. If it was
under the dead Gotch Ear, it might as well be at the
bottom of the sea.

He could think of only one refuge where no one could
come at him except from the front. He started off for the

cabin of his grandfather. He wasn't fooling himself. If they were Apache renegades from Camp Verde or, very unlikely, broncos still on the war trail, and if they wanted him, he wasn't going to lose them. He didn't even say, silently to himself, "Whitey. Whitey and Eddie Burke," but the certainty was screaming inside his head.

No, he couldn't shake Whitey off his trail, but he might do a lot better than most white men could, and gain a little time—to think, to plan, to invent something . . . something . . .

Using every trick, every stratagem he had ever seen, it took him over four hours to reach the cabin, six miles of travel from the dead mule, which was less than two miles from his goal. He waded in rivulets which would be dried up in a few hours. He walked on bare rock. He left faint tracks to misdirect, which only an Apache would see, then with utmost care, returned to his general course. He crossed patches of sand deliberately, where tracks would be seen by anyone, then wiped them out so thoroughly with a handful of grass and loose sand spilled slowly from his hand that he, himself, couldn't see them. But Whitey would. He bent twigs, several pointing the same direction, then went cautiously the other way. All the while, he knew full well that Whitey would work it out, Whitey and whoever else it was. The bleached side of a tiny dried leaf turned up to the sun, long grass bent down by his moccasin, a twig stepped on, a pebble the size of a grain of corn pushed out of its embedment in the earth—a dozen things Whitey would read as easily as Neil could read newsprint. Whitey would find him. Whitey and Eddie. He accepted that, but he fought for time.

The cabin showed no sign of occupancy since night before last. The charcoal of his fire was undisturbed, his moccasin prints were there—and the bear trap was there.

If the two men who rode into the brush were white bummers on the dodge, they might have shot at him just for the hell of it—or have been ready to murder him for his pistol and the mule—but they would hardly have bothered to try to puzzle out his trail. He doubted that there were a half dozen non-Indians in the territory who could do it, anyway. And two renegade Indians being already well mounted and trying for distance from Camp Verde would hardly go to the trouble for one lone man on a mule. And maybe he was just spooked, huddling here, trying desperately to concoct a plan of escape. But he had that feeling—that sense beyond sight and hearing and smell that he had seen operate with his Apache Scouts and had experienced himself—that feeling that told you which of two likely passes a band of broncos would take through a range of hills, or that you were getting close to your quarry, or told you to get the hell out of someplace fast, but for no reason you could pin down. Somebody was out there for sure. Or somebody was getting mighty close and it almost had to be Eddie Burke and Whitey.

The doorway and window opening were both in the front wall. Maybe if he made a club of a corral pole, or waited in a dark corner with a rock in one hand and his knife in the other—but he knew that these were the false plans of desperation. Then he looked again at the bear trap, and the plan began to form. He wouldn't survive, but maybe he could make one of them sorry he had tracked down Neil Douglas—sorry with a mangled foot. And anything was better than waiting like a penned steer in a slaughterhouse.

The trap was two powerful springs about two feet long, shaped like hair pins, or maybe like flat tongs, each end having a circular opening a couple of inches across. The lower circle of each spring was hooked over the short, bent-up ends of a flat bracket in the form of a very shallow U with short ends which terminated in hinges for the trap jaws. The jaws themselves were big. inverted U's eighteen inches across, with terrible saw teeth. The ends of the paired jaws passed down through the upper rings of the springs, where they were hinged to the bracket ends.

All you had to do was depress the two springs at the same time, let the trap jaws fall open like the jaws of a shark, raise the bait pan in the middle of the trap and hook that little latch across one of the jaws and into the notch on the arm of the pan. Trouble was, it took two big C-clamps to compress the springs and take the pressure off the jaws so they could open—and the clamps were gone.

He hauled the trap out of the corner and stood on one of the springs, and his hundred and eighty pounds pushed it down far enough, but the other spring still held the jaws firmly clenched.

If he could set the trap, and if he could toll one of them into it, maybe the odds would be cut down to man to man—and maybe a man would drop a pistol or knife if a bear trap cut his foot half off.

Cautiously he looked out through the small window opening, its sill at shoulder height.

There had to be a way!

CHAPTER 15

He lay watching over the door sill, studying the tangle of growth beyond the clearing for any movement, trying to contrive some way, no matter how hopeless, to make use of the bear trap. There was no knowing how much time he had—probably enough, considering the false trails he had left and the real one he had tried his best not to leave; but with that pair of two-legged wolves unraveling it together, he might have no time at all. They had seen him, and knew he had no rifle, and very probably they had found his pistol.

He hauled the trap into the middle of the room and went out to collect flat rocks. When he had brought in what looked like enough, he began to pile them on one of the springs, the biggest rock first, then the next largest, and with the addition of each one, the spring bent down a little farther, until the ring at its end had slid down far enough to free the jaws. Then, with great care, he stood on the other spring. It, too, bent with his weight, but the jaws didn't flop open as he expected. It must be the accumulation of rust jamming the hinge pins.

Balanced on the spring, he squatted slowly, drew his skinning knife, and with utmost care pushed it between the trap jaws, down close to the hinges where the shanks were sufficiently far apart. Slowly he exerted pressure sideways, and they separated grudgingly, the vicious, toothed sections moving only an inch apart, the knife being too short a lever; but it was enough for him to get his fingers between. He pulled slowly, increasing pressure gradually and evenly, sweating with fear. The jaws moved apart, and if he had lost his balance, they'd have had him by both hands, and it wouldn't matter whether Eddie and Whitey got there or not—his death would be as slow as anything they could devise.

The trap jaws were down flat, opened wide, and again with utmost care, he moved the little hinged arm with the pan on one end and the latch on the other, and hooked the latch over one jaw, and the end of it into the notch. He stepped off the spring, and the latch held. He wiped sweat out of his eyes, and removed the rocks one by one. The trap was set.

Then he waited, knife in hand, with his back against the wall, staring out through the door. Shadows were lengthening. Dusk was gathering. And somebody was out there.

The old feeling was on him, the unexplainable certainty, the crawly feeling that his back hair was rising. He knew.

And he knew Apaches, and in that lay his one slim chance, his thousand-to-one gamble, with not a thing to lose by trying. Well, really, no gamble at all, because he was going to die. The only uncertainty was how long they would take in killing him, and whether he might possibly hurt one of them badly enough to make them kill him quickly. But knowing him to be defenseless, they would first enjoy his agony of mind, drawing it out, maybe taunting him all night, playing on his fears, relishing the building of panic into hysteria, if he proved not strong enough to stand the mental pressure. Then the sudden, silent attack at dawn, and the slow, drawn-out, terrible death. That was the Apache way—particularly if there was personal animosity involved beyond the impersonal cruelty to all white captives, or if a captive had managed to really hurt one of them, or kill him. And Neil had certainly given both of them their lumps, and in public, which shamed them all the more.

The back of his neck and his cringing back muscles could feel the impact of their eyes as he got up and dragged the trap to the doorway. It was heavy, and he didn't want to set if off, and he wanted them to see it. As he stooped to position it behind the flat rock that served as door sill, his stomach muscles cramped slightly, and he had to exert all his control not to shove the trap quickly into place and jump back.

It was much worse when he forced himself to step out and cut an armful of long, dry grass, taking his time, stopping to look and listen, because they would know he feared pursuit. He took his time, too, scattering the grass on the trap to conceal it, rearranging a handful here and there, stepping back to study the effect from outside, while his back muscles flinched and he could feel the eyes on him. He pulled another handful of grass and placed it carefully on the trap, and went inside to the far corner and sat down to wait.

It grew dark, and nothing happened. Maybe his whole elaborate scheme was a waste of effort born of his fear. He thought about Jennie, and *her* fears. Maybe those two riders—well, let's not fool ourselves—maybe Eddie Burke and Whitey, or Whitey and some cousin or uncle, had found the dead mule. and knowing Neil to be afoot and helpless, had gone on to the Citadel. Maybe they had her, now. Maybe they had killed Whitman, if he'd dredged up enough guts to resist, or even if he hadn't, and had already taken her.

It was full night now, and he mustn't wait any longer, whatever had actually happened, and wherever they were.

He sat another moment or two, straining to listen, concentrating on sound—the light movement of branches in the breeze, his own breathing, nothing else. Nothing moving out there.

An owl hooted just overhead, in the branches of the piñón, or maybe on the roof of the cabin. He was foolish, and he knew it, but that owl hoot shook him, and brought the sweat to his neck and armpits. He had lived with Apaches too long. When an owl hooted on top of your wikiup, somebody was going to die.

His vision had adjusted as the light diminished, and he could see, faintly, a lighter square in blackness at the upper part of the doorway, and another, at the window, but no actual object, inside or outside. On hands and knees he crawled to the trap and got hold of the chain with the ring on the end, riveted to one spring, and slowly pulled the trap across the packed earth of the floor until it was under the window, about eighteen inches in from the wall. He crawled back to his corner and sat waiting, knife in hand leaning against the wall, staring at the faint light of the doorway. They might come by door and window at the same time, or both come charging through the door, leaping over the sill and the place where they had seen him hide the trap—that is, if anyone had been out there at all.

He breathed normally, like any man asleep, and moved arms and legs for comfort when he had to, and stared at the faint, dark blue-black of the doorway. His eyes watered with concentration, and he wiped them repeatedly on his torn and dirty sleeve. He waited. An eternity, he waited.

Almost imperceptibly, the faintest lightening of the blackness came. A bird twittered and was quiet.

There was a whisper of sound, a faint scrape of movement at the window, and the next instant the trap clashed shut and a man squalled in agony.

Neil plunged out through the doorway, slashing right and left blindly, in the dark. The man in the trap might have managed to hang onto the pistol or knife he would have had in his hand. The other, if there was another, might be waiting, gauging his actions by what happened inside.

The sounds in there made Neil's skin crawl—the gagging of a man trying to suppress groans of hideous pain, the thrashing around, the clinking of the trap chain, the hoarse grunting.

No one else came. No one called a question. The noise inside quieted down, except for the labored breathing. He waited while the light grew stronger, then went silently to the window opening.

Whitey sat rocking back and forth, hugging himself, eyes squeezed shut, lower lip bitten through and bleeding onto his quivering chin. Both ankles were in the trap, one foot jutting at an odd angle. A heavy revolver lay on the floor out of his reach.

Neil walked in and picked up the revolver. Whitey didn't open his eyes or stop the steady rocking on his buttocks. He said, "Kill. Duggles kill Whitey."

"Who was with you?" Neil demanded. "Where is he?"

Whitey groaned and jerked his head back convulsively, bloody lips drawn back, teeth clamped shut.

"Where were you going?"

Whitey mumbled something, but all Neil understood was "woman."

"Talk Spanish, Whitey!"

Whitey's Spanish was crude but fluent, better than Neil's. *"Voy pa' mujer,"* he said. (I go for woman.)

He drew a shuddering breath, and for one weak moment Neil had the impulse to pile the rocks on one trap spring and stand on the other.

"Con quién?" Neil said. *"Con quién, alla en la carretera?"* (With who, there on the road?)

"Kill Whitey! Please, Duggles!"

His ankles weren't bleeding much, but a jagged piece of bone stuck out, and sweat rolled off him like rain. He sat up straight, then rocked back, teeth bared.

Neil asked, "Are you going to talk?"

Whitey didn't answer. He might not talk, even if he died slowly in unimaginable agony. He was as good an Apache as any—white blood, blue eyes, and all.

Neil picked up the chain and gave it a sharp jerk.

Whitey almost screamed. Almost, but not quite. But he couldn't hold back a moan of agony. And he talked.

"Burke," he said. He pronounced it "Book."

He stopped often, to breathe raucously and because he couldn't speak in connected sentences, just bits and pieces between his agonized writhing and grunts of pain.

It had all been Burke's idea, but Whitey liked it. He liked the white woman. He was going to take her to his people and never come back. He had paid for her, and the father had accepted. Then Eddie Burke said he wanted her, first. It would be a funny joke on Neil, and would pay him back for the laundry woman and for everything else. Whitey didn't care. It wouldn't spoil her. Nobody as old as Jennie was virgin, and anyway, who cared?

Then Neil came back to Camp Verde with the wagon, and Whitey knew Jennie and her father were alone at the ruin. He stole the horses from the reservation and took them to the ruin, and waited in the brush until Whitman led them to the corral. Whitey went back to Camp Verde, but Eddie Burke had gone to Prescott; and when he came back, he couldn't leave that day, so they left the next day, yesterday, for the ruin. They were going to kill Neil, and Whitman too, to shut his mouth. It would look like the work of renegades, or maybe wandering prospectors.

Then they heard Neil's mule on the road, and they didn't want to be seen, so they rode through the brush and up the little hill. When they saw who it was, Whitey took a shot at him, and they followed the mule's track, and found it dead. Burke told Whitey to track Neil down and kill him, and Burke would go after Jennie. He told Whitey to take all the time he wanted. Whitey was to meet him at the ruin after he killed Neil. And now would Neil kill him? Because there was nothing more to tell.

Neil started to leave to find Whitey's horse, but outside, he couldn't shut the ceaseless, low groaning in the cabin out of his ears or his mind.

He went back in, laid the revolver on the floor well away from Whitey, so Whitey couldn't grab Neil's pistol from his holster, and picked up the largest rock to lay it on the trap spring. Whitey couldn't possibly make it, with both ankles broken and a piece of bone jutting white out of the dirty skin, but Neil could put on a couple of tourniquets, and give him a piece of pole for a crutch and give him the one absolutely hopeless chance, merely to ease his own conscience. He regretted that he didn't have the guts to shoot the son of a bitch.

As he went to place the second rock, Whitey took a cut at him with a knife he got from under his breechclout. It slashed his shirt and burned across his ribs, and he jumped away. Like a sidewinder with a broken back, Whitey would still strike, even if it meant he'd be three days dying. Apache through and through, that was Whitey.

Neil pulled out his shirt tail, and there was a long, red mark with droplets of blood oozing like a string of little red beads, but it was no more than skin deep.

He said, "Where's your horse?" but Whitey couldn't talk anymore, and Neil went to look for it. It whinnied at him—no doubt neither fed nor watered since early yesterday—and he saw it far back in the brush. There was a rifle in the saddle boot. If Whitey had any more little tricks, Neil could use the rifle on him.

He got it and went to the door of the cabin, took all the cartridges but one from the revolver, and tossed the weapon down where Whitey could reach it if he would crawl a few feet.

He stepped back and waited and heard the chain clink, and in about a minute the click of the hammer on two empty chambers, then the shot, curiously muffled.

Whitey had stuck the muzzle in his mouth. Neil picked up the revolver, loaded it, and went to the horse.

He was too late, by far. He knew it. A few minutes or an hour one way or another would make no difference— but on the chance that she might still live, he drove the horse without mercy stumbling through brush and rocks until it faltered. When he reached the road, he eased up, because he would still need the animal. He let it blow for ten minutes, then let it walk a while, then trot, and repeated this, and twice got down and let it rest. He reached the open space in front of the ruin about eleven o'clock, and got down and tied the horse. He took the Long Tom, and from a screen of brush, he looked the setting over. Nothing moved except two mules on the other side of Beaver Creek, which saw him and discreetly moved away.

The ladder was in place—not hauled up out of reach. He couldn't see over the rim of the patio, so he moved out into the open and called Jennie's name, and called again, and there was no answer, and nobody came out of a tent, or out of the entrance of the ruin. Two buzzards rose heavily from the corral, a hundred yards farther on, and flapped away.

He tried not to do any thinking as he walked to the ladder. There were moccasin tracks around the bottom of it in the damp earth, and others to and from Beaver Creek. Eddie Burke's moccasin tracks. Nobody could prove they were Eddie's, but they were. He knew it. He leaned the rifle against the rock face and climbed the ladder and saw Dr. Whitman's prone body with flies buzzing around its head and a dark stain on the rock.

He turned Whitman over, and saw where the bullet had taken him just over his right eyebrow. There were no weapons, but two spent cartridges from a Spencer carbine showed that the doctor had tried.

Had Burke taken her away, or was she inside there? He didn't want to know. He didn't want to go in there.

He wiped sweat out of his eyes with his forearm and walked toward the low, T-shaped doorway. The sun poured through the door, cutting a sharp line of light on the earth floor. Dust motes swam in the sun and flies buzzed, and her legs were in the patch of light, naked except for a torn stocking, and a scuffed shoe on her right foot.

Numb, feeling nothing, he waited for his vision to adjust. She was almost naked. Her shirtwaist and camisole and breast band torn away. There were the parallel marks of fingernails across her left breast, and blood on the corner of her mouth, and her face looked puffed. Near one stiffening hand lay the derringer, and around her neck was the necklace of Apache Tears. In the lower, inner swell of her left breast was a small, powder-burned hole.

Dully he wondered whether she had shot herself after Eddie raped her, or before. He said aloud, "You little fool, I told you to do it if Apaches got you. I didn't mean just one man, didn't you know that? You could kill one man, with the derringer. You didn't have to kill yourself, did you? Just because of what I told you? And suppose you got raped. Is that the end of the world?"

Be he knew. And maybe she had known, too. Maybe she hadn't just blindly done what Neil had ordered her to do. Because Eddie would have killed her, after. He had to, just in case she might ever get loose from Whitey someday, just in case people heard about a white woman captive of Whitey's clan down there in the Dragoons.

But why, why, hadn't she shot him! Panic? Hysteria?

Unable to think in her wild terror, in the horror of what Eddie was doing to her?

He made himself look closer, and saw that the corner of her pocket was torn, and the spur of the hammer of the derringer had a little tatter of cloth caught on it. So maybe she had tried and the hammer had caught, and had cost her the chance to kill him before he caught her and beat her and threw her down and ravaged her.

He felt like some sick kind of freak looking down at her nakedness, feeling that she would be horribly embarrassed, even in death. He got a blanket from her bed and covered her. He knew it hadn't hit him yet. It was like someone had said that got shot in the Salt River canyon fight—you didn't feel it. You didn't even know it, maybe, for fifteen or twenty minutes, and then you wished it had killed you.

He went out and got Dr. Whitman by the wrists and hauled him inside. Then he brought a bucket of water and a dish towel, and made himself uncover Jennie and wash the blood and dirt from her face and her body.

He unhooked the Apache Tears necklace. He was going to put it in his pocket, but instead put it around his neck and fastened the clasp.

He got the two tarps he had folded and used for a mattress out on the patio, and came in and washed Dr. Whitman's face. He straightened Jennie's legs and crossed her arms on her breast, the way he'd heard you ought to do, and smoothed her hair. He couldn't stand to look at the way her mouth hung open, so he found a clean bandanna and tied it around her head to hold her jaw closed, before he wrapped her in a blanket and then in a big tarp, like a huge, clumsy envelope. He wrapped Whitman up the same way. And after that, he was so exhausted he could hardly manage to toss down a slab of bacon in its sewn cloth to the ground, and a can of tomatoes and a couple of blankets, and make his way down the ladder.

Neil stripped the horse and watered and fed it and took it to the corral. One of the mules was lying there, and the buzzards had been at it, and a hunk of meat slashed off one haunch, wild Apache style. Apaches loved mule meat, and this was just a dodge of Eddie's to set people's minds on the wrong trail.

He wondered how long Eddie had waited for Whitey to come. Maybe he thought Whitey was still having fun with Neil, as much fun, maybe, as he'd had with Jennie if she hadn't shot herself; and maybe Burke had gone back to Camp Verde to act normal and wonder why Whitey hadn't showed up, after he found his woman dead.

Well, at least, she was where the buzzards couldn't get to her.

He went to the creek and saw where Eddie had ridden across, out of sight of the ruin, had tied his horse, and crept behind the big log at one end, and waited. There was a splintered place where a bullet had hit, which meant maybe Eddie had missed his first shot, or maybe Dr. Whitman had been alert enough to see him first.

He didn't believe Whitman had let the ladder down, not this time. But after Eddie had killed him, it wouldn't have been hard to rope an outcrop of rock and get up to the ramp. Jennie could have had him cold, then, if she hadn't lost her head, or tried to hide, maybe.

Now it began to get to him. If he hadn't been Neil

Douglas and a tough boy—not a real hard case, but tough enough—he might have cried.

The black rage took him like a dog with a rat, and shook him almost blind. He began to swear—vile, dirty obscenities he had almost never used, and got the lariat off the saddle and trotted toward the corral. Tomorrow was too long to wait. Eddie Burke had no right to live that long.

Then the blurred heat in his head cooled a little and the rage subsided, glowing unseen like a banked fire, but hot—hot! He went back and picked up the can of tomatoes and the slab of bacon.

He had to climb to the ruin again to find a clean shirt and socks and underwear. He was able to walk past her bundled body and into the second room where she kept the clean laundry and soap and towels, then back and down the ladder.

A bath in the creek cooled somewhat the heat of mind and body. The shallow slash from Whitey's knife bled again, but soon stopped. He fried bacon and made coffee, and exhaustion hit him like a blackjack. He had been sure he'd lie awake again tonight, but it was all he could manage to stay awake until he could pull off shirt and pants and moccasins, unroll the blankets in the big tent, and fall onto them.

CHAPTER 16

For a few moments after he awoke, he felt fine. He wasn't really awake yet, having slept as though drugged, and the long sleep and the clean underwear he had slept in and his clean body made him feel new, rested, ready.

Then it hit him like a mule kick in the belly—what was

up there in the Citadel—and the banked fire of his fury broke loose. He had to fight for control, to think, to plan. But there really wasn't anything to plan. He was going to ride to Camp Verde and kill Eddie Burke. And if Eddie had got a hunch that anyone knew about him—maybe he had found Whitey in the trap by now, maybe he had made a run for it to his mother's people, or to Mexico— Neil would run him to earth. If it took a year. Five years.

He lit a fire in the range, took the horse to water and grained it, while he warmed up the coffee and fried bacon and ate canned tomatoes. He had slept later than was his habit, and it was eight o'clock before he left.

During the ride, he managed to push his emotions to the back of his mind, and began thinking again. I just can't walk up and shove a gun in his car and kill him. I'd do it, but how do I explain it after? Who saw him kill Whitman and her? Nobody. Not me, either. I'll kill him one way or another but there's no use to hang for it, to trade myself for him. For all anybody but me would know, Whitey did it, and I can't prove he didn't. I can *say* he did, but who'd believe me? Who'd believe Whitey didn't go there and kill them, and then try to ambush me on the way back? What's to prove anybody passing through didn't do it? No way I know to do it all legal and aboveboard, but by God, he's gonna tell somebody all about it.

Alternating a walk and a lope, he was in Camp Verde, dismounting at the administration building, just before noon. He tied the horse and crossed the veranda and went in. Lieutenant Underhill passed him in the doorway, going out, saw the horse at the rail, and followed him back into the room.

"Where'd you get the troop horse, Douglas?" he demanded truculently.

Neil ignored him and crossed the room to shake hands with Major Trumbull, who had just got up from his desk to go to his quarters for dinner.

The major said, "Didn't expect you back so soon. Any trouble out there?"

"Yes, sir, there was. Eddie Burke can tell you about it. Is he on the post?

"Eddie Burke!" Major Trumbull was astounded and skeptical. "Neil, I know he and that white Apache gave Jennie a bad time, the damn fools, with that head they showed her. But I talked to him about it. I laid into him, good. Now don't tell me Eddie is tangled up in any trouble out there!"

"No, sir! It'd be just my word against his. An' he's Regular Army, and Underhill, here, is Regular Army, and you're Regular Army, and me . . . I'm a civilian ex-employee that never got near West Point. So you're gonna hear it from Eddie, himself."

The major stared at him. "I don't much like the implication of that, Neil."

Neil's temper was barely under control. He said, "The hell with implications! Is Eddie on the post, or is he out rambling around on his own as usual, like he never had a duty or a detail in his life?"

Lieutenant Underhill, behind him, tapped him on the shoulder, and Neil turned. Underhill said, "Douglas, you aren't going to talk to Major Trumbull like that!"

"God damn you! Is he here, or isn't he?"

Some of Underhill's righteous indignation drained away at what he saw in Neil's eyes. He said, to the major, "Why, yes, he's here. He asked for leave when he got back from Prescott, and I gave permission. Your own policy, sir, with everybody so restless and all. Somebody said he went hunting, with that white freak he's so partial to. But he's back, I saw him this morning. He should be having his dinner in the noncoms' mess right now."

"He went hunting with Whitey, Wilbur? Seems I gave Whitey permission to go visit his people, down in the Dragoons."

Lieutenant Underhill's forehead wrinkled in puzzlement. "Why, that's right, sir. Well . . . I don't know . . . I'll never understand these savages."

Major Trumbull wasn't dull-witted. He sensed something in Neil's mood, something that chilled him. He said,

"Well, all right, Neil. I'll send somebody for Eddie right after dinner."

"No, sir! Now! Before he finds out I'm here. And you won't want the whole post in on this—just maybe us three and Captain Eastwood. I'll fetch him to your quarters." Neil pushed Lieutenant Underhill out of his way and started to leave.

Major Trumbull said, "Hold on, there! My quarters? Why not right here?"

"Not to your house, sir. I'll bring him to your back yard. It's private, with that board fence."

He went out and slammed the dooor. Walking fast, he looked back. The major and the lieutenant were in the doorway, staring after him.

Because it was mealtime, few people were about as he crossed the parade ground. Nobody looked up when he stepped into the long adobe barracks where the noncommissioned officers lived. There were about thirty sergeants and corporals, four to the bench, on eight benches flanking the mess tables. They had all left their pistols on their bunks. Mess attendants were coming and going, and there was a gabble of talk, and no one looked up when Neil entered. His moccasins made no sound on the plank floor as he stepped behind Eddie Burke at the second table.

He had Whitey's Colt in his left hand, and he got a good handful of Eddie's hair in his right fist and pulled him over backward. The bench and the other three on it came with Eddie, crashing on their backs onto the floor. For an instant there was silence, and Neil dragged Eddie away from the overturned bench. Then the gabble broke out, loud and mixed up, laughter, shouted questions, a lot of profanity, and Eddie's voice cursing above the uproar.

Neil hauled him to his feet, and when Eddie reached for the knife sheathed at his hip, Neil whacked his hand with the gun barrel. While Eddie's voice rose higher in outrage, Neil released his grip on Eddie's hair, pulled Eddie's knife free, flipped it, caught it by the blade, and threw it whirling at the wall, where it stuck three inches into the adobe. Eddie turned, and Neil slammed the muzzle of his pistol hard into his belly, and he doubled over, gasping, with no wind left for cursing.

Most of the noncoms were on their feet, some silent now, some advancing threateningly. Neil seized Burke's left ear and jerked him around to face them, himself behind Burke. He said nothing, but as with Major Trumbull, something about him got through to them, and the yelling and laughter and swearing stopped. Nobody approached, and he got Eddie by the hair again and hauled him, stumbling backward, out of the barracks, into the noon glare. Eddie, with his head bent back, jerked and swung his fists, and Neil released his grip and said, "To the major's place, Eddie."

For once, Burke had the sense to estimate Neil correctly, and he marched along without further objection. A few soldiers and a couple of Apache Scouts saw the gun at Eddie's back and followed.

Major Trumbull and Captain Eastwood and Lieutenant Underhill were waiting in the back yard of Trumbull's quarters, enclosed by the five-foot board fence. As Neil marched his man through the opened gate, and Captain Eastwood closed it after them, Mrs. Trumbull came out onto the rear veranda and said, "Claude! What's going on? What are these persons doing here?"

The major had the reputation of being henpecked, but now he said, "Get back in the house, Ella!" and she looked insulted, but said not a word, and slammed the door behind her.

A few soldiers and Scouts were looking over the fence, and the major said, "You boys clear out! You Scouts, too. Tell them, Eddie."

Burke's perspiring face was red. He massaged the hand that Neil had whacked with the gun, and said loudly, "Major, I swear to God, what the hell's goin' on here?"

"Run those Apaches off, Eddie!"

Burke spat three words in Apache, and the Scouts' heads vanished behind the fence, as had the soldiers'.

Burke swung back to Neil. "Gahdamn you gahdamn

little bastard! I'll break yer gahdamn neck this time! What the hell you think you're——"

Neil hit him hard on the mouth with the heel of his hand and Eddie staggered back, not so much from the blow as from sheer astonishment.

Lieutenant Underhill grabbed Neil's arm, Captain Eastwood strode toward them. Major Trumbull said angrily, "Here! Here! None of that! This will be a fair hearing, whatever the hell you've got in mind!"

"It'll be a hearing all right, Major, but what's fair got to do with it? I'm gonna beat the truth out of him if I kill him doing it. Here! Hold this!" He shoved the pistol into Major Trumbull's hand and turned to meet Eddie's rush.

He slipped inside a vicious hook and hit Eddie on the mouth, stopping him as though he'd run into a wall. And while Eddie stood there a little befuddled, fingering his bleeding mouth, Neil jerked open the throat of his own shirt. Buttons flew and Eddie stared, and they all saw it— the necklace of Apache Tears.

Eddie's ruddy face, running sweat, seemed to go gray. He looked right and left and at the ground, anywhere but at the necklace, and Neil knocked him flat with an overhand right, flush on the mouth again.

Everyone now was silent, sensing something more than just the well-known Eddie Burke–Neil Douglas feud, everyone except Lieutenant Underhill. Again he grabbed Neil's arm and tried to pull him back, yelling, "That's enough now! Don't you hit him again, Douglas!"

Neil turned on him, snarling, and what Underhill saw in his face sent him back a couple of steps and kept him quiet.

With Neil's back to him, Eddie charged again, and Neil suddenly bent at the waist and Eddie went sprawling over him onto the ground. As he rose, still on one knee and with a hand steadying himself, Neil got him in the face with his knee and knocked him onto his back.

Captain Eastwood said. "Now, Major Trumbull, sir, that's enough! That's brutal!" but Trumbull said, "We'll let it go awhile, Charlie."

Burke got to his feet and lurched sideways, and caught his balance. His left eye was swelling, and his nose and mouth were bloody. He blurted, "I never, Neil! Honest to God I never! It was Whitey, Neil! Whitey! Honest to God, Neil!"

He came toward Neil with his hand out. "You gotta believe me!" When he spoke, little bubbles of blood were on his lips, and suddenly he kicked at Neil's crotch.

Neil sidestepped the worst of it, but took it on the thigh, and as he stumbled sideways, Burke dove at him, arms spread wide, hands clutching. Neil stepped into him, between the outflung arms and smashed his elbow into Eddie's face, halting him, straightening him up. He drove Eddie stumbling back off balance, with three, solid overhand rights to the face. Burke brought up against the fence.

Neil stood, feet spread, chest heaving, and said, "Tell them, Eddie. Tell the major what you did to her, in that room in the ruin!"

Nobody said anything. There were distant voices and laughter, and Eddie Burke leaned back against the fence, gasping, sweat soaked, with one eye shut and his mouth smashed and his nose broken, and somehow found the strength to charge like a grizzly, mouthing incoherent obscenities. Neil took him coming in—a terrible hook in the belly, and another, and another. Burke's knees buckled and he sprawled forward and rolled over, gagging. He struggled to a sitting position, leaning back, braced on his arms.

Neil stood over him, wondering if his hands could stand up to hitting him anymore. He said, "Tell the major, Eddie. She shot herself after you got through with her. After you murdered her father."

Burke was whimpering. He wiped his sleeve across his mouth, and it came away bloody. He said, "Whitey! Whitey done it, Neil!"

Captain Eastwood said softly, "My God! My God!"

"Not Whitey, Eddie," Neil said. "Whitey's dead with both feet in a bear trap in my grampa's cabin, where you sent him to kill me. Tell the major, Eddie."

Burke got up slowly, blunderingly, turned and staggered to the fence, caught the top with both hands, and tried to haul himself up and climb over. He couldn't make it, and Neil got him by the hair and slammed him to the ground on his back. He lay a moment with his eyes closed, then painfully rolled over, braced his elbows, and dropped his face into his hands.

Lying there with the four of them around him, he told of the murder of Dr. Whitman and the ravaging of Jennie, told it to their appalled silence and open mouths and unbelieving ears.

Neil edged toward Major Trumbull, and Trumbull, holding the gun, held him at arm's length and pushed the gun under his belt and held on to it.

Sniffling and whimpering, Burke finished by saying, "But she got away from me, Neil. She was yelling for you, and she got away an' I couldn't hold her down. She kep' squirmin' an' kickin', an' draggin' at that derringer in her pocket, an' I didn't know she had it, and she jerked it loose an' shot herself."

So what did it matter now, if it was before or after? Neil walked to the rear veranda and sat down, elbows on knees, face in his hands. With little interest, he heard Major Trumbull order Underhill to get the guard.

The major and Captain Eastwood came to sit with him on the veranda; they were silent for a long time. Mrs. Trumbull opened the door; her shocked face peered out for a moment, then disappeared.

Major Trumbull said, "That's the worst I ever heard. Well, I mean from a civilized man. I guess we've all seen what the wild ones are capable of, but this . . . . Well, he'll stand a general court-martial, and he'll hang. I'm not saying your way was legal or ethical, Neil—but I have to say I don't know how else you could have got it out of him."

"If the Army don't kill him, I will," Neil said.

"You won't have to, I guarantee. The general court will hang him."

"Will you send and bring her in?" Neil asked. "If

you need anything to back up the story, take Chalk Eye and Limpy. They'll read the signs out there like a book."

"We'll handle it, Neil. We'll take them to a funeral parlor in Prescott."

"All right, sir. I have to ask you a favor. I didn't get paid, and I left my money and gear with the quartermaster at Fort Whipple. Could you lend me twenty dollars, and a horse? And maybe a blanket for tonight?"

"You'll stay here, Neil. We've got a spare room. What you need is a drink and a bath."

"I thank you, sir. But I'd rather get going. Anyway, Mrs. Trumbull don't want me around here."

"Mrs. Trumbull doesn't run the household unless I let her," the major said. "I'll have our striker heat some water, and you can use my razor. You look like you could spend some time in bed."

"Sir, I don't think so."

"Can't he helped, Neil. I've got to hold an inquiry. Have to have some officers over from Whipple, and we'll get your story in writing and have you sign it."

He got up and yelled, "*Ella!*"

She opened the door, stuck her head out, and said timidly, "What is it, dear?"

"Bring the bourbon and three glasses, and a pitcher of water."

"Yes, dear."

Captain Eastwood said, "I can still hear him telling it, and still can't believe it."

He had two days of rest before officers arrived from Fort Whipple. Most of it he spent in the room in Major Trumbull's quarters. The major had lent him the twenty dollars, and he walked to Shanty Town and got a new hat and shirt, and tobacco, and a shave and haircut, and a few shots of whiskey.

Mrs. Trumbull, under duress, treated him with icy politeness, both of them hating the necessity of his presence there. Because he had no stomach for meeting Molly Killian, he borrowed a washtub and washboard from Mrs. Trumbull and washed his shirt and underwear, sweated and bloodied during his beating of Eddie Burke.

He saw the Trumbulls only at meals, and wanted no contact with anyone. The afternoon of the second day, the major brought him what little gear and clothing he had left at the Citadel, and told him the bodies had been taken to Prescott, and General Kautz, Crook's successor, was getting in touch with the Smithsonian Institute and relatives of Whitman. Trumbull also said the officers had arrived from Fort Whipple for the board of inquiry, which was set for the next day.

Whenever Neil dressed or undressed, the Apache Tears around his neck kept Jennie sharply in his mind. Not that she was ever out of it, really. He didn't want her there. She spoiled his sleep, and, awake, his peace of mind; but he missed her deeply, which surprised him, because he had not realized how much she had come to mean to him, and in the camp he had become a little weary of her open devotion those last couple of weeks. Now he kept remembering her innocence, her dependence on him despite her education and social position—but most of all, he kept thinking of the horror of her ordeal at the hands of Eddie Burke. And himself, Neil Douglas, at the time running for help, or cowering in the cabin, waiting for Whitey to come and kill him. If he had only stayed with her after he got back with the supplies and found those ratty horses with which Whitey had bought her! All he had to do was run Whitey off, or gun him down the minute he showed his freak face. On the other hand, he couldn't have foretold that Whitey was already on the way, and Eddie Burke with him—that he would run into them on the road.

It *had* been important—in fact, desperately necessary —to get help, to tell the authorities, to get Jennie out of the deadly tangle her father's ignorance and vanity had got her into. No, he couldn't honestly blame himself. But he did, and he couldn't stop.

Early in the morning, in the administration building, the officers of the post and those from Fort Whipple questioned him endlessly. Clerks wrote frantically, trying to keep up; and Eddie Burke was brought in, his eyes swollen blue and yellow and his face like dried chopped meat. He wouldn't talk. Not a word.

Tired of the repetition, the stupidity of many of the questions, Neil signed a long statement purporting to be his story, without reading it. She was dead, and Eddie had killed her as surely as if he had pulled the trigger himself, and it began to look like they were going to say Burke actually did, in the board's findings, and avoid any awkwardness about suicide during the general court-martial.

Neil said to Trumbull, who sat at his desk alone for a few moments, "Sir, it's all been said. All I want to know is, are they going to hang him?"

"Never doubt it, Neil. Sure as the sun will come up to-morrow. We'll see him hanged like you'd step on the head of a rattler."

At dinner in the major's quarters, a captain and a major from Fort Whipple morbidly fascinated by what had happened, wanted to keep on talking about it—what Neil had seen when he got to the ruin, what condition he had found her in, things like that. Mrs. Trumbull was distressed, Neil's temper began to boil, and Major Trumbull said, "I think we've been over all that, gentlemen."

Neil excused himself and went out to the privy, then up to his room.

CHAPTER 17

It seemed he had hardly got to sleep when someone was pounding on the front door, yelling for the major. Neil got up and hurried to the window and looked down at an excited trooper, barely distinguishable in the gray dawn.

Major Trumbull, in his nightshirt, opened the door, and the trooper said, *"He got loose! He's gone! Stole a horse, and he's gone!"*

Trumbull grabbed his arm. *"Burke? You mean Sergeant Burke?*

"Yeah, him, Major!"

Neil got his clothes on fast, buckled on his gun, jammed on his hat, and ran down the stairs. He passed the major coming up, yelling orders over his shoulder at the departing messenger: "Get Captain Eastwood! Tell him blow Boots and Saddles, and he can pick the men he wants. Three days' rations. He'll know!" He trotted along the upstairs hall, yelling, "Ella! Get up! Light the lamp!"

If he had seen Neil when they crowded past each other on the stair, he gave no indication, and Neil sprinted from the house, then slowed to a trot as he crossed the parade ground, heading for the tent where he had lived with his five Indians, hoping they weren't all away visiting relatives, or hunting. The bugle was blowing and horses neighing and men running. The sun would be up in a few minutes.

When he went into the tent, Limpy said, "Hey, Duggles!" and old Chalk Eye grinned at him, buckling a belt heavy with cartridges around his skinny wrinkled middle. Chiquito was woodenly noncommittal as always. Only Yellow Face was absent, and they really didn't need him— that is, if Chulito had gone for horses, as Neil supposed. Eddie Burke was as smart and devious and tricky on a trail as any full-blood Apache, but not more so. Neil said, *"Bueno! Muy bueno! Chulito va pa' caballos?"* (Very good! Has Chulito gone for the horses?)

Chalf Eye said, *"Listos afuera."* (They're ready outside.)

Chulito, the girlish-looking killer, was holding the horses behind the tent—two saddled for Limpy and Chiquito, one bareback for himself, one with two grain sacks strapped on, for Chalk Eye. A big bay, for Neil, already had all the equipment he needed hung on the saddle—not too much, but much more than theirs, including a picket rope, saddle bags with grain and extra maga-

zines, and a two-quart canteen which his Scouts considered a somewhat effeminate indulgence. Chalk Eye
handed him a Spencer carbine—he could tell by the weight
that it had a full magazine—and they were off, cutting
across the parade ground at a lope while Camp Verde
boiled with shouts and orders and men running around.

Chalk Eye led them along the road to where a deep-
cut arroyo crossed under a wooden bridge and meandered
past the south side of Camp Verde all the way to the
river. They slid down into it and went very slowly along
the bottom. Neil was puzzled by the maneuver, but knew
better than to question it. Then it came to him—if Burke
had gone south—the logical expectation if he was trying
for Mexico, or perhaps to reach Whitey's people in the
Dragoons or broncos still in the Chiricahuas—he would
have to cross the arroyo, if he hadn't gone down the
river. And if he had done that, they could find where he
had gone in.

Staying behind so as not to mess up any tracks, Neil
said in Spanish, "How did he do it, Chalk Eye?"

"He got the guard to come to the window, maybe to
light his cigarette. Probably got him by the collar and
slammed his head against the bars. Didn't kill him, but
he's in the hospital with a broken head. Well, you know
the guardhouse. He broke a leg off the bunk and pried
three bars out of the windowsill. It's just adobe. You
could almost do it barehanded. He got the guard's Springfield and cartridges, and sneaked down to the stable and
hit the guard there in the back of the head with the gun
butt. The other one never even heard it. Never heard
him lead the horse out, either."

Shadows still filled the arroyo, but the sun was slanting
over the Mogollon Rim, and the visibility was now ample
for the Scouts. They ambled along the sandy bottom for
half a mile before Limpy, in the lead, held up his hand.
A shod horse had slid on its rump down the side of the
arroyo, and hadn't been able to make it up the other side,
carrying a rider. A booted man had got off and helped
his mount to scramble up the other side. Limpy led the
five of them in the same maneuver, and when they were

on top and mounted again, the tracks led southeast toward
Twin Buttes, five or six miles away, and presently disappeared into a stretch of waist-high manzanita so thick
and tough and springy that a man couldn't have fought
his way through it on foot, and Neil doubted that any
horse could, for very far. The growth was interspersed
with leads of bare sand, and a stretch of malpais, islands
of manzanita varying from a few feet in width to a
quarter of a mile— a maze, a puzzle, which might have
let Burke double back, or go east, west, or south.

Chalk Eye said in his guttural and rough Spanish,
"He's not going to waste much time. He has to go for distance, so he wouldn't stay in the manzanita long. Chulito
and Limpy can go left around the outside, and the three
of us go right. First one that sees sign, yell."

He grunted a sentence in Apache, and Limpy and Chulito split off and went east, while Neil and Chalk Eye and
Chiquito swung the other way. The going was incredibly
rough, scrambling up arroyos, sliding down the sides of
hills in a shower of gravel, long detours around some
impossible arm of the manzanita growth that stretched up
a talus slope. Neil was sure they missed where Burke had
come out, but Chalk Eye led them on, half the time on
foot. Limpy and Chulito caught up with them, having
been stopped where the manzanita grew up to the face of
a cliff and was impassable.

Neil said to Chalk Eye, "We're wasting time. Which
way you think he'd go? East Fork of the Verde? Or maybe
cut across the mountains from Verde Hot Springs and try
to make it down the Agua Fria?"

"No. Shortest way for him is down the Verde to the
Salt River. But how you know he didn't double back, out
of that manzanita?"

"It doesn't grow tall enough to hide a man on a horse,
not even a man walking," Neil said.

"That's right. But what if he killed his horse and is
just lying low to double back after we leave?"

Then Chulito found the track, coming down a bay of
sand and gravel between two tongues of the manzanita
growth, plain and sharp, until it hit a stretch of hardpan,

and for another ten minutes was lost again. That's the way it went for three or four hours, but Neil's Indians had a fourfold advantage, there being only one smart half-Apache trying to hide his trail, and four Apaches to find it.

Neil said, "You're so sure, why don't we quit this running back and forth and head for the East Fork?"

Limpy answered that one. "That's the best way for him to go, and he knows we know it, so that's where he doesn't go."

"Maybe he doesn't know we're on his track."

"Of course he knows. Even without the dust, he'd know it."

Chalk Eye seemed to track by inner communication with himself as much as by the physical signs of a pebble knocked loose, a twig cut by a horseshoe, the bend of a few blades of dry grass where the rest grew straight. Most likely he had put himself in Burke's place, in Burke's mind. They all knew Burke well, from many a campaign, many a pursuit with him, and a few retreats, and maybe they couldn't read a newspaper, but they could read a man and the country, and no matter how Burke twisted and turned and backtracked and took advantage of terrain, and used every trick and stratagem he knew and even invented some new ones, he couldn't shake them.

It was mid-afternoon, and the trail let into the powder-dry foothills of the Mazatzal range. The horses, pushed hard all day, were suffering for water and beginning to falter. So far as Neil and his Indians knew, Burke had carried no water, and he would be in bad shape, and no doubt looking for water now. The Scouts began to look for indication of a seep or spring. They were going up a steep arroyo, and hadn't found any track for a half an hour. Considering the condition of their horses, they went afoot, leading the exhausted animals, with Chalk Eye first in line, all scanning the surrounding steep slopes, which were choked with dusty, dry brush and chaparral and a few palo verde trees and a lot of saguaro and cholla and ocotillo. Chalk Eye stopped, and his horse blundered into him. He pushed the horse back and carefully moved aside, looking down. He signaled for Neil to approach, and pointed at the mark of a boot heel. He had stepped on it, and recognized it through the sole of his moccasin.

"Horse gone," he said. "Back of us, somewhere. Chulito, go find it. We'll wait."

"Maybe fighting his way through that manzanita took too much out of it," Neil said. "Or he thinks he can hide his trail better without it."

They waited for Chulito, and Neil saw the first sign of possible water—three pairs of whitewing doves flying fast, all in the same direction. He jogged Chalk Eye with his elbow, and they looked along the line of the doves' flight and saw, a mile ahead, across thickets of stunted mesquite and catclaw and cholla, and way up the side of a steep slope, a little patch of green where there had to be a seep of water, maybe a small spring.

They tied the horses to bushes, and Chulito rode back to them. He had found the horse, a quarter mile to the side of the arroyo up which they had come. Burke had led it there most cunningly with hardly a mark of passage, and cut its throat. Probably he had seen the green spot, the sign of water, and he knew he couldn't get the horse up there, and was afraid to leave it for fear it would whinny to any other horse approaching.

Chalk Eye led off again, and they rode a half mile up the steepening and narrowing arroyo, then dismounted and went carefully afoot.

A small wash cut into the arroyo from up the hill. The little area of green was clear now, high above them and still a hundred yards or more ahead. Limpy went up the little wash. Chalk Eye slithered on his belly into the chaparral, cradling his long rifle. Chiquito nestled down behind a jumble of small, round boulders and began to scan the thickly grown hillside, and Chulito, climbing out of the arroyo, got shot in the upper arm. He grunted and almost fell back, but managed to cling to an exposed root and haul himself up over the edge with his left arm, and squirm into the brush.

Neil stayed in the arroyo, scrambling up its steep side

to just below the crumbling edge, where he dug in his toes and elbows, and propped the carbine on his hands, staring upward through a fringe of brush until his eyes watered. Three Indians were working their way through dry brush, and one was lying up there bleeding, but there was not a sound, nor the lightest puff of dust.

Neil saw what he was looking for—a wisp of gray smoke lying like a bit of cobweb on the still air, against the inky black shadow under the overhang of a slab of rock.

He fired into the shadow twice, as fast as he could work the lever, and Eddie Burke screamed and lurched out of the shallow depression under the rock, clutching his smashed left shoulder.

Neil shot him in the chest and he folded in the middle and plunged sprawling off the ledge down into a tangle of brush.

Neil slid to the bottom of the arroyo, and Chulito rolled over the edge and landed with a thump. Neil was tying his bandanna around Chulito's wound, when Chalk Eye came sliding down in a shower of sand, grinning at Neil with his sole two upper teeth showing like the blunted fangs of a senile lobo wolf. He went trotting off out of sight down the arroyo.

In a while, the others came down carrying Burke's rifle and boots and hat, and presently Chalk Eye came trotting back, slick with sweat, leading his horse. He unfastened the cinch strap and rolled up one of the grain sacks he used for a saddle pad. He stuffed it under his cartridge belt and climbed the side of the wash and disappeared.

The rest sat waiting, and in half hour, he returned. He offered the grain sack to Neil. It was bloody, and no longer empty.

Chalk Eye, grinning, reverted to what he thought was English. He said, "Fo' you, Duggles. Gib to Maje Tumble, eh?"

Neil understood him. "You give it to him," he said. "Tell him I'll leave the horse at Fort Whipple. Limpy, take my canteen up there and fill it for me."

Limpy said, "Sure. You bet! First we gonna have

smoke, eh?" Deftly, he lifted the sweat-soaked Bull Durham sack from Neil's shirt pocket.

Neil took a room above the Palace Bar, right there in the center of all the whiskey and poker tables and faro layouts and girl entertainers who really weren't whores, but were far from chaste if they liked a man. Mickey Free came in from Fort Whipple, and they went on a three-day drunk. Neil won eighty dollars playing faro. He rented a horse at Daugherty's O.K. Corral and rode out to Lynx Creek and over to Lion Springs. He drank late and got up late and tried his best, but none of it helped.

Every time he dressed or undressed, there it was, that string of Apache Tears around his neck, whose weight he had felt all day, keeping the memories going, the good ones and the bad ones, and his guilt at not having been there when she needed him. He kept telling himself that he had done the right thing—he didn't have second sight and couldn't tell that Eddie Burke would come back to the Citadel, or that Whitey and Burke would be on their way there at the very time he was riding for help. But he had told her that under certain circumstances (which, of course, could never happen) she would have to kill herself. And it *had* happened—or she thought it had. No matter that simple rape wasn't what he feared most if she fell into the hands of wild Apaches or renegades—but what would precede and follow rape. Just rape alone wasn't necessarily fatal—but then, it might have been for her, or more likely, would have driven her stark crazy.

So one cool September morning he rode his hired horse out to Point of Rocks and laid the necklace of Apache Tears on a boulder and took a stone and smashed the obsidian beads to bits.

Now maybe he could settle down and go to work punching cows again, or go prospecting up in the Bradshaws, and be again what he had been, a self-sufficient loner, like three-quarters of all the men in the territory, with no ambitions, and no future and no need of one.

But the thought of Jennie Whitman was still in his head as he passed Fort Whipple, returning. Here was where he had seen her first. Here was where he had brought her the Apache Tears. Here was where he should have returned her safe and sound. Here was where he had given her the Apache Tears that had meant so much to her.

With no further consideration, he rode back to Fort Whipple and tied the horse in front of the administration building. He went in and saw the man with the general's stars on his shoulder bars.

A corporal clerk eyed him sourly and said, "What you want?"

"I'd like to speak to General Kautz."

"State your name and business."

"Neil Douglas. I was Sergeant of Indian Scouts, at Camp Verde."

The man with the stars at the big desk said, "Sergeant Douglas, have a seat over here." He shook hands with Neil, and Neil sat in the chair by the desk.

General Kautz said, "Terrible thing about that girl and her father. Terrible."

Neil stiffened. He wasn't going to take anything from anyone in uniform over what had happened out there. He had the weight of it on him, but nobody else was going to pile any more on.

"Well, it's over and done," the general said. "I'm glad the son of a bitch broke out. Saves a lot of trouble. What can I do for you?"

Relieved, Neil relaxed and said, "Sir, I've had a lot of experience under General Crook, and I was wondering if the cavalry could use me. Somewhere else. Not here in Arizona."

"I know about you, Douglas," General Kautz said. "No question about your competence. Now up in Montana and Dakota the Sioux and Cheyennes are raising hell—Sitting Bull and Crazy Horse and Red Cloud and Gall—and there's a big campaign under way with Crook commanding, and Terry and Custer. You know of General Custer? Fine officer! Youngest brigadier in the Civil War. Custer's got a body of Scouts, mostly Crows, almost as good as Crook's Apaches. I can reenlist you. No doubt about approval from General Crook for a raise in rank and ten dollars more a month. You want to go to Fort Abraham Lincoln up in Dakota Territory, as First Sergeant of Custer's Crow Scouts? I guarantee Custer will welcome you."

Neil stood up. "Sir, how soon can I leave?"

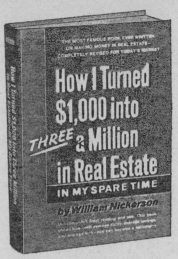

"Is it still possible today to make a million by my formula?"

People are always asking me this question. And in spite of tight money and high taxes, I answer, "Yes—more than ever!" The new updated edition of my book (*How I Turned $1,000 into Three Million*) **shows you how.** by William Nickerson

In my book I reveal—and tell how to use—these 4 basic principles of traveling the surest road to great fortune still open to the average person:

1. How to harness the secret force of free enterprise—the pyramiding power of borrowed money.

2. How to choose income-producing multiple dwellings in which to invest your own (and your borrowed) capital.

3. How to make your equity grow.

4. How to virtually eliminate the "tax bite" on your capital growth.

▼ AT YOUR BOOKSTORE OR MAIL THIS COUPON NOW FOR FREE 14-DAY TRIAL ▼